beautiful

RUSSELL

the linden press

NEW YORK

SYDNEY

islands

MARTIN

simon and schuster

LONDON   TORONTO

TOKYO   1988

Copyright © 1988 by Russell Martin
All rights reserved
including the right of reproduction
in whole or in part in any form
Published by The Linden Press/Simon and Schuster
A Division of Simon & Schuster Inc.
Published by Simon & Schuster Inc.
Simon & Schuster Building
Rockefeller Center
1230 Avenue of the Americas
New York, NY 10020
THE LINDEN PRESS/Simon and Schuster and colophon are registered
trademarks of Simon & Schuster Inc.

Designed by Liney Li

Manufactured in the United States of America
1   3   5   7   9   10   8   6   4   2
Library of Congress Cataloging-in-Publication Data
Martin, Russell.
Beautiful islands.

I. Title.
PS3563.A7285.B43   1988   813'.54   87-37823
ISBN   0-671-64662-1

for Joe Allen,

who took me to space, and
encouraged me to pay attention

We had the sky, up there, all speckled with stars, and we used to lay on our backs and look up at them, and discuss about whether they was made, or only just happened.

—Mark Twain
Huckleberry Finn

beautiful islands

one

Seeing Colorado from space was like looking back with new uncertainty on a place you've known forever but have never understood. Late spring snow still draped the high spines of the San Juans and the Sangre de Cristos, and the valleys spread like disheveled rugs between the ranges. Yet I couldn't see the towns that I knew were tucked into the folds of the mountains and that sprawled across the sage-strewn plains. I couldn't see Durango, my hometown, couldn't gauge by a gridwork of streets where the house must be. My father had joked with me over the phone before the launch, promising he would go outside and wave into the sunlit sky; and I bet he actually did wave a time or two. But I never waved back because it was hard to imagine that he was actually somewhere in my field of vision—

an indiscernible speck in faded jeans and house slippers standing on the cement slab by the back door. And it was hard to
imagine that the entire rumpled and wind-scoured region
wasn't just some glorious gas station map that had been
wrapped around the sensuous curve of the earth. That can-
yoned and summited corner of Colorado was profoundly familiar to me, but from the silent vantage of space it looked like
someplace that was worlds away, forever inaccessible.

Colorado had seemed plenty far enough away from Houston as well, and I had considered flying up for a visit, but I
finally decided to drive. We had spent about ten days in de-
briefings following the flight, and then NASA sent Bill
Grimes, Cathy Cohn, and me out on the promotional circuit
for a couple of weeks, so the idea of throwing some quarts
of beer into a cooler and heading across the hard, anvil-hot
prairies of Texas sounded strangely appealing. I stopped at
Pe-Te's for lunch on the day I left, mentioned I was heading
north for a few days, then chewed on pork ribs while Pe-Te
told me about the time he almost froze to death hunting elk
above Pagosa Springs. I laughed, told him I figured Cajuns
ought to stay the hell out of the high mountains for the
general safety of us all, then had him make me a couple of
barbecue sandwiches for the road.

I hadn't seen the kids since the day before the launch and I
wanted to stop in Austin to take them out for a hamburger or
something, but Peggy had made it clear that I was never to
stop by unannounced, and I was afraid that that *Texas Monthly*
jerk would be there, so I simply blew the kids a kiss as I drove
up 290 into the Hill Country, promising myself that we'd have
a real reunion on my way back. I had been a father *in absentia*
for only a couple of months, and it was a role I wasn't very
good at. When I was away from Matt and Sarah, as I was most
of the time now, it was hard not to convince myself that I was a
bastard for not being with them. Yet when we were together, I

always seemed to be glancing into mirrors, wondering if I appeared to be a good father to the rest of the world, rather than simply paying attention to those two remarkable little people. Peggy and I had at least succeeded with them, hadn't we? At least our children were evidence that our twelve years together had had some meaning, a more precious legacy than simply a couple of fat photo albums too painful now to open. As I drove through Dripping Springs and on through the secure and sultry darkness, eating Pe-Te's sandwiches and listening to a country disc jockey dedicate songs to "all you boys high-ballin' out on I-20," it seemed to me that driving those whining eighteen-wheelers on all-night hauls wouldn't be a bad occupation. But by the time I got to San Angelo I was so road weary that I was already looking for a new line of work, and I stopped at the Holiday and got a room.

The bar, called the Branding Iron as I recall, was still open, but empty except for a guy who looked as if he had rough-necked for ninety years and his girlfriend in vinyl pants. The bartender probably would have been just as lovely even it it weren't after midnight and if I weren't alone and awkwardly lonely. We talked while I drank better scotch than I usually drink and while she began to clean up the bar. I told her I was from Houston and she told me about the time she and her best friend, who lived there now, had gone to a club on Richmond called Cooter's, how they had quickly discovered that every male in the place was rabidly on the make.

"Did you take anyone up on it?" I asked.

She grinned, shook her head, and dipped two glasses into the rinse sink. "It's quite a world out there, isn't it?"

When she asked me what I did for a living I told her I was an engineer, my standard reply, but I was immediately sorry I hadn't tried the truth. It was late; she just wanted to get home, no doubt, and I was just another engineer. I finished my drink, went to my room and fell asleep with what seemed to be the

undeniable knowledge that had she known I was an astronaut
she would suddenly have found me irresistible and certainly
would not have gone home.

•

In the morning I was glad to be waking up alone, glad to avoid
saying a cold and sober good-bye in the unforgiving fluores-
cent light of a motel room, anxious to drive as fast as I could
across the sere sweep of west Texas. I ate breakfast in Big
Spring, made Lubbock by eleven, then rolled northwest toward New Mexico among the polled Herefords and Brangus
cattle, the stubbled cotton fields, and the scattered, persistent
pump jacks sucking oil out of the smooth skin of the plains.

My father would be full of questions, I knew, and I wanted
to get to Durango before it got late. He and Mom had gone to
Canaveral to watch the launch that Tuesday in May, and I was
able to have lunch with them and the kids in the crew quarters
the day before, but it was an awkward way to see them. They
both seemed surprisingly nervous and I was paying most of my
attention to the kids. When I got back to Houston, Dad told
me over the phone that Mom had decided she just couldn't
watch the liftoff, shutting her eyes and squeezing his hand until
that crackling roar of the solid boosters reached them. She
opened her eyes, he said, expecting to see the orbiter augering
into the alligator marshes. But all she saw was those beautiful
sun-bright streams of exhaust as we arced out over the Atlantic.

When I got to Durango, I wanted to tell my parents how
glad I was that they got to see that sight—knowing their son
was sitting atop those shrieking rockets. I wanted them to
know that I owed them a lot and that I really was trying to be a
decent adult, but I didn't know how to say it without my
words sounding like the maudlin verse in a greeting card. Still,

I hoped I would find something I would be brave enough to say.

By the time I got to Albuquerque, the stupefying Texas humidity was gone, the sooty air in the city was hot and powder dry. Just outside Bernalillo I picked up a young Navajo who was standing by the side of the road with one arm outstretched, the other clutching a paper sack. He wore a T-shirt that said KISS ME in red paint that was meant to look like lipstick, blue running shoes, and his long hair, black as space, was folded and wrapped with a cotton ribbon. He said he was going to Nageezi and I told him I could take him that far. When I asked if he was a student, he said no and then was silent.

"Where are you going?" he asked as we passed the turnoff into the Jemez Mountains.

"Home," I said. "Durango."

"What do you do for a job?" he asked, now seeming ready for conversation.

"I'm . . . an astronaut. I work for the government." This time I told the truth.

"Oh," he said, then was silent again. I could see a flannel shirt and the brown spine of a book in his sack but I couldn't read its title. The red hills were spotted with squat piñon trees, and the dark layers of the distant mesas were distinct in the evening light.

"Do you go to the moon?" the young man asked after a while.

"No. No, we only go into earth orbit these days."

"Why do the other astronauts go to the moon?"

"Well. I think the main reason they went was to see if they could get there. It was exploring."

"Oh," he said. "Do they like the moon very much?"

"I think they were glad to get back."

"I bet," he said.

When I stopped on the shoulder of the road across from the trading post at Nageezi, I asked him if he lived nearby.

"Over behind that round hill," he said. The spare ground, covered with small sage and saltbush and dry chamisa, stretched away in a series of shallow depressions and stunted hills. I held out my hand and told him my name was Jack. We shook hands and he said, "Good luck if you go to the moon," before he shut the door.

As I drove on in the advancing darkness, I couldn't help but wonder what the moon means to a Navajo teenager who lives in the barren, lunar landscape of the San Juan basin. I wondered whether he was the sort who would figure all we got out of Apollo was the boxes of rocks, or whether flying out to another world would seem as reasonable to him as hitchhiking to Albuquerque and back. I looked out the window for the moon and found a pale crescent in the western sky—not a cratered sphere caught in the empty sea of the solar system, just a new moon, small and intangible, suspended above the Carrizos.

I was tempted by the Lottaburger in Bloomfield but realized I could get to Durango in less than an hour, so I stayed on the road, anxious and wide awake, glad to be arriving in the enveloping and quiet night. I stopped on the bridge at the base of Cedar Hill and peed between the rusted tangle of trusses into the river, the same river I'd grown up beside, then crossed the state line and headed for town. Yard lights like the pinpoints of stars spread across the flat farm country, and the bright streetlights at the southern edge of town lit the new shopping mall and the five acres of asphalt that surrounded it, its empty parking lot making the whole enterprise appear out of place, unneeded. The sight of it also made me realize that this wasn't a town I knew well anymore. It would always be home; it would always belong to me in a strange, emotive sense. It was probably a possession I would never really know again, yet I could never sell it or give it away.

•

It looked as if every light in the house was on when I turned off
Seventh Avenue into the steep driveway. The sagging basket-
ball hoop and the backboard with a rectangle outlined in elec-
trician's tape had been gone for fifteen years, but it still
surprised me to find them missing. And there was a new Su-
baru they hadn't told me about. But just as I was about to get
in to investigate the new car, Dad opened the back door.

"Don't leave," he hollered. "You just got here."

I closed the door of the car and walked over to give him a
hug. He had taken his collar off and his white T-shirt was visible through the open front of his black shirt. His eyes were
bright in the dim light, but it was obvious that he had tem-
pered the wait with a tall highball or two.

"Hi, Dad," I said while he held me. "Nice car."

"Wonderful to have you," he said, and when we pulled apart
his eyes were wet. "Come on. Your mother's anxious to see
you. Yes, we're really going to enjoy it. I'll take you for a ride
tomorrow."

My mother met us in the laundry room. I gave her a kiss,
assured her that I had done nothing but eat all day, then wan-
dered through the house, sizing it up like some sort of prospec-
tive buyer. Dad handed me a drink in the living room, and
there was one for himself in his other hand.

"Sit. Sit," he said. "How was the drive?"

"Good. Just what I needed. But it's a big trip."

"You've had your share of those lately," Mom said, her voice
and her smile betraying a pride in me I didn't think I deserved.
"Did you stop in Austin?"

"No. They weren't expecting me. Peggy's pretty firm about
me scheduling my visits."

"But they're your children as well," she said. "Sometimes I

don't think she's as aware of that as she should be." She seemed
startled by what she had said, a little embarrassed, then quickly
added, "—but the kids were thrilled with the launch. Matthew
tried to be the picture of nonchalance about it all, but by the
time they got us up on the roof of that building to watch he
could hardly stand still. I think he was really kind of afraid."
"Sure he was," Dad said. "We all were. But then you were
off and it looked like everything was going to be all right. It
was hard to believe you were really inside it."
"How did Sarah react?" I asked.
"She was a real trouper," Mom said. "I don't think she expected all the noise and so much steam and smoke. She asked
me if it hurt you, and I told her it didn't hurt a bit, which was
probably something of a white lie, wasn't it?"
"Not really. You are pretty well crunched into your seat for a
bit, but it's all so quick. I hope neither of them got too upset. I
probably should have been more careful to explain to them
what to expect."
"They were fine," Dad said. "Just fine." He paused to sip his
drink. "You and their mother have put them through all kinds
of new experiences in the last six months, and that launch was
undoubtedly one of the better ones."
"It didn't take you long to bring that up," I said. "You're
welcome to give me your usual pastoral line about how these
things are so hard on the children, Dad, but you ought to give
us a little more credit."
"Don't you two start in," Mom said. "Let's leave that alone,
Richard. Jack's barely in the door."
Dad stared at the print of the Georgia O'Keeffe painting of
the church at Ranchos de Taos, a Christmas gift from his parishioners a few years before, then took a long drink of his
scotch. He had always played silence to great effect, its tension
his reliable ally. I had learned long ago to give him as much of
it as he wanted, so I said nothing, but I winked at Mom as she
went out to the kitchen.

When he was ready to speak again, he cupped his glass in his hands, leaned forward in his chair, and spoke quietly, his words coming as if they had been rehearsed: "Your mother and I went through some very difficult times during the years I was in seminary. You and Mary were barely out of diapers; she was still nursing Michael. We had to live on next to nothing. But the worst of it probably was that I felt that if I was going to be a priest I had to somehow prove my sainthood. I was going to be wearing a collar and that was going to change everything. When we fought, I tried to make her feel guilty for fighting with a holy man." He smiled. "I'm sure I was a real joy to live with. I've kind of assumed that something similar happened last year with you two. You being too busy getting ready for the flight. Peggy feeling that you had abandoned her for a spaceship."

"She was the one that did the abandoning, Dad. I didn't run off with some asshole from Austin."

"No, I don't think you abandoned her, Jack, and I doubt she really meant to abandon you. But now that your flight's over, things might seem rather different to both of you."

"You are a nosy bastard, aren't you?" I said, grinning when I said it. I knew I wasn't prepared to have him solve my marital problems so early in my visit.

"I'm in the nosy business. We clerics begin with the presumption that absolutely everything is our vital concern. That's probably why we seem so damn overbearing."

"What about that?" I asked, obviously changing the subject. "Are you really going to retire?"

"I've decided not to decide. If the Holy Spirit wants me to stay at St. Mark's after I'm sixty-five, he'll just have to let me know by keeping me alive. I guess Mom told you we buried Hal yesterday?"

"No . . ." I didn't know what to say. "The cancer?"

He nodded, his eyes got wet again, and he pulled on his nose. "They thought they had it licked. Then about a month ago they did a biopsy of a little spot in his stomach—positive —and they sent him to Denver for more tests. It had spread all through his lungs and liver. He was in the hospital here for about three weeks." Dad ran his fingers through the thick hair at his temples. The skin on the top of his head was taut and pink. "When I went to see him on Saturday, he asked me whether I would rather see him die in a hospital bed or die catching trout. So Sunday afternoon I got him dressed and snuck him out a service entrance. We drove up to Rockwood and I put him in a lawn chair next to the bank. He fished for almost an hour before he got too weak. The river seemed like such a tonic."

"Did he catch anything?"

"No," Dad said, "but he didn't mind. He died back at the hospital that night. Asked all about your flight, Jack. He was looking forward to seeing you. He said he sure would put that on his list of things to do before he died."

"It ought to be on everyone's list," I told him, wishing I could say something about Hal and how I was so sorry.

"I told Hal they ought to send burned-out priests on space missions. I bet one weightless orbit would be better than all the retreats you could ever stand. Say. I was kind of hoping that at coffee on Sunday maybe you'd talk about it a little. Everyone is very interested."

"And that way you'd cleverly get me to church."

"You can't blame a fellow for scheming a little."

"I guess it wouldn't hurt me," I said. "You sure you don't mind having a heathen address your flock?"

"Oh, I'll be keeping my eye on you," he said, then smiled as Mom came back into the room. "He said yes to my proposition, Dorothy. I only had to agree to a five-figure sum."

"Perfectly reasonable," she said, "if you'll really let him talk. No annoying interruptions."

"Dorothy!" Dad said. "You've got me confused with one of your other men of the cloth. I—"

"You be still," she said. "That kind of talk doesn't become you. And I think I'll call it a night."

"We haven't even heard about the flight yet. Come sit down. Your son has grand things to tell us."

"I'll hear everything in the morning. Good night, Jack," she said, bending over to kiss the top of my head. "And good night to you, Father Healy."

Dad blew her a kiss, then watched her disappear down the hall. I refused his offer of another drink, then changed my mind when he got up to help himself to another. He had always preferred to let my mother go to bed without him, it seemed, staying awake, drinking and reading until his head collapsed into the corner of the recliner and he slept. I remember that when I was still home I would often get up in the middle of the night and find him slumped in his chair and snoring, a book by Teilhard de Chardin lying in his lap. I always wanted to close his book, to take his watery drink to the kitchen, to nudge him and send him off to bed, but I never did. Time after time, I just turned off the lamp that stood beside the chair, then slowly made my way across the carpet, leaving him alone in the darkness.

But that night there was my mission to discuss, and his book stayed shut, and I drank with him into the early morning. He wanted to hear about the reason for the countdown delay, wondered whether we were aware of how much media attention we were getting, asked me all about the EVA, how the backpack worked, and what it felt like as I flew away from the orbiter. I remember that when I was in high school kids used to tell me what a good listener he was, but that ability to listen always seemed limited to the hours he wore the collar. I don't think Mike or Mary or I ever thought he paid any sort of rapt attention to us. But that night, he was undeniably entranced by my descriptions of the flight. Space seemed to be a subject that tapped the inveterate tinkerer in him as well as the starry-eyed theologian. He was enthralled with the thought that humans could go to inhuman realms, and the idea of seeing the earth spin in the blackness seemed almost sacramental to him.

"When we saw those first pictures on TV of you and Bill Grimes out there, completely away from the shuttle, I couldn't believe it. Your mother and I both had big tears streaming down our faces. I mean, good heavens, there you were in ab-solute space. I thought, what a very lucky man he is."

"I know I am," I said. "Whenever I had a second just to drink it all in, that was what crossed my mind. Why do I get to do this? I felt so damn...fortunate. Why not Mary or Matt ...or Hal McGinnis?"

"Matthew's time will come. He'll have a hell of a life. And Hal...I'm going out to see Jane tomorrow, by the way. Losing her dad on top of everything else has been quite a blow. Hal's brother and his wife were going to leave today. Come with me. I told her I'd try to drag you along."

"Sure. I'd like to," I said. I told him about how we had finally snared the satellite, and then I demanded a bed.

"Off you go," he said. "I'll be along in a bit."

•

The next morning, I asked my father if he had heard from Mike recently as we drove west out of town, crossing the run-off swollen river, then twisting through the bare canyon that was still and shadowed in the morning light. Mike had called from Denver on Tuesday, he said, and he seemed to be doing better. He was working at a bakery in the mornings and spend-ing his afternoons at St. Andrew's, helping in the kitchen and cleaning the room where the street people slept, their canvas pads strewn across the checkered linoleum floor.

"As long as he stays on the Thorazine, he seems to do just fine," Dad said. "But then for no reason he'll stop taking it, and I'll get a call that he's threatening Father Long with a Buck knife because John takes his mind away while he sleeps. John

Long has been tremendous with Michael. You remember John, don't you? We wanted to bring Michael to the Cape with us, but since he finally seems to be getting settled, we decided we'd better not. And I'm sure Mary was sick about not being able to come."

"She called a couple of days after I got back to Houston," I said. "Vintage Mary. She was certainly not going to be overly impressed by some expensive federal enterprise that smacks of militarism, but she did say she wished she could have seen the launch. I told her I hoped there'd be another one sometime. The next time, she said, she could guarantee she wouldn't be strapped with a ten-month-old."

It was still hard to imagine Mary as a mother. She had not married Robert until she was thirty-three, and the daughter, named Adrian, had not arrived until a few days following Mary's thirty-ninth birthday. She would be devoted to her child, I was sure of that—she would be patient and endlessly understanding, and her fascination with Adrian's progress would smother other, less captivating concerns. Yet Mary was utterly independent, and it was hard to imagine her surrendering to the mundane commitments of motherhood.

The eldest of the three of us, Mary had very decidedly emancipated herself at seventeen when she went to college in California. She seldom wrote or telephoned our parents, and her Christmas visits were always short, plagued by a kind of unspoken argument about her responsibility to her family. When Mary had her first one-person show in Berkeley a couple of years after she graduated, she didn't tell any of us about it until the show had already come down. Mom and Dad were crushed that she had not wanted them to see it, or to come to the opening, but she professed shock at why they would have even considered it, telling them her work was tentative and unfocused, missing the point entirely.

I had always struggled with the question of what I wanted to do with myself, with what would ever be worth doing for dozens of years; Michael had struggled with the neurochemical chaos inside his brain; but Mary had always been resolute. Painting was, for her, not so much a decision as an obligation. She was very critical of her talent, never satisfied with a specific piece, yet she painted, year after year, as if she were meeting the terms of a demanding personal contract.

I had never understood what she and Robert shared, nor did I know how this zoology professor and the abstract painter had ever managed to meet. When she spoke of him—on the few occasions when we talked on the telephone—she would only refer to him in the most cursory way, always saying how busy he was, how his job at Cal was all-consuming. About young Adrian, however, I was happy to discover that Mary was willing to talk at length. Adrian, it seemed, was her first creation in which she was willing to take some pride.

My father said he was sure Mary was still painting, but that since she had stopped teaching when Adrian was born, he was worried that their financial situation was getting rather pinched. Yet he was gratified and a little relieved to hear from Mary that a gallery in San Francisco had recently sold two of her large paintings.

The highway met Cherry Creek and followed its twisting course beneath the snow-shrouded peaks of the La Platas. The aspen were in leaf; the trees swayed in the warm breeze of early summer, their white trunks straight and thick and knotted. Dad turned onto the dirt road in Thompson Park, the tires of his new blue car churning a column of dust behind us. He waved at a rancher in a straw hat and tall rubber boots who was irrigating a green hay field, then drove another mile before turning into the lane that led past the barn and the hay shed to the house. Jane, dressed in jeans and a snap-button shirt, her dark, gray-streaked hair held up with a silver clip, was tossing scratch to red chickens when she saw us. She emptied the grain from her bucket and came over to the car, hugging Dad first, then holding her arms out to me.

"Hello, spaceman," she said, "You don't look like it's harmed you." Her broad face was tan and smooth, her smile as disarming as ever. "Welcome back to solid ground."

I told her it felt good to be back. Her shirt was rolled up to her elbows and she saw me glance at the smooth stump at her right wrist. I had heard about the accident, of course, and I knew that her hand was gone, but the visual evidence was nonetheless an unsettling surprise.

"Oh yes, you haven't seen this," she said, lifting the stump up to my eyes. "What do you think? Some people pierce their ears. I chop off my hand." Always brash and uninhibited, Jane had no doubt thrust the evidence of her misfortune into dozens of people's faces in the months since she had lost her hand and her husband.

"Very becoming," I said. "I like it. How are you getting along?"

"Well, if it wasn't my goddamned right one it wouldn't have been so bad, but I swear it's like trying to work with five toes and an ax handle this way. But . . . all things considered, I—"

"She's doing beautifully," Dad said. "I saw her saddle a horse when I was out the other day and she didn't seem to have any trouble."

"But you didn't see it roll off his back when I stepped in the stirrup, did you?" She grinned, told us to follow her into the house, and I watched her as she turned and marched toward the back door. I had always been attracted to Jane; we had even dated—both of us feeling a weird incestuousness about it—during one summer when I was home from college, but I was surprised to find that as a one-handed widow now pushing forty Jane seemed so strong and so alluring.

Kenny had been dead for almost a year; she had been hospitalized for two months and had worn a back brace for two more. Her hand was severed by the hitch of the horse trailer when it landed beside the overturned truck. Kenny was also thrown out of the pickup and was crushed by the side of the

trailer. Both horses lived for over an hour before a state patrol-
man finally took out his revolver and shot them. The neighbors got the last cutting of hay in, and Jane hired an illegal
from Chihuahua to feed for her that winter. Dad said she
wanted to sell the cows and half the place. As we sat down at
the kitchen table, she told me she planned to keep the horses
and to stay out in the park indefinitely.

"I had thought about finding a house in town for Dad and
me, but I didn't really want to live in town. Now that he's
gone, I'm sure I'll stay put. I saw you on TV, Jack. Couldn't
really tell it was you out on your spacewalk, but you looked
great floating around inside the shuttle. You guys must have
had a terrific time."

"I doubt they got a lick of work done," Dad said.

"Strictly recreational," I told them; then I said something to
Jane about her dad. Hal and my father had been friends since
Dad first arrived at St. Mark's. But unlike Dad, Hal was always
as captivated by the skies as I was. He and I used to spot con-
stellations and watch lunar eclipses in my parents' backyard,
and I was fascinated by his stories about the Northern Lights
from his years spent in Alberta. I got a telegram from him in
Houston years ago on the day the first Viking lander touched
down on Mars. It just read, WE MADE IT! BEST, HAL.

"He watched your launch at the hospital," Jane said. "He
told all the nurses and technicians that he had a friend flying on
the shuttle and that they, by God, couldn't sedate him."

"When we got back," Dad said, "he had to hear every last
detail about the launch. I brought him one of those souvenir
hats that says NASA, and he wore it in bed while we watched
the landing." He paused. "I'm going to miss that man."

"Me too," Jane said; then she got up from the table. "Shoot,
it's after eleven. It's not too early for a beer, is it?" She went to
the refrigerator. "Come on. We'll take these out to the porch."

"I'll meet you there," I said. "I want to go look at your
horses." I took a beer and walked through the corrals by the

barn and out into the pasture. Four horses grazed on the
bromegrass near the south fence. They picked their heads up
and studiously watched me approach. A bay mare finally took
a few steps in my direction, then stopped when she noticed I
wasn't carrying a grain bucket. When I reached her, I rubbed
her neck and let her smell the bottle to prove it was nothing of
interest. The other three, still wary of a hatless man in khaki
pants, kept their distance. A second mare, surely ready to foal,
had a big, bell-shaped belly, and her steps seemed labored as
she moved along the fence. I ought to be a horseman, I
thought. I ought to trim hooves, attend the births of pinto
colts, spend weekday afternoons in smoky sale barns, and tell
inquiring strangers that I was a stockman when I hung my hat
on the racks in the local cafés. The bay mare, still not convinced, grabbed at the neck of the bottle with her mouth and
hit it against her teeth. She stepped away, and I turned back
toward the barn. I could see Jane and Dad sitting in a swing on
the porch, and I waved but they didn't notice. The sun was
high in the cloudless sky, and the sweet aroma of the cottonwoods wafted up from the creek. A magpie scolded me from a
fence post, and the horses went back to the grass.

I couldn't hear what Dad was saying as I came around the
corner of the house. Jane nodded and said, "Yes, I suppose so,"
then waved to me to join them.

"That mare looks like she's about ready," I said.

"I hope so, poor thing. She's so uncomfortable, especially
now that it's getting hot. She's a sweetheart. This is her first
foal. I'm a little nervous about it. Knowing me, I'll probably
end up with a huge vet bill for having him come watch a perfectly normal birth. I told your dad I'm going to ride the roan
up to the cabin tomorrow to get some of Dad's things. You can
have Brenda, that bay that likes you, if you want to come."

"The cabin?"

"That hunting shack of Dad's up in Echo Basin. Want to?"

"Yes. I do. But you have to promise not to laugh at me when

she makes me look ridiculous. I haven't been on a horse in ages."

"I thought all you Texans could cowboy," Dad said.

"Maybe all those Texans can," I said. "I just use their license plates. What time?" On the way to the car, Jane suggested I come out about noon; she said she'd have the horses trailered and the whiskey packed in the saddlebags.

"Don't get him too relaxed," Dad told her. "I've got him reserved for Sunday morning."

"I'll take care of him," she said. "And thanks, Dick. You've been awfully sweet to us, to me," She pushed the door of the car shut, and the way she looked at my father in that instant made me aware of how close the two of them had become. Something in her face, too—perhaps it was the sorrow it still reflected, perhaps it was a nascent hint of happiness—made my feelings for her seem like a sudden infatuation.

•

At dinner that night, my mother was worried about Mike, about whether he would end up in the hospital again, and I told her I had thought about going up to Denver before heading back to Houston. I hadn't seen Michael in almost two years, and I wasn't particularly anxious to see him again and to hear his incoherent stories. But Mike was doing very well, they said, and I admitted that it would be good for the two of us to be back in touch.

Mike was only two years behind me in school and we had been close until I was a junior or senior in high school. I was student body president and was, no doubt, rather impressed with myself, and I began to be horribly embarrassed by a brother who would lean for hours against the tiled walls of the science-wing restroom because, he said, the kids in the hallways wanted to steal his clothes. Mom remained Michael's great ally during the two years he tried to go to college, and although Dad had read a seemingly endless series of articles and books about schizophrenia, he, like me, responded to Mike with a certain exasperation.

"It would mean a lot to Michael if you could stop for a day or so," Mom said. "He really needs to know he has a family who cares about him." My mother's voice always assumed a terrible sadness when she talked about Michael, the child to whom, for reasons I doubt even she knew, she had always been closest, the son whose private anguish had deepened her love and protection. When she spoke with concern about Michael, I always wanted to give her a kind of comic hug and to tell her with unfounded optimism that he was going to be just fine. But I never did, perhaps because I somehow sensed that she knew a contradictory truth.

"I'll call and find out when I have to be back. I'd enjoy the drive through the mountains. Mike and I could catch up on a lot of things. And doesn't Jane's offer to ride up to Hal's cabin sound great?" I asked, getting away from the subject I knew they were desperate to talk about, but the one that I somehow couldn't address.

I borrowed a pair of boots from Dad on Saturday and he insisted that I take his straw hat as well. I told him I'd feel a little stupid in a cowboy hat, but he convinced me that without it the sun would burn me up. When I got to Jane's, the horses, as promised, were in the trailer, and she had sandwiches for us to eat in the truck. She asked me to drive, and I'm sure she noticed how timidly I negotiated Mancos Hill. I was more at ease on the Forest Service road that led into the basin, but pulling the heavy trailer was unsettling and the conversation was often cut by my silent attention to the road.

"I could see the La Platas from orbit," I said to break the silence. "They were just a minuscule white group of ridges, but they were easy to spot. It's funny. I felt so proprietary about this place, seeing it from two hundred miles up."

"Do you want to go again?"

"I'd love to. But working for the government gets pretty gruesome. You never know what in the hell they've got planned for you. And ass kissing is the only real talent you're required to have. If Peggy and the kids moved farther away, I'd have some real second thoughts. There was a time when all I ever imagined doing was teaching astronomy at some little college somewhere. Now that possibility seems so remote I can hardly imagine it. Maybe I'm destined to become a beer distributor, like all the other ex-astronauts."

"I was sorry to hear about you two splitting up, Jack. I always assumed that you two really had made that pact that everybody aims for. But... did it have something to do with her finally deciding she had to see if she could walk without a net? Not that it's any of my business."

"What do you mean?"

"I know what it's like to live in somebody's shadow. Kenny was Mr. Wonderful around here, on every committee and invited to every social event, the heartthrob of all the horny young wives whose husbands were getting fat. They all thought I was just this weird complication in his life, an aloof bitch who wouldn't even join the bridge clubs. I was in the hospital, but they told me that at his funeral they had to set up loudspeakers in the parish hall and out in the courtyard so everyone who came could hear the service. Poor Kenny. He would have loved to know he could draw that kind of crowd. He wanted to run for county commissioner. Now that he's gone, people just can't associate me with him anymore. It's the first time I've ever really felt like an individual, I guess."

I pulled the truck to the edge of the road when Jane motioned toward the sign that marked the trail. "You and Peggy probably do have something in common," I said. We backed the horses out of the trailer. Their saddles were already on, so all I had to do was to fumble at getting the curb bit into Brenda's mouth and tie the nylon bags to the saddle skirts. I watched Jane tie a rolled canvas pannier behind the cantle of her saddle, anxious to help but afraid to offer. She mounted the roan gelding, then held the reins in her teeth while she struggled to adjust the stirrups with her left hand.

"Son of a bitch," she said. "I forgot that my irrigator used this saddle last week." She turned to me, her voice softened as if she was telling me something she wouldn't have shared with everyone. "Doctor keeps telling me it's time for a prosthesis, but, God, I don't want to wear some stupid hook or a plastic hand. I don't care how much easier it would be." I didn't know how to respond, so I was silent again.

The trail was wide as it led into the timber, and the horses walked abreast. Brenda was a good walker and seemed relaxed in the trees, but the roan, named Sport, snorted and seemed to hunt for an excuse to spook. Jane held him on a tight rein and slapped his ears with her handless arm a time or two before he abandoned his hopes for chaos. "So," she said, "you want to become a beer distributor."

"Maybe a cowboy," I said. "This seems to suit me."

"I like your hat. Makes you look like Smiley Burnette."

"It's my father's fault. The image would be more like the Lone Ranger if it was my own hat."

"That's the astronaut coming out. You want people to think you're perfect."

"But you don't buy it in my case, right?"

"This whole space business...I don't know," she said. "I just have never got it. I'm glad for you, Jack, I don't mean that, but isn't it just a big show? All for the patriotic glory of it?"

"My Rotary Club speech about the space program would put you to sleep," I said. "But no. I think it's pretty important. Even going to the moon made sense if you accept the idea that you ought to go wherever you can get to."

"So now we know the moon is rocky and gray and wouldn't be much of a vacation."

"There's an old book by Oriana Fallaci about the space program in the years before the first moon landing. She began her research as this outrageous skeptic, but by the end she seemed to think space travel was some sort of valiant symbolic quest. She interviewed Wally Schirra, who is your classic right-stuff kind of guy, Spartan and tight-lipped as they come. But old Wally ended up gushing to her that the moon and Mars are ugly islands. Nobody would want to live there, he said. But the reason for going to the ugly islands was to prove you could do it, so you could keep searching for the beautiful islands."

"Assuming there are some."

"Oh, they're there."

"An act of faith?"

"An act of a telescope. I mean, I don't know if we'll ever find one that has oxygen and aspen trees, but that doesn't bother me. We have to look because that's what we're programmed for—I mean, maybe even genetically. Basically what we do as a species is poke around, snoop, isn't it?"

We rode out of the trees into a small meadow, its grass still matted by the weight of the winter's snow. A doe that was drinking in a quiet meander of the creek looked warily at us, then bounded into the stand of spruce that swept up toward the barren rock. The trail narrowed at the far side of the meadow, then made two switchbacks as it climbed through the damp floor of the forest. Sport was winded enough to be steady now, and Brenda followed so obediently that I had nothing to do but sit. The cabin, built out of pine planks that must have been hauled up thirty years before, stood on a small bank of bald rock. Loose tar paper on the roof flapped in the mountain wind, and the one window was covered with cardboard. We tied the horses to a fallen log, then looked inside.

The small room smelled musty but strangely sweet. It was dusty and dark and the mice had made themselves at home; their dry turds were scattered across the table, the long counter, and the plastic sheet that covered the bed. Hal had left four boxes of split wood next to the rusted Ashley, and the dishes were carefully stacked beside the washbasin. Jane looked inside a three-legged chest of drawers for the things she had come for—a deerskin jacket, an old revolver, a thick roll of topographical maps, and a stack of books. She took them outside, sat down on the west side of the shack in the late-afternoon sun, and put them inside the canvas pannier. "I didn't like the idea of these things that were important to him sitting up here where they could be stolen now that he's gone," she said. I sat down beside her and could see Ute Mountain in the west, and off to the southwest, the high plateau of Mesa Verde, cut by its finger canyons. "He only liked to come here alone," she said. "I used to suggest that the two of us ride up here occasionally, but he always had some lame excuse. Then out of the blue one day he'd call and say he was on his way out the door, headed for the cabin. Always a great urgency about it. He kept that little telescope here too. But he brought it down last fall when he discovered some hunters had stayed here." She finished the packing, then took a pint of scotch out of her jacket pocket.

"You'll join me, I trust," she said before she put the bottle to her lips. "This has become quite a habit since the accident. I used to wonder why people drank alone, but I don't wonder anymore. I suppose I count Johnnie Walker among my best friends these days." She grinned, and considered before she spoke again. "What's it been like for you alone, Jack?"

"I've been lucky," I said. "With the mission, I've been busy enough, gone enough that I haven't really had to face it. I'm sure that's part of the reason why I decided to drive up. I still wasn't ready to face the office routine and that god-awful empty house of mine."

Jane stared into the distance. "I haven't washed my windows for nearly a year," she said. "I leave the newspapers in rolls and stack them like kindling in the kitchen closet. Maybe this is what they mean by mourning, but I think it's inertia. It's a sort of weird inertia caused by being left alive. Like I'm numb. Like

I just don't give a damn about anything. Even when we knew it was just a matter of days for Dad, I couldn't cry. I couldn't tell him the things I always assumed I would say."

I put my hand on her leg, smoothing the faded fabric of her jeans, and Jane turned to me and kissed me. She smelled wonderful, like my memories of Peggy, and she pressed herself against me. She lifted my hat off when we looked at each other again. "I'm not so inert that I couldn't make love to you," she said, her voice quiet now, its cynical edge evaporating. "I don't think I could have till . . . well . . ."

We stood and went inside the cabin. I sat on the edge of the table while she pulled the plastic from the bed. She sat on the edge of the bed, kicked off her boots, and unbuttoned her shirt with her single hand. Her breasts were tan and round and lovely, her nipples hard. "You stop wearing bras when you lose a hand," she said with a shy smile. "Come here, for heaven's sake."

I was glad to follow instructions. She must have known how much I wanted her, but for some reason I preferred to pretend I was merely compliant. I went to the bed and undressed before I touched her again. We stared at each other, saying nothing while I stood, then I curled beside her on the cold cotton bedspread. I reached for her head and found her mouth again. It had been nearly two months since I had made love to anyone, too much aching time since that strange weekend in April when Barbara Collingwood, another astronaut, and I had gone to Padre Island for the expressed purpose of coming to each other's carnal rescue. There was something similar happening with Jane and me, but bound up in it too, for both of us, were the accident and her dad and our strange connection to each other shaped by that backwater corner of Colorado. We held each other desperately, shouting and sweating, almost fighting, before we were finished and were again aware of the cold.

I pulled the bedspread over us; Jane dozed with her head on my shoulder. Her handless arm was stretched across my chest and I could see the pale, precise scar that curled around the stump. I kissed her forehead. "Let's stay," I said. "The night. There's lots of wood."

"We'll bother the mice," she said. "Won't be much of a dinner. That . . . was the first time since Kenny. God, it seems like ages ago."

"You think your dad would mind us staying here in his private retreat?"

"If he knew you were here I think he'd arrange some sort of dispensation."

Before we got up, Jane mentioned the accident again, telling me it had been a long time before she realized she was mourning the loss of her hand as well as her husband. "At first, it seemed like such a little thing. Kenny, the horses were dead— gone forever—and my hand, well, it was nothing in comparison. Then, after a few months, I started to get angry, really mad, about being left with this stump. I was alone, and I was damn lonely, I suppose, and to top it all off, now I was some sort of freak."

"No," I said, "you don't—"

"You don't realize what it does to you, Jack. Everything you do is a big procedure, and you're reminded a million times a day of how incompetent you are. Then, finally, the resignation sets in, and that's the paralyzing part."

"But you haven't really had to give anything up, have you?" I asked, as if I had to counter with a feeble optimism.

"I've given up taking my abilities for granted," she said. "That's something more than you'd guess it would be. Before, I basically assumed I could do anything I chose. There weren't any limits. Now, the limits are the first things that cross my mind."

I built a fire in the Ashley when I got up from the bed, and at dusk I built a second fire in a ring of stones that lay off to the side of the cabin. We unsaddled the horses and Jane tied their lead ropes to a snag that looked as if long ago it had been hit by lightning. We sat by the campfire in the thickening darkness, ate two apples and a candy bar, and finished the scotch. I took Hal's deerskin jacket out of the pannier and put it on; Jane wrapped herself in a wool blanket. The crescent moon, looking as if it had leaped above Ute Mountain, had grown to nearly a quarter, and the serpentine stars of Hydra hung above it. I pointed out Betelgeuse and the bears and tried to spot the dim outline of Pegasus, but could not. Before we went inside, I told Jane that from orbit, the only way we could locate the earth at night was to find the arc where the stars stopped. It seemed so strange that that sweep of total darkness, of emptiness, was the familiar earth itself, just a rocket's throw away.

Brenda and Sport began to whinny in the dead of night. When I opened the door nothing seemed to be wrong, but I waited until they were quiet before I went back inside. I don't think I slept again. I remember lying in Hal's bed until it grew light, imagining how improbable it was that I was there in his mountaintop retreat, his daughter asleep beside me.

●

I didn't realize what I had done—or what I'd forgotten to do —until Jane was awake, kidding me about spending my Sunday morning with an old widow-woman instead of attending my father's church. By then it was too late to make it back to town to give the talk I had promised him I would, but we hurried anyway, closing up the cabin and riding the horses back down to the truck in a flurry of preoccupied and guilty activity. At Jane's ranch, I tried to slow down long enough to thank her for the outing and the night, but she hurried me on my way, knowing better than I did, I suppose, how disappointed my dad would be.

My mother was in the kitchen when I got back to the house; she didn't say anything when she looked up from the letter she was writing at the table. I sat down in a chair across from her and asked her where he was.

"He's in the backyard. Trimming roses. But don't go out. I'm not sure he'd speak to you."

"I completely forgot," I said. "I'm so sorry. We decided to stay up at the cabin. I didn't remember until this morning, and by then it was too late to get down in time."

"He told them you suddenly had been called back to Texas. He was so embarrassed, Jack. That was the worst of it."

"Jesus. That was probably the cruelest thing I could have done to him."

"Well... just leave him alone."

"I guess I ought to go ahead and go now that he's told people I have."

"Did you have a good time?"

"Yes... very, but I ought to apologize at least."

"Wait till this evening. You two can talk after dinner. Just let him garden for now."

"I better just say something and go," I said, and I got up and went out the back door. Dad was kneeling in the brown soil of the rose bed, his shirt off, his hands in cotton gloves. I sat on the grass beside him and watched him work before I spoke. His back was moist; his belly looked bigger than I had imagined it was.

"I just wanted to say that I'm terribly sorry," I said. "It wasn't intentional. We decided to stay and I forgot. I just forgot."

He turned the soil with a hand spade. "The worst thing about being a parent," he said, "is that it's irreversible." The dark soil was damp; it stuck to his ragged gloves. "I don't want an apology; don't want to accept one. It didn't matter."

"Yes it did. You asked me to do something for you and I let you down."

"You're thirty-six years old, Jack. You're free to let down

anyone you want to." He still did not look at me. "That cabin meant a lot to Hal. Now I guess the wind and snow will have it ruined before long. Come back and see us, Jack."

"I guess I ought to go, shouldn't I?"

"We've had a good visit. Find your mother before you go. Give the kids a big hug for us."

"I'll give you a hug."

"Let's wait till next time," he said, patting the soil with his broad hands as I turned back to the house.

My mother was still at the table and I told her I was on my way to Denver. "I'd like to see Mike in good shape," I said.

She got up, embraced me and held me for a moment. "I'm sorry, Jack," she said. "This family is funny, isn't it?" It was something I had heard her say dozens of times before. Whenever one of us fought with my father, whenever Mary's correspondence dwindled to months of silence, whenever the voices began to shout inside Michael's head, my mother would smile sadly and tell us what a funny clan we were. She knew, of course, that our troubles were much like any other family's. In saying we were funny, she meant to tell us how readily we could break her heart.

I got my things, drove through the quiet Sunday streets and out of town to Jane's. No one answered the door. I checked the barn and the outbuildings and walked through the near pasture. God, I wanted to see her again. I left a note taped to the door, and went back through town, drove east into the tall ponderosas and over Wolf Creek Pass. I found a phone at a gas station in Del Norte.

"Come to Texas," I said to Jane when she answered.

"How was he?" she asked.

"Hurt. Furious. Sad that he had to have kids. Will you come?"

"I'll keep you posted," she said. "And thank you."

I was in Pueblo by dusk. The interstate was almost empty and the bare brown plains rolled away in the darkness. The moon at last lifted above the high hump of Pikes Peak, but it couldn't keep me company, couldn't keep my mind off what I had done to my father, or the way he had hurried me out of his garden. Even the recurrent image of Jane—her shirt unbuttoned, her arms opening out to me—couldn't convince me that I had ever done a damn bit of good for anyone.

two

The dark air that hung over Denver in winter like the lid of a heavy pot had been washed clean by summer rain; from the running path I could see the thin swirls of snowfields that still hugged the peaks of the Front Range, and beneath the mountains the city sprawled across the sloping prairie. I had spent the night in a dreary motel on South Colorado Boulevard, eating Fritos, drinking beer, watching three former Playmates on the Playboy Channel discuss whether orgasm was always essential. I woke up early, drove to Washington Park, and started to run, my legs still stiff from the trip on horseback. The morning was cool and still, and it felt surprisingly good to be back in Denver—a place where I had never actually lived, but the one large city where I nonetheless felt I might belong. I had gone to

school twenty miles away, in Boulder; Peggy had grown up
here; I had had a variety of friends who were based in Denver
at least briefly; and in recent years I had made a steady series of
trips up from Houston to the Martin Marietta plant, first to test
and comment on the prototype manned maneuvering units,
then to train for our mission on the MMU simulator—a machine that really did have an uncanny ability to convince you
that you were flying a rocket backpack through the empty sea
of space.

Running at the edges of the park's small and glassy lakes, I
kept thinking about Jane, about how she had kindled a kind of
unrest in me, about how now we had to settle whatever it was
we started—and I tried to convince myself that the abrupt end
to my visit with my parents was nothing to brood over. But I
knew from three decades of experience that I would have to
harbor my familiar filial guilt until Dad's tone on the telephone
told me I had been forgiven. Maybe Mike and I could call them
together; surely that would please both of them. My penance
for standing up my father in front of his entire parish simply
would be to make contact with my brother, my brother the
crazy, to have an honest talk with him, to let him know I really
did love him, and to give Dad some glimpse of my continuing
concern.

But I didn't want to go to St. Andrew's and to see all the
blank-eyed old boys who lived in heavy, ragged coats in the
hot weather of summer, who stood in line at the kitchen as if
they had already given up the ghost, their lives so hideously
quiet. I wasn't one of those people who could serve them stew,
or work at the Goodwill once a week, and feel invigorated by
the experience. People like Mike or the derelict men at the mission somehow seemed like cruel and uncomfortable challenges
to my success and my material ease. They were capable of
making me feel even more guilty than my father was, and the
questions they inevitably raised about why I had not suffered
the same fates as they had were questions I couldn't confront. I

was dazed by their desperate conditions, by their crumbling hopes, and never did any more in response to them than to write modest, occasional checks at my desk in the calm seclusion of the family room.

But for once, perhaps, I could do a bit more. Maybe Mike and I could go watch the Zephyrs play, or climb the Flatirons; maybe have dinner and a few beers at the Brewery Bar and reminisce about the days when we conspired to build an invincible raft we would launch into the languid waters of the lower Animas and that would take us on to the silty San Juan, to the boiling brown Colorado, and at last to the shimmering Sea of Cortez. Maybe it would be good for both of us just to remember those secret plans and pacts, the boyhood hopes that bound us together until Mike began to torment himself and I pulled away, afraid.

The commuter traffic began to get thick before long and the number of runners increased, their sweating faces flushed and serious as they nodded when we met. The sun rose high enough to begin to be hot, and I ran for just thirty minutes or so before I got back into the car. At the motel again, I showered and dressed, putting on a tie for the first time since I'd come to Colorado. But when I studied myself in the mirror I realized that it probably made more sense to meet Mike without one, so I took the tie off and zipped it inside my bag. I wasn't sure where I would spend the next few nights, but I knew I didn't want to keep staying out on that commercial strip with all the red-nosed traveling sales reps, so I checked out of the motel and eased my wheezing Honda—its injectors tuned for the soupy, sultry air of Houston—into the traffic on the Valley Highway.

•

The air seemed damp in the shade of the small, spireless Gothic church, and I rubbed my hand against its smooth brick, dark-

ened by age and the city's soot, as I walked toward the door of
the two-story rectory that was connected to the church by a
breezeway. I pushed open the massive wooden door and
walked into a room that was empty except for a long, low,
threadbare couch and a lovely old Navajo rug that lay on the
polished terrazzo. A wooden crucifix hung on one white wall;
on another was a framed poster—a photograph of a chalice and
a loaf of bread with the words JESUS OF NAZARETH REQUESTS
THE HONOR OF YOUR PRESENCE AT A DINNER TO BE GIVEN IN HIS
HONOR. I could see down the dark hallway toward the doors to
two rooms where the lights were on, and as I started toward
them, a man in a black cassock emerged. He wore leather sandals and a clerical collar; his close-cropped hair stuck out in
every direction, and his short, narrow beard did not conceal the
sharp cleft in his chin. He smiled when he said, "Hi. Can I help
you?"

"Yes. I'm looking for Michael Healy."

"I'm sure he's down in the kitchen right now. I'll show you
the stairs. Are you...?"

"I'm his brother."

"Well, then you must be Jack," he said. His eyes brightened
as he put out his hand. "John Long. I think we met here several
years ago."

"I think we did briefly. Good to see you again."

"How are your folks?" he asked.

"They're well, thanks. I was just down there."

"Your dad's one of my favorites. I always look forward to
the clergy conferences so he and I can catch up. We're bridge
partners—not very good, I'm afraid. But I've spent several
memorable evenings at the bridge table with him, drinking
sherry and laughing, no doubt annoying our more serious
competitors. Say, we've heard a lot about you lately. We don't
have a TV here, but from what I read in the paper, I guess
your—what? flight or mission?—went very well. Congratulations."

"Yes it did," I said. "Thank you. It went real well. And how are things here?"

"Hectic. With our ongoing projects; some new things we're trying to get started. We get tired, but we know this is what the Holy Spirit would have us do, and we try to do it joyfully. Michael gives us a lot of help."

"How is Mike?"

"Well, you'll see for yourself, but I think he's doing quite well. There's no question that he still has some of what the doctor calls psychotic episodes. He may always have them. But I think he feels he has a home here, a niche, and Michael's faith is very important to him. Come on. Let's go find him. Cup of coffee?"

I followed Father Long down the hall to the head of the stairs. He didn't look as though he could be any older than I was, but there was something in his manner, in the way he spoke, that made him seem like one of my dad's contemporaries, and it was easy to see why they were friends. Although no one ever considered Dad to be any sort of radical priest, he did have a reputation for being more readily sympathetic with what you might call the socially conscious wing of the church than with those who considered "street ministries" rather seamy and ill-advised. At the foot of the carpeted stairway, John Long stopped at an enormous stainless-steel coffee machine, filled a Styrofoam cup, and handed it to me. "He's back in the kitchen," he said, pointing across the long, empty tables that were covered with butcher paper. "I'll let you make your own introduction. By the way, you're welcome to stay here while you're in town. We have a guest room, a guest cubicle really. Michael can show you where it is."

"Thanks," I said. "I'm not sure yet what my plans are. And . . . I know my dad appreciates all you've done for Mike. They don't worry about him here."

"They shouldn't. Stop by my office later. I'd like to show you a letter I got the other day from Michael's psychiatrist.

Perhaps you ought to see it." He put his hand on my shoulder before he turned to go up the stairs.

I wound my way across the concrete floor, between the low wooden benches covered with peeling red paint, tucked under the tables' edges. The swinging door that led into the kitchen was propped open with a number-ten can of corn, and I stood in the doorway before I entered. A plump man in a white uniform stirred a large kettle on top of the Monarch range; a young woman was slicing heads of iceberg lettuce with a chef's knife, a scarf pulled low on her black forehead and tied at the nape of her neck. Michael stood at the deep commercial sink, rinsing baking pans, stacking them on the counter. He wore jeans and a white sleeveless T-shirt. The dark hair that he had worn long for more than a decade was pulled back and held in a single braid. I had forgotten how handsome he was—tall and muscular, his face smooth and pale, his square jaw as sharply defined as Dad's. "Mike," I said, and he turned to look at me. He didn't smile; he put down the pan he held and dried his hands on a towel as he came toward me.

"Well, Jack," he said, as if he had been expecting me. "So here you are." He looked at my hand for an instant before he took it. I started to hug him, then stopped.

"So here I am. It's good to see you, Mike. Did you know I was coming?"

"You told me, didn't you? You must have told me the other day when you were floating around out there."

"Oh..." I said. "Well, good. I'm glad it worked out so our paths could cross. It's been a long time. When was the last time we saw each other?"

"I guess it was at home. You and Peggy brought the kids up from Texas while Mary was home one time. I was there. I don't think Robert was."

"No. I think he was in Costa Rica that summer. Three years ago, I guess." I took a sip of coffee, then awkwardly fingered the white cup. "Listen. Am I interrupting you right now?

Maybe I ought to come back after lunch; we could take off for a while."

"I should help Wendell and Lucy get everything ready." He turned to them. "Wendell, Lucy, this is Jack, my brother, Jack." Wendell nodded; Lucy smiled and said hello.

"I'll let him get back to work," I said.

"You can eat lunch here," Mike said in his familiar monotone. "Then we can go for a walk. I used to work here in the afternoon, but that was when I worked at the bakery in the morning. But they were way too jealous of me at the bakery. Especially that girl who was pregnant, so I stopped going."

"Why were they jealous of you?"

"I don't know. I guess she wanted me to be her baby; it was still inside her and she tried to get me to be it. I wouldn't though. I don't want to be a child all over again."

"No. I don't blame you," I said. "I'll come back down after while. Father Long said he had something he wanted me to see." I set the Styrofoam cup on the counter; Mike picked up the cup, drank the last of the coffee in a single gulp, then threw the cup in a trash can.

"Good, Jack," he said.

•

The wall behind Father Long's desk was filled with books, and I noticed a copy of Martin Buber's *I And Thou,* a book my father often referred to, as he handed me the letter he wanted me to read.

Dear Father Long (the letter began):

I saw Michael Healy in evaluation today. He had been referred to me by Wells Walker, a general practitioner who attends your church. My understanding is that he has lived at the church since his release from the state hospital eight months ago.

I found Michael, a 34-year-old white male, to be pleasant and cooperative, although he does have a rather flat affect. His records show that he was diagnosed as suffering from a dementia praecox (schizophrenia) as early as 1969. Based on my examination today, I would certainly concur with that diagnosis, although I might add that I noted, in addition, some rather pronounced paranoid elements. Michael denied having had success with drug therapies over the years, but he did agree that while he stayed carefully on his medication (principally Thorazine), "the voices quiet down sometimes."

I was quite intrigued by Michael's discussion of his brother, a man who he tells me is an astronaut, and who Michael seems to regard as being mysteriously powerful. While I did not note any information in Michael's records to confirm whether the brother is, in fact, an astronaut, I presume that he actually is. Michael explained that during a recent shuttle mission, his brother was much more capable of controlling his thoughts from space than he normally is on earth. When the brother was on a spacewalk, he said, he "pulled my mind up there with him, then wouldn't bring it back." When I asked him how he was able to get his mind back to earth, he said that you and his mother were able to intercede with the brother and finally to convince him to bring Michael's mind back in the shuttle.

Although this sort of history is not particularly unusual with schizophrenics, I thought it might be valuable to make you aware of it. He obviously trusts you and his mother (although I did note that he has felt that you were tampering with him in the past), and I would say he has repressed a great deal of anger and feelings of inferiority toward his brother. In our subsequent sessions, I plan to attempt to get some of these to surface, and I would appreciate any insights you may have into the nature of their relationship. I would, of course, also welcome communications from the parents and/or the brother if you are in touch with them.

As you may know, there is not a particularly bright prognosis with many of the schizophrenias, but in Michael's case, I feel confident that he won't have further need of hospitalization and that we may be able to make real progress in dealing with his fears of his brother.

Thank you very much for your assistance and concern.

Yours sincerely,
Donald Yelland, M.D.

"Well . . . ," I said, setting the letter on his desk.

John Long didn't respond for a moment, seeming comfortable with the silence. "I hope you don't mind me showing that to you," he said as he folded the letter and put it back in its envelope. "I thought perhaps you might want to get in touch with Dr. Yelland—if there's anything about you and Michael from the past that you think he should know."

"Well, I . . . I'd be glad to talk to him, but I don't think I'd throw much light on anything. We never had any big blow-ups or anything. I mean, everything was fine, we were just normal brothers until high school when he started to get . . . withdrawn. I'm sure that as he got stranger, I got more distant."

"Maybe that's where the anger comes from—if it is anger."

"He didn't seem angry just now. He wasn't overjoyed or anything, but we talked. He seemed willing to take off for a while after lunch. I don't know. Has he ever said much to you about me?"

"I've gotten the impression that he's very proud of you. I've heard him talking to people about you, about what you do. But then, I've never talked with Michael about his voices—the ones he hears. I probably should, but since they're not real, I don't feel like I should pretend with him that they are—though I know they seem real enough to him."

"Evidently. Dad said something about him thinking you were one of the voices, or that you were controlling him or something?"

"A few times when he first came to stay, before he had got-

ten to know many people, Michael had some real torments. I
was pushing to get him organized, too hard probably, to find a
job and so forth. One night he came into my room with a knife
he'd taken from the kitchen. When I woke up, he was sitting
on the edge of my bed, stroking the knife with his fingers, and
speaking in a soft but very eerie kind of voice, something about
how could I, of all people, work for the devil."

"God. I'm amazed you didn't ship him back to the hospital."

"I don't think he really planned to hurt me. He was just
afraid that I was going to become one of the regular voices. I
tried to be careful not to nag at him, or push him too hard from
then on, and things did get better."

"I'm never around him; we hardly ever talk on the phone. I
don't understand why he thinks I'm his big controller or something."

"I guess that's what the psychiatrist is interested in. From
what little I know, schizophrenia is a kind of deterioration of
the personality and of the means of making logical connections between things. Michael's weird association of his mind
and your space flight, for instance, must seem ultra-real to
him."

"He told me that some girl that works at the bakery tried to
get him to become her fetus."

"Yes, I heard that. Imagine how the world must seem to him
sometimes," he said before I left his office.

•

In the hot early hours of the afternoon, Michael and I walked
east on 20th Avenue, past rows of neglected brownstones, their
windows shielded by heavy, drooping curtains and fading cotton blankets, their screen doors standing ajar. Old men in pairs
sat on the shaded porches; children with crayons drew pictures
on the steaming sidewalks and dug into the squares of dirt that
surrounded the trunks of elm trees. Mike said hello to everyone

we met; he didn't know the people, I was sure, but he offered his flat, almost unfriendly, greeting to each of them as we passed.

Mike asked me about the kids as we angled our way through the parking lots at St. Luke's Hospital, the car windshields reflecting the searing sunlight into our eyes. I remembered the summers when Michael and I would hold a plastic magnifying glass above each other's forearms until the pinpoint of pain, the small solar burn, was too unbearable and we would pull our arms away, laughing, sometimes with tears in our eyes. He knew that Peggy had gone to Austin, but he seemed surprised to hear that Matt and Sarah had gone with her. "You live in that house all by yourself?" he asked.

"Me and the cat," I said. "And the cat's giving serious consideration to making a permanent move next door."

"You should get some roommates," he said, seemingly troubled by the image of empty rooms.

The tall trees on Pennsylvania Street gave us some shade, and I could smell the sprinklers on the small lawns that sloped down to the sidewalk. At Colfax, we turned left onto the stained cement where people with satchels and paper sacks walked slowly, aimlessly, stood curled over parking meters, or sat with their knees pulled up, their backs bent against the hot brick of the buildings. The traffic was steady, noisy, and we wound through clumps of young men who asked for money in quiet voices, or offered us lids of marijuana and grams of uncut coke. "No, thank you," Michael would say to each request for charity, to each offer to buy. He pointed across the street to the bakery where he had worked, then stopped in front of the open door of a sex shop, its racks of magazines visible on a red pegboard wall, seemingly every cover a photograph of a woman with an enormous penis in her mouth.

"Have you ever seen the quarter movies in here?" he asked.

"Not here. But I've seen some quarter movies."

"You have? Where?" He seemed intrigued.

"Oh, I don't know. Other places."

"I go in here sometimes," he said. "But when I do, then I'm ashamed that people see me walking out."

"Nothing to be ashamed about, as far as I'm concerned. They're usually kind of grim places though." We started to walk again.

"But that kind of thing is sinful, Jack. You can't be proud of it."

"I didn't say I was proud of it. I said I didn't think you need to be ashamed of it. As far as sin goes... I don't know what I think about sin, Mike."

"I didn't think you were a very sinful person, Jack. It's hard to imagine you going into those little booths to watch all that fucking."

"Well... I've done it. Most people probably have. You shouldn't be so surprised. People are people. You want to get a Coke or something?"

I held open the glass door for him at the Wendy's, but Mike reached behind me for the door and insisted that I go first. He studied the brightly lit menu board as though it were an examination, then finally told the teenager in the checkered cap he wanted a large Dr. Pepper. I paid for the drinks, and we sat at a small square table near the salad bar. Mike asked me how long I would be in town.

"Just a day or two. I've got to get back to Houston, but it was a good chance to come up for a short visit. I probably should stop by to see Peggy's folks, but... I don't know. I don't really want to explain anything to them. She said they both have been pretty upset by everything. They might just as soon not see me."

"They called me when I got to St. Andrew's," Mike said. "Well, she called. She said to let them know if there was anything they could do for me, but I wouldn't call them back. I could tell they just wanted to spy. You must have told them to watch me."

"Mike. I didn't even tell them you were here. I haven't talked to them since before you came. I don't know how they knew. Mom, maybe."

"Don't lie to me, Jack. I'm aware of a few things, you know." Mike stiffened. I could see small beads of sweat standing on his upper lip.

I took a deep breath. "They live way down by DU. They couldn't spy on you."

"They could if you told them to. The thing that worries me . . . now that you've been up in orbit, there's no place I can go where you can't watch me." He seemed to speak to the table. "You . . . you could try to grab me no matter where I was in the whole world. I don't know why you think I'm so terrible that you can't leave me alone."

I remember rubbing my eyes with my fingers, my fingers cold from cradling the cup, trying to come up with something to say. "I doubt I can convince you, Mike, but I don't think you're terrible. I think you're a hell of a good guy, as a matter of fact. I have never wanted to change you, never wanted to control you, never caused you any kind of trouble."

"You tried to keep me in the hospital," he said, his voice rising, his words coming in quakes. "Then you got together with Father John to make me get a job where they could watch me. He finally figured out what you were doing, but you still wouldn't stop. You just keep talking. Telling me this, telling me that, every single day. But you're not so perfect, Jack. You're just as bad as I am."

I waited before I spoke again. I looked at Mike, but he had turned his head away, his eyes held on the far wall. He seemed to suck in air, and his chest heaved with each big breath. "Mike," I said slowly, "I'm probably about ten times worse than you are, and I am not your goddamn problem! You can't lay all of this shit on me."

Mike stood, tipping his chair backward; it rocked on two legs for an instant before it came to rest, upright. "I can't stand liars!" he shouted, raking his strong, bare arm across the table, driving the paper cups of Dr. Pepper into the couple seated next to us, soaking their table and their pants legs, before he ran out of the restaurant.

The thin young man and his girlfriend were shocked for a second, then angry. "What the fuck is—?"

"God, I'm sorry," I said. "I'm really sorry." By the time I got out to the sidewalk, Mike was already half a block ahead of me. I tried to catch up, dodging a car as I crossed the street, shouting "Excuse me" as I ran through the parade of people, running as fast as I could until Michael slipped out of sight. I slowed to a walk, shuddering, then turned the corner, trying to catch my breath, searching the shaded street for Michael.

●

Mike wasn't at St. Andrew's when I got back; I wasn't really worried about him, but Jesus, I wanted to finish the conversation. I had never known before that I played such a role in his demented nightmares, in his bizarre conception of the way things were. I was mad, and I was hurt—wounded enough by Michael's accusations that I decided I very much wanted to see my in-laws. Now that Peggy and I had separated, my relationship with them would have to be a bit abnormal too, but even if they held me completely responsible for what had happened, at least they wouldn't think I had done it with some kind of mind control. Michael made me feel alienated from so much that had once been vital to me, and I didn't want to think that because of the separation, or the divorce or whatever was in store for us, Peggy's parents would have to slip away from me as well.

Marge was surprised to hear my voice, but said they would love to see me. She said Buddy usually got home from the cleaners at about five, and I said I would see them then. I drove to Argonaut Liquors, a converted supermarket on Colfax a block away from the Wendy's, and ambled through the aisles, looking for a bottle of wine to take to Buddy and Marge. I found one, and also bought a tall can of beer, drinking it as I drove down Washington Street in the tangle of traffic and the steady hold of the heat. I thought I heard the word "Canaveral" as I turned the radio dial; I scanned back for the station, found it, and heard the end of a report about the successful test firing of *Discovery*'s main engines. I had seen *Challenger*'s final pre-flight test a year and a half before, and I remembered what an astounding sight it was—the pale blue fire suddenly spewing from the three exhaust bells, the billow and swirl of steam and rocket smoke as the heat boiled the thousands of gallons of water that were dumped at the base of the pad to dampen the vibration, the orbiter swaying and straining against its bolts like a captive bird struggling to free itself. Congratulations, *Challenger,* I thought as I watched. You'll be a spectacular ship.

I could see that Buddy's small white truck with QUALITY DRY CLEANERS emblazoned in blue on the door was already in the driveway when I turned onto Pearl Street. I pulled in behind the truck, twisted the paper around the neck of the wine bottle and took it with me to the door. The screen door was closed, but the wide wooden door was open and Marge called, "Hello, hello," as she crossed the living room to greet me. She had gained some weight, which suited her, in the more than a year since I had seen her; her hair had been permed, and she looked tanned and happy. She wore a blue skirt and gold sandals and I noticed that her toenails were painted a surprising shade of orange. She gave me a big hug, kissed me, and said, "Isn't this a treat?" then said, "Oh, you shouldn't have," when I handed her the wine.

Our wedding photograph—Peggy looking lovely and me looking young and ugly and uncomfortable—hung with others in the entryway, and as we walked into the living room, Buddy came in from the hall, rubbing his cheeks with his

hands as if they were wet with after-shave. His yellow sport
shirt was tucked into brown trousers and he wore a pair of tan
running shoes—not the kind of footwear I would first associate
with Buddy. "Son of a gun," he said as he shook my hand,
both his broad palms in a firm and friendly grasp of my hand.
"So. Do you feel any different?"

"Not a bit," I said. "I grew an inch while we were in orbit—
everybody does—but unfortunately I lost it as soon as we
landed."

"Well, you look great," Marge said. "Doesn't he, Frank?
He'd probably like something to drink, though."

"I got a bottle of Chianti open, or beer, or what else? Probably some bourbon back there."

"Beer, thanks."

"And a glass of wine for the landlady," he said as he went to
the kitchen. Marge sat down with me on the sofa; she smiled
—that tearful smile of hers that was so sudden and so much a
part of her—and she squeezed my hand. "Frank and I are so
proud of you, Jack. We always have been, of course, but this is
just great."

"I appreciate that. Especially coming from you. I was afraid I
might not be terribly welcome this time."

"Shhh, that's silly," she said, big tears now running down
her ruddy cheeks. "You're family. You're always welcome
here. If you hadn't called, then we would have been upset,
wouldn't we, Frank?"

"I think he's probably a pretty busy man," Buddy said as he
handed me a bottle of beer. Marge set a cardboard coaster with
a picture of the shuttle on the table in front of me, whispering,
"I got those in Houston that time," while Buddy asked, "When
they going to let you go up again?"

"I wish I knew. The earliest would be at least two years or
so. Could be a lot longer though. There are a lot of people
waiting to fly."

"I made a scrapbook," Marge said, "with all the newspaper articles, and the things in *Time,* and all those photographs that you very nicely sent us, by the way."

"I was sorry that you couldn't come to the launch."

"Well... so were we," she said. "But... since Peggy decided not to go, we felt it probably would be best to just stay right here and watch it on TV. And it sure was something to see. Frank took the morning off from work, and his brother and his wife came over to watch with us. I fixed a big ham omelet and a nice fruit salad."

"Peggy said the kids are still talking about it," Buddy said. "We talked to her and the kids—when was it?—Thursday night, I guess."

"How is everybody?"

"Said Sarah can't keep any teeth in her mouth. Poor tooth fairy is going to go broke."

"They're just fine," Marge said, "swimming every day because of the heat. Peggy said a friend of hers is teaching her to water-ski. I suppose knowing how to ski on the snow helps a lot. The girl probably doesn't have much teaching to do."

"Peggy's an athlete," I said. Evidently Buddy and Marge didn't know about the magazine writer, and it wasn't my job to tell them. If I had been in Peggy's position, I probably wouldn't have said anything either. It would have been interesting to know how she had explained the move to Austin. "I'm anxious to see them—and I will in a few days. Hopefully the kids and I can spend some time together before school starts."

"Well, if they aren't going to let you go to space again for a while, maybe you can all have a real vacation," Marge said. Her hopes for some sort of reconciliation were impossible to hide.

"I... I'm not sure what's in store for Peggy and me. I guess I should say that. I wish I had good news for you—for all of us—but everything is still completely up in the air."

"Sometimes these things take a lot of time," she said, "a lot of work and a lot of patience. We know you both, love you both. We think things will work out for the best. Our nephew Jim; you remember Jim. He and his wife split up, then got divorced, then took up together again—not married—and just last week they went to Reno and came back married again. So you never know."

"That Jim just didn't like cooking for himself," Buddy said. "Ate at his mother's table every night for nine months. Never a nickel or a 'nice to be here.'"

"That's none of our affair, now," Marge scolded. "And neither is this with Jack and Peggy. We don't want you to think we're meddling, Jack. You kids have to make your own decisions. We just pray for the best, don't we? And you're staying for dinner, of course."

"Well, I do need to get back to see Michael before too—"

"Frank already has the charcoal going; the chicken's ready to put on, and I made a potato salad. Just a quick little dinner."

I stayed for dinner, unwilling to refuse food from Marge, happy to have the company, and buoyed by their support and good spirits. Buddy got me another beer and I followed him out to the backyard, watching from a lawn chair while he attended to the chicken. He said business had been good, but confessed he had begun to consider giving it up. "Trouble is," he said, "I'd just have to close the doors. Nobody'd buy a little dry cleaners; nobody wants to work that hard." Buddy was only in his early sixties, but both his parents had died of heart attacks at his age, and Peggy had said he never expected to live to be very old. "I'd like to have a little retirement—just go to the Bronco games and bullshit with the guys down at the Oak Alley; go fishing once in a while. But, hell. All I've ever done is work. That's all I know how to do."

Marge carried plates and silverware in her hands as she came out the back door, and a tablecloth was tucked under her elbow. I helped her spread the checkered cloth on the weathered wooden table and tried to help her set the places, but she wouldn't let me. "Scoot,"she said, "this is my job." She asked me how my folks were, and asked how hot it had been in Houston before she went back inside.

"That Peggy," Buddy said. "I don't have to tell you that she's every bit as headstrong as her mother. Seems like the two of them are more alike every time I see her. But Marge and I have been lucky—knock wood. I don't think I'll trade her."

I looked up, expecting to catch Buddy's eye, but he was staring at the grill, watching intently as he turned the chicken.

"We'll save your wine for something special, something to celebrate," Marge said as she cleared the plates. I had finished the potato salad and had turned down the last piece of chicken. "And you're sure you don't want to use the spare bedroom? We could give you a key so it wouldn't matter when you got back."

"No. But thanks. There's a room I can stay in at St. Andrew's, and I may try to have a long talk with Mike." I hadn't told them about what had happened that afternoon, but they knew something about Mike's situation, and they seemed to understand. Buddy suggested that we call Peggy and the kids before I left, but Marge quickly said no, adding something about how this was the night, wasn't it?, that they were going to see that new Indiana what's-his-name movie.

Marge showed me her scrapbook when we went back inside the house. On the first page was an article cut out of the Denver *Post,* headlined COLORADO ASTRONAUT FLIES ROCKET PACK TO RETRIEVE STRANDED SATELLITE. A *Post* reporter had called me in Houston on the day after we landed. He was friendly, and seemed well informed, but he kept calling me John, as if we were friends, and as if that were the name I was known by. A few pages later, I noticed my official NASA portrait, the one that the astronaut office mails to every kid from Colorado who writes in hoping to find an astronaut for a pen pal. In the photograph, I am wearing a space suit with an

American flag on the shoulder and emergency evacuation instructions stitched onto the sleeve. I had written on it in bold
ink: "To Buddy and Marge, who let me fly away with their
darling daughter. Love, Jack." Marge could tell that something
about reading those words really got to me. I closed the scrapbook and stood up to say good-bye.

•

I could hear the clear, quiescent sound of plainsong as I locked
the car in the small parking lot across the street from the
church. The last band of orange light hung on the western horizon, silhouetting the ridges and peaks of the mountains, reflecting off the the smooth steel-and-glass facades of the
buildings downtown. The church's stained-glass windows,
long rectangles of radiant color, seemed to stand out from the
dark surface of the brick, and the sound of the single chanting
voice grew sharp as I walked up the steps to the open doors.

Only a few people stood in the long rows of walnut pews;
John Long was at the side of the altar, a long white surplice
covering his cassock, a heavy brass Celtic cross hanging from
his neck. Michael faced Father Long from the opposite side of
the altar, dressed like the priest except that he wore no cross.
Only two of the altar's tall beeswax candles were lit, their
flames fluttering in the breeze that curled in from an open window.

Father Long began the *Magnificat* as I stepped into a pew at
the back, and after the first versicle, the rest of the people
joined him, chanting the evensong canticle that flooded me
with memories, its lilting and lovely melody sharply etched in
my mind, my father's voice suddenly coming to me, his steady
baritone so full of emotion and strength. I watched Michael as
he chanted, crisply enunciating each word, singing with an assurance that was also reminiscent of my father. I thought I
could make out his voice among the other voices:

*"... And his mercy is on them that fear him, throughout all
generations.*

*He hath showed strength with his arm; he hath scattered the
proud in the imagination of their hearts.*

*He hath put down the mighty from their seat, and hath exalted
the humble and meek.*

*He hath filled the hungry with good things; and the rich he
hath sent empty away..."*

Following the *Magnificat,* everyone sat while Michael read the
New Testament lesson, the Genesis account from St. John. Michael's voice was loud, his monotone broken by the unusual
words he chose to accent: "... and the Word was with God,
and the Word was *God.* The *same* was in the beginning with
God. *All* things were made by *him;* and without him was not
any thing made that was made..." I watched Father Long casually scan the church as he listened, and when he caught my eye,
he smiled.

I stood with the others for the Creed, but did not recite it;
and for the first time in at least three years, I knelt when the
priest began the collects, chanting each short prayer in simple
plainsong. I could see that Michael's eyes were closed; I saw
Lucy, the woman I had met in the kitchen that morning, in a
pew near the front, a boy about Matt's age beside her. Just
before the Thanksgiving, I could see John Long turning the
pages of his missal to find another prayer. When he found it, he
read it in his speaking voice: "O most glorious God, whom the
heaven of heavens cannot contain; whose mercy is over all thy
works; we praise thy holy name that thou hast been pleased to
conduct in safety, through the perils of space, thy servant Jack
and his fellow crew members. May they be duly sensible of thy
merciful providence toward them and ever express their thank-
fulness by a holy trust in thee; through Jesus Christ our Lord.
Amen."

After Father Long gave the blessing, Michael genuflected in

front of the altar and followed him down the chancel steps to the communion rail and out through an arch at the side of the church. As the scattered congregation began to go, Lucy and the boy walked down the wide aisle and stopped at the pew where I sat.

"Hello again," she said. She wore a cotton print dress; her scarf was gone and her short black hair capped her head like a halo. "This is my son, Simon. And this is Michael's brother. He was hoping he'd get to meet you."

I gave him my hand. "I'm pleased to meet you, Simon."

"Pleased to meet you," he said in a shy voice. Then he added with more confidence, "Is it true that there are black astronauts?"

"It's true. There sure are. Would you like me to have one of them write you a letter?"

"No," he said. "You're good enough."

Lucy laughed and cradled Simon's head against her side. "His daddy was a pharmacist, but this one says he wants to be an actor or an astronaut."

"Actors make more money, I'm afraid. But we do get some nice travel benefits."

"We think a lot of Michael," she said. "Nice you could come visit him; he seems kind of lonely so much of the time. I've invited him over to the house for supper a few times, but he doesn't seem to want to come. Always says he thinks Father might need him here."

"I think Mike is lonely," I said. "But, I don't know. It's such a strange kind of loneliness."

"Sometimes I kind of get the feeling that the memory of who he is just kind of vanishes from him," she said. "Like he doesn't even have himself. That would scare me to death."

"Me too," I said. "I appreciate your being so kind to him."

"I appreciate him being good help to me. Guess help is what we all need, isn't it?"

Lucy asked me how long I planned to stay, and I said I had to leave tomorrow. But I told her I hoped to see her again before she and Simon said good-bye.

I waited for Michael outside, near the breezeway that connected the church to the rectory, assuming that he and Father Long would walk by on their way back from the sacristy. I felt like having a drink and considered whether I ought to try to get Mike to walk down to the Broadway Grill with me. But we couldn't even make it through a soft drink at a Wendy's, for God's sake. What made me think we ought to try our luck at a trendier establishment? And I knew too that the last thing Mike would be interested in would be sitting in a bar with the boozy professional set, keeping a practiced eye on the tables of talkative, unescorted women, or the inevitable woman in a silk dress who would be sitting alone at the bar, drinking a wine spritzer and smoking a cigarette.

I waited there in the darkness, the night air cool and moist, the scattered sounds of the city seeming like a steady assurance that everything was in order, then I finally decided to try to find my brother. I checked his room and the kitchen and John Long's office before I found him at the back end of the basement, near the small rooms that had once been used for Sunday school classes and that now had become sleeping rooms for people who came in off the street.

An outside door was open and I could see a line of people on the cement steps that led up to the alley. Michael and two young men I hadn't seen before were busy in an alcove near the door, Mike collecting quarters from each person in the line, the others handing each man and woman a canvas pad and a green army blanket. I watched a grizzled man in a gray coat, his head shaved, his beard growing down into his shirt, carry his pad into the large, linoleum-tiled room. He put his nylon athletic bag against a wall and curled the top of a paper sack to close it. He laid his pad perpendicularly to the wall, then slowly tucked the blanket beneath it before he took off his coat, folded it, and placed it carefully on the pad for a pillow. Several more men soon followed him into the room, placing their narrow pads in rows, each sleeping with his head against the wall, leaving a big, bare patch of linoleum in the center of the room. I only saw three women, each of them surely under thirty, carry pads and blankets down the short hallway and through the swinging door to the small, secluded room where they slept.

Mike closed the coins inside a metal box, and one of the men he worked with closed the door to the closet where a high stack of pads still stood. I heard the other man say, "Okay, guys, lights out if you're all set," as I said hello to Mike.

"Jack," he said. "You're back."

"I'm back. I had dinner with Buddy and Marge. I decided I really should see them. Are you finished now?"

"Finished. I'm never on duty all night. Just Benny and Jim do that. I just help them check people in. It's easy in the summer. We only have crowds in the cold weather."

"Why do they have to pay?"

"I don't know. I guess just so it's not free. Just a quarter, though. I always loan them a quarter if somebody doesn't have one."

"Do you think we could find someplace to sit and talk for a while?" I asked. "I kind of think I'd better head home tomorrow."

"We can sit outside here," he said.

I followed Mike out the door and up to the top of the steps. He sat on the steel rail that surrounded the stairwell, his shoulders hunched, his hands gripping the rail at his hips. I sat on the top step; I could smell the sweet rot of the food scraps in the dumpster across the alley, and I dimly saw a white cat bound up to the dumpster's lip, then disappear inside it. "I heard you read at evensong," I said. "I've always liked that, the 'in the beginning was the Word.'" Mike was silent. "I used to imagine that that's how the Big Bang began—that at the point when the whole universe was just a pinpoint of matter and energy, it began its expansion with a spoken word. Course, from a physicist's point of view, that's a little crazy, but I still think it's an appealing thought."

"What would the word have been?" Mike asked. I was surprised he was really listening.

"I don't know. I don't know what it could have been; and even if you figure that God was the one who spoke it, where was God when He spoke? Outside the pinpoint that made up the whole cosmos? Or was He the pinpoint? Maybe the word was . . . *now.* "

"I saw something on TV at the hospital about the universe," Mike said; he turned to look at me. "They said that some of the stars you look at, maybe even some of the ones everybody knows about, may have already been dead for thousands of years, but there's no way we can find out except wait. That really seemed strange to me. It made me feel kind of weird, like you never know. Maybe so, maybe not."

"You just put your finger on the essence of modern astronomy. Those are the words we live by. Listen . . . I'm sorry about this afternoon. I sure wasn't trying to badger you. But . . . it's important to me that you try to understand that I'm not telling you how to live your life."

"I don't want to talk about it. Maybe you don't know it when you do it. Just like that light from the stars."

"No. There's a difference. That light is real; you can measure it, study it. The voices, or those feelings you have that you get from other people, are imaginary. They're imaginary."

Michael was silent, and I didn't say anything again until he slid off the rail and sat on the step below me. The light from the doorway gave a glancing illumination to the side of his face that I saw, and his dark braid seemed to split his white shirt in half. "Do you remember watching Apollo 13 through my old Celestron back when we lived in Boulder?" I asked. "I'm not sure what year it was; I think Peggy and I had just gotten married, I know I was still in grad school. You must have just been

roaming around that spring. We were watching from the yard
of that little carriage house we lived in at the edge of Chautau-
qua Park."

"You mean when you saw the explosion?"

"I had tracked enough flights that I thought it would be easy
to show you guys. I remember I got the command module
sighted—just a bright speck of light—and then all of a sudden
it flared for an instant, much brighter, like old light bulbs
would do before they burned out. I couldn't figure out what it
was, the flare, but it seemed pretty strange. Then Peggy went
to get the transistor and we heard about twenty minutes later
that the LOX tank had blown. The radio made it sound like
Lovell and Haise and Swigert were goners. The Denver stations were all trying to get Swigert's mother to tell them how it
felt to have her son be a sitting duck. I think I stayed out in the
yard all night, watching the light reflecting off the module,
whenever I could find it, listening to the reporters in Houston
who all sounded a little shaken. Peggy went to bed finally, but I
think you stayed up with me, didn't you? There wasn't a thing
in the world we could do but sit out there with our sleeping
bags pulled up to our armpits, but there we sat till the sun came
up."

"It was called the *Odyssey*. That was the name they had given
to the module."

"Yeah, I think it was, wasn't it? I guess the reason I even
remembered that night is that I end up feeling that same way
with you sometimes. It's like you're two hundred thousand
miles away. We can see you and we can tell that something's
bothering you, but there's not a damn thing anybody can do
except just sort of keep the night watch. That probably sounds
dumb, but I don't know what else to say—just that I'm not the
one that's causing the explosions. I'm just one of lots of people
who are pulling for you. Does that make any sense?"

"They called the other thing, the lunar landing thing,

Aquarius, I think. They all crawled inside it on the way back to the earth. It kept them alive, but then they had to pitch it so they could do their reentry."

"Mike, do you see what I . . . what I'm . . ." I stopped. Mike was running the fingers of both hands through his hair. I leaned forward to try to catch his eye. "I'm . . . I'm just trying to say that I'm on your side."

"Oh, I'm with you astronauts a hundred percent," he said. "You're the new explorers. You're at the head of the line."

I didn't know what to say. It probably didn't make any sense to keep at it, and I didn't want to let things slide into another fruitless fight. I tugged at his braid and put my palm on the back of his neck. "Thanks," I said, "I appreciate it." And I did appreciate it; I appreciated the fact that he could still be civil with me, that he still seemed to count me as a brother, when all I could ever offer him was a handshake or a hug and a couple of hours a year. "Can you show me where that room is?" I asked. "I don't have to leave too early. Let's go get some breakfast before I go."

We both stood up, and I followed Mike down the concrete steps. "It's a nice room," he said. "It's right by the room where I sleep. They're tiny, but from the window you can see the skyscrapers. Sometimes I watch, and you can see the lights go out, one by one. When I see one, I wonder, you know, who it is that's leaving and where they live and how long it will be before they get home."

At Mike's suggestion, and after he had left me alone in the little room, I watched the lights in the Republic Tower for a time, but none of them ever seemed to go out. I wondered if Mike was watching, and if he was, I hoped he wouldn't worry about those people who couldn't yet go home.

three

I-25 angled up through scraggly stands of piñon and juniper trees, then rolled over the low summit of Raton Pass, and Colorado disappeared behind me as I started down the southern slope. The New Mexican llano, the searing short-grass plains that stretch away to Texas, seemed to float in the hot afternoon air, and thick, dark thunderheads had gathered above the sharp peaks of the Sangre de Cristos.

During the three-hour drive from Denver, I had considered turning back several times, not so much because I couldn't bear the prospect of the impending humidity, or the return to the dull days in the astronaut office, or the nights alone in that empty, eerie, air-conditioned house. It was a sense of failed obligation that tempted me to turn the car around, to go back and get Michael, to take him away from the kitchen and the daily services and his job dispensing canvas pads, and to hike up into the Gore Range, or the Mosquitos maybe, to make camp at the edge of a noisy, cascading creek, to talk by a smoldering fire, and to sleep under a sky so clear that the Milky Way would look like a bright celestial brush stroke. But I didn't turn around. I was good at imagining how Mike and I could spend time together, how we could become brothers again after years and miles and his mysterious disease had turned us into distant relatives, but I could never pull it off. When it came down to actually *being* with Mike, I was inevitably too perplexed, too sad and selfish to stick around.

While we were eating breakfast at the Eggshell that morning, Mike had asked me again about how I managed living alone. He seemed worried about me, worried about what the solitude would do to me. "I don't think it's good to be by yourself too much," he told me. Then for the first time since I had arrived, he asked me about my flight. Telling him about the launch, about the retrieval, and about the wry pleasures of weightlessness, I felt as if I was finally able to give something small but significant to him; I was finally doing more than simply putting in an appearance. I was surprised by how much Mike already knew and by how eager he was to hear; his eyes came alive as he listened, and we sat in the restaurant until almost eleven o'clock. I drove him back to St. Andrew's, told him to take it easy, as he stood on the sidewalk with his hands in the pockets of his jeans, then pointed the car toward Texas.

The highway widened as I crossed the cattle guard outside of Clayton that marked the Texas border, and I counted four DRIVE FRIENDLY signs in the forty miles to Dalhart. I had gained an hour at the cattle guard, and it was seven o'clock by the time I got to steamy, sprawling Amarillo, the air outside the car still hot enough to startle me. I was hungry and thirsty and had driven downtown to Van Dyke's, but the door to the café was locked; a sign said that they closed at three, and I walked away feeling a bit betrayed by the vagaries of vagabond travel.

At a Stop-N-Go near the interstate, I bought a paper and a quart of beer, then dialed Jane's number from the phone that hung on the west wall of the small brick building. I pressed the receiver against one ear and stuck my index finger into the other. "Jane?" I said when she answered the phone. "It's me. Here I am in Texas, and you're nowhere to be found!"

"I know. I'm right here in my own little house. How are you?"

"Pitifully lonely," I said, but she could tell I was kidding. "No, I'm fine. But my favorite café is closed and Amarillo is hotter than hell and I'm still an awful long way from the sultry shores of Clear Lake."

"Poor thing," she said. "You've sure been on my mind since Sunday. That was quite an event for an old woman like me, Jack. How was Denver?"

"Denver was quick. I didn't last long. Mike seemed good in some ways, and I could have stayed another day or two, but I don't know. I always feel like I run out of conversation. Seeing him is such a blunt realization that I'm not much of a brother. I'm pretty much batting zero these days, aren't I? Failed husband, errant father, shitty son—then I go to Denver and find out that Mike tells his psychiatrist that his brother bosses him around from outer space."

"My mare foaled this morning, Jack. A colt. She didn't have a bit of trouble. He was already standing by the time I went out to the barn to check. Looks just like his daddy. How about if I call him Pegasus?"

"Does he have wings?"

"No, but . . . I may call him Pegasus anyway, or Peg."

"Not Peg," I said.

"Oh. No, no, I guess not."

"Now that he's born, you can come to Houston. I need some help to keep from rattling around inside that house of mine."

"How many days do you think we could get along if I came to visit?"

"I think I'd give us pretty good odds."

"But you've got things to settle yet, Jack. I'll be patient." She said something else, but I missed it because a pickup suddenly roared out of the parking lot.

"I don't want to let this get away," I said. "I know it was just a night, but we've known each other forever. I don't want to wait another year to see you again."

"Oh," she said with a long sigh, "I wish I had pocketed a little wisdom somewhere along the line."

"I'll call when I get home," I said. "I'll put a Stouffer's dinner in the oven and we'll have a nice long talk."

"Hey. I'm no cook," she said. "Seriously. And wear your seatbelt."

I hung up wishing I had told her how much the trip to Hal's cabin had meant to me, or that I'd said *something* vaguely appropriate, but I didn't know what else to say. I had to settle for dinner at a Chi Chi's, eating franchised Mexican food, and drinking one more margarita than I probably should have, but Highway 287 was wide and ran straight as a rifle shot; it crossed the slow and ruddy Red, then nearly nicked the corner of Oklahoma as I drove, pushing eighty, all the way to Dallas.

•

The tall towers of downtown Houston, rising like clusters of monuments in a crowded cemetery, were visible from as far away as Conroe, their boxy outlines dim in the bayou haze. Driving in steady midday traffic, I could see a succession of jetliners, seemingly silent, lift up from the tarmac at Intercontinental, and off to the southwest, the Transco Tower stood like a sublime sentinel above the jumble of shorter buildings surrounding the Galleria. Out near Aldine, I passed a Houston city limits sign; I was technically home again, but I was still an hour away from the house.

"Houston," Neil Armstrong had radioed a decade and a half before, "Tranquility Base here. The *Eagle* has landed." The first word that was spoken on another world was *Houston* and the city's captains of commerce had seen great symbolism in that fact. But Houston had never really seemed like a space city to me. Sure, Johnson Space Center did fill a whole section of bottomland between Mud Lake and Cow Bayou, and dozens of private space contractors rented glassy office space nearby, but the city of Houston was actually much more committed to the enterprising hustle of the earth. Its icons weren't the display rockets that rusted at the entrance to the space center, but the concrete business complexes that flanked its web of freeways. The notion of space was hardly more than a mirage, a faint image in the humid, entrepreneurial air.

A wall of mirrored skyscrapers soon loomed directly in front of the interstate, but the road avoided a confrontation, quickly curling its way around downtown, then aiming itself at the gulf. As I passed beneath 610, I turned on the radio just in time to hear Paul Harvey reading a list of people from Indiana to Idaho who were celebrating their seventy-fifth wedding anniversaries. Harvey seemed to think they deserved the Congressional Medal of Honor or something, but I couldn't help but wonder how many of them still actually spoke to each other. Then I gave some thought to whether people in their nineties could still screw once or twice a year. I wished them the best of luck as I passed the huge billboard advertising the Alibi, a slightly sleazy topless club with which I, unfortunately, had some passing familiarity.

I had spent the night at a Rodeway Inn in Irving within sight of Texas Stadium, which looked in the night like some sort of civil defense bunker big enough to house the combined populations of Fort Worth and Dallas and all the duplexes in between.

It was after one o'clock by the time I checked in; I remember taking a long shower, pouring myself into the king-sized bed, then falling asleep in the middle of that old Charlton Heston movie in which he plays an aging and arthritic cowboy, old enough to be riddled by self-doubt, but still young enough to by God get the job done. I think I slept until ten the next morning, waking up feeling a little foolish, eating a quick breakfast at a McDonald's and getting back on the road, anxious to get home in time to make it to the bank and drop my laundry off before I faced the silence inside the house.

It had been almost two years since Hurricane Alicia had turned the bayous into a battle zone; the stately old oak that we had lost in the front yard long ago had been cut into cordwood, and coarse new grass covered the spot where I had dug out the stump, but the house still looked strange, a little uncertain of itself, without it. The boy who had been watering for me had neatly stacked all the yellowed newspapers by the back door, and I noticed that the cat's dish was full enough of food that it looked as if he had been attended to, empty enough that I presumed he was still on the premises.

The house was dark and cool. The cleaning lady had come while I was gone; I noticed the familiar and funny way she spread the magazines on the coffee table, the top edge of each one carefully positioned below the banner of the one beneath it. The soured milk in the refrigerator looked like tofu when I poured it into the sink; I opened a beer, then opened the living-room curtains and sat down to thumb through the mail. I threw all the catalogs and the envelopes marked YOU MAY HAVE ALREADY WON into a pile on the floor, set the bills on the sofa beside me, put Peggy's mail in a separate stack, and opened three letters hand-addressed to me. Two of them were congratulatory notes, one from a former physics professor who now lived in New Jersey, the other from a technician at Martin Marietta, a spectacular woman with whom I had been flirting in vain for more than a year. "Why didn't I get this before I went to Denver?" I asked out loud as I tore into the third letter, typed on letterhead I didn't recognize. The letter was from some guy I had met at a NASA reception in Washington a couple of weeks before. It had been an honor to meet me, he said; he was proud of the whole space program, and he wanted me to know that if I ever gave any thought to entering the private sector, he would be very happy to discuss his company in detail with me. They were one of the nation's foremost fire-arms manufacturers, he said, makers of machine guns and in-fantry rifles and a whole array of modern military weapons. His final paragraph was all about how these were bullish times in the war business, what with the international scene being so unstable and the Reagan administration thankfully being dedi-cated to rebuilding a strong defense. "Hey, good news," I said to the empty house, "I can become a machine-gun maker." I think I shouted the word "asshole!" before I shut up, a little embarrassed at already having started to babble.

I realized as I finished my beer that I had not spent an eve-ning at home doing nothing in almost two months. The pros-pect didn't sound particularly appealing, but neither did sitting by myself, sipping scotch and trying desperately to appear at ease in the midst of the stereophonic cacophony at J. Larkin's, or, for that matter, bumping into fellow astronauts and their families eating hamburgers at Fuddrucker's, the wives politely asking me to join them, the husbands joking about how many women I no doubt was currently seeing. I turned on the televi-sion to watch the early news, then put on a pair of shorts and went out to mow the lawn. The sun was still high in the sky and sweat was pouring off me by the time I finished the strip on the north side of the house and put the mower away. Gus, the tabby cat that Sarah thought she simply had to have a cou-ple of years before, was lounging on a derelict deck chair inside the garage when I rolled the mower back inside; he gave me a jaded glance, then got up, stretched, and followed me into the house.

I opened the cold tap in the tub in the back bathroom, then went out to get another beer and the current *Newsweek*. I rolled a slim joint in the bedroom, then eased my way into the shallow tub, smoking most of the thin, poorly rolled cigarette before I tossed it into the toilet and started to read. The cover story was about the kidnapping of children, not by thugs in hopes of ransom, but by desperate, perhaps deranged, fathers and mothers. It wasn't something I needed to read; not because I had ever given any thought to trying to run away with Matt and Sarah, but because it all just seemed so sordid, the lives of people who were once in love now filled with rage and the need for revenge. I read a review of a Jack Nicholson movie in which he plays a hit man hired to kill his hit-woman wife, and something about how the home rental of X-rated movies had become the year's big growth business. The water was cool and comforting; I threw the magazine onto the carpet, dunked my head under the water, then rested it against the lip of the tub, my eyes closed, my hand around my penis. I imagined the woman from Martin Marietta while I masturbated, and I remembered how Jane's body had felt just a few nights before, about how she had tasted, about how she cried when she came. Then I thought about nothing at all until I finished myself off, my temples soaked with sweat, my breath heavy and broken.

I walked into Matt's bedroom as I dried off. About half of his posters were gone, but I couldn't remember which ones were missing. The door to his empty closet was open; his bed was made, and his plastic shuttle model sat in a cardboard box by his dresser. I looked around but didn't find the photograph Peggy had taken of Matt and me when we were skiing in Telluride two winters before; I was pleased when I realized he must have taken it to Austin. The door to Sarah's room was closed; I started to open it, then changed my mind and went back into the bathroom.

I called Jane from the kitchen phone after I had put on a pair of sweat pants. Her line rang ten times before I gave up. I told

her I'd call, I thought, stupidly miffed that she had something
else to do besides sit by the phone and wait. Then I dialed my
parents' number without first thinking about what I would try
to say.

"Jack!" Dad said after I said hello, "where are you?"

"I'm at home."

"Already? Did you go to Denver?"

"Yeah. I stayed at St. Andrew's. We had a good visit."

"You did? How did you think he was doing?"

"Well, pretty good, I guess. He's quit that job at the bakery.
He just works there at the church now. He's agreed to see a
psychiatrist regularly again. I think that's a good place for
him."

"Did you get a chance to talk with John Long?"

"Yes—who seems like a good guy. And he obviously takes a
lot of interest in Mike."

"I'm glad you saw him, Jack."

"Dad," I said, stumbling over what I was trying to say, "I
think I ought to try to apologize again. That was a pretty rotten way to end the visit."

"Never mind," he said, and his voice conveyed the certainty
that he meant it. "Let's put that little business behind us. I'll
still claim you if you'll claim me."

"Deal. But you'd think I'd be capable of—"

"So you're back to work, are you?"

"Tomorrow. I wish I was looking forward to it. Is Mom
home?"

"No. This is her P.E.O. night. Very important. I wonder
what those gals do that's so secret. Do you suppose I ought to
investigate?"

"I bet it's pretty tame, Pop."

"No, can't really imagine your mother conspiring against the
government or sitting in a seance or anything."

"Dad," I said, then I stopped.

"Jack?"

"Oh...nothing. This...this is just a hell of a big house for one person. You know, I never would have guessed I'd be on my own at this age. I'm not sure I'm suited to it."

"I doubt you are, Jack. I know I wouldn't be, but...Jane stopped by the church this morning. I think she kind of felt responsible for everything, but I hope I made her feel a little better. She gave me a stack of Hal's old engineering texts and this ancient leather jacket that he used to wear when we went camping. It's a lovely old thing, but it smells like twenty years of wood smoke. Smells like Hal really."

I tried Jane again after Dad and I said good-bye, after we had promised each other we'd stay in touch, again assuring each other that we had made a deal. I just let Jane's line ring four times before I put on my running shoes and ran out into the motionless evening air.

•

A clean sport shirt was hard to come by the following morning, but I finally found one and put it on; I put my chain of IDs around my neck, and thirty minutes later the guard at the gate waved the Honda past the checkpoint. I gave her a sleepy smile and she returned it with the jazzy little salute that I'm sure she offered to all the employees she recognized. Driving past the supine Saturn V, a rocket longer than a football field, a splendid machine that was built to fly to the moon but that only got to go as far as Texas, I thought the space center looked like some sort of sedate new university, a quiet campus devoid of fraternity houses and beer parlors and boys playing frisbee, a school so unimaginatively run that each of its buildings got numbers instead of names. I parked in the lot in front of Building 4, went inside, and climbed up the stairs to the third floor, where I shared a spartan office with two other astronauts, Rob Torrington and Bob Simons, the Rob and Bob show, both of whom were training for a fall mission and would probably be off in the simulators or stuck underwater in the WETF tank. As I opened the door at the third-floor landing, I nearly collided with Mary Lee Yost, a longtime acquaintance who worked in the astronauts' public relations office; she and her cohorts were the busy bunch that made us all look as if we were dedicated correspondents.

"Well, hello, stranger," she said. "I thought maybe they'd forgotten to bring you back."

"No such luck," I said. "How are you?"

"We've been crazy. You've damn near worn out an autopen for us since your flight. I didn't know you were such a popular guy, Healy. But I guess that's what happens when you let somebody go swimming around out there. I could probably get you, say, thirty speaking engagements in the next month, several visiting professorships or whatever you call them, and you can have all the girlfriends you can handle."

"Let me look at all the amorous inquiries," I said, grinning, a bit embarrassed, "and kindly decline everything else."

"We're way ahead of you. Where've you been?"

"Colorado. Just a few days. Not long enough. How are things around the plant?"

"Oh, you know, same old shit, I guess. But I just hear the rumors. Seems that they're shaking up flight assignments again and everybody's getting pissed off. Rob and Bob will fill you in, no doubt."

"Are they around?"

"Beats me. They could be, but I haven't seen them," she said as she started to go. "Hey. Take me to Colorado with you next time. This weather is giving me a bad rash in the most embarrassing places."

"I'll be glad to examine you," I said.

She aimed for my cheek with the back of her hand. "You're awful," she said with a coy smile; then she started down the stairs.

The door to the office was closed; Rob and Bob were elsewhere. A couple dozen phone messages were held by the clip that had my name on it, and my desk was loaded with all kinds of stuff that various people had decided I ought to see. My photos of Matt and Sarah were taped to the side of the khaki-colored filing cabinet, and no one had pilfered the poster from the wall above the desk—a painting of the shuttle poised for launch, the orbiter mounted on an enormous bottle of Lone Star beer instead of the external tank.

Getting back into the swing of things was plainly going to take some time. I did not want to sift through the mail and the memos and the assorted administrative directives just yet. Compared with the long months of labored training for the flight, the excited anticipation and the sense that I was finally doing the kind of work that suited the title "astronaut," becoming just another of the dozens of space bureaucrats again was going to be a letdown. I had noticed many times how so many of my colleagues seemed perfectly happy with their earthbound jobs until they got to fly; then, following a flight, they almost inevitably would begin to grouse about having to make the PR trips to the contractors, or having to sit on some dumb efficiency committee, or worst of all, doing color commentary for one of the networks at the launch or landing of a subsequent flight. I had hoped that following my mission I would quickly be assigned to advance planning for the deployment of the space telescope, but what would actually happen to me was anybody's guess. All I could do in the meantime was to patiently keep my ears open, and to be exceedingly polite to everyone who had a hand in deciding my fate.

At the top of the stack of letters that had been left for me was one from the president of Telcomm, the company whose satellite I had snared and that we had brought back in the orbiter's bay for repair of its transfer orbit stage. It was a nice handwritten note, and I had never before actually realized that the job that was, for the most part, the great challenge and adventure of my life was very definitely reducible to a dollars-and-cents

deal for the people at Telcomm. I liked the notion that all I had
been was a deliveryman, or better yet, a space-suited cow-
puncher out to gather a stray. Whatever I was, I still couldn't
escape the realization of my astonishing good fortune. As I had
flown away in the MMU from the bay's front bulkhead, I was
very literally a satellite myself, as separate a component of the
solar system as an asteroid or the moon or one of the puzzling
planets. My adrenal glands were no doubt going crazy, my
heartbeat hit 110, and I remember being very clearly cognizant
of the fact that I was *alone* in a way that no other human being
had ever been. When I got out to the stranded satellite, a little
more than three hundred feet away from the orbiter, I had a
hell of a lot to do and to pay attention to, but there were a few
moments in which I got to savor a kind of clarity of perspective
that I might never know again: *Challenger,* my beautiful life-
boat, sailed beside me in the near distance, and the enormous
earth, an elegant arc of clouds and water, filled nearly half my
field of vision, but it was the stark, sloe-black emptiness of
space that seemed to take precedence over everything else.
Alone in that seminal darkness, I was just a watery mass of
molecules, very fragile and totally insignificant. But if nothing
else, I was an observer, a spectator at a vantage point that had
had few visitors, and I had a fleeting sensation that I might be
centrally important in the cosmic scheme of things.

I slogged through the rest of the stack of mail, read a short
report on a proposed change in the launch evacuation contingency plans, then, on an impulse, called Peggy to see if I could
drive over to Austin on Saturday. I was surprised to catch her
at home late in the morning, and she seemed to be in good
spirits.

"I was hoping you'd call before long," she said.

"You remember my phone number, don't you?" I asked.

"Yes, smarty, I do remember the number, and I called about
four times before I decided you must have left for Colorado."

"I told the kids they could reach me at Mom and Dad's. I'm

sorry. I asked them to let you know where I was."

"Don't worry," she said. "I had a good idea how to find you if I needed to. How were things up north?"

"It was a real quick trip, but I was glad I got to go. Saw your folks for dinner in Denver. They both seem well."

"I'm . . . kind of surprised you stopped to see them. Did you talk much about everything?"

"Hardly at all. They were just very nice and didn't seem disgusted with me or anything. Your mom's such a character. I'm just calling to see what's on tap for you all on Saturday. I thought I might drive over."

"Saturday would be good. We'd love to hear about the flight. I think the kids are anxious to see for themselves that you're still in one piece. What time?"

"I'll leave early. How about if I get there about noonish and take them out to lunch?"

"They'll be ready,"she said, then she added, "We'll look forward to seeing you, Jack."

I wasn't sure if the "we" meant her and the kids, or her and the magazine writer, but it didn't matter; I hung up feeling happy to be back in touch.

Steve Ehrlich stuck his head in the door an hour later, looking for Rob or Bob, I suppose. He seemed surprised to find me back in town, and suggested I join him for a bite to eat. I was willing to do anything that would get me out of the office, and we walked across the street to the noisy cafeteria, waiting in line for cheap government food prepared by plump gals whose short hair was held under nets, women who genuinely seemed to enjoy their work, who probably had learned how to cook in towns with names like Needville and Alvin and Alta Loma. While we waited, I could see the tourists in the little gift shop at the edge of the dining room who were scanning the hundreds of people with badges on their breast pockets to see if they could spot someone famous. Most of them quickly gave up, buying a few postcards or place mats before they left.

"Are they keeping you busy?" I asked Steve as we sat down. Steve and I had been a part of the same incoming class nine years before, a group of ten pilots and seven scientists who were only now beginning to get their first flight assignments. Steve had flown three months before I had, and I assumed he was jockeying to go again.

"What bullshit," he said, shaking his head. "I'm currently charged with the critical task of drafting new menu recommendations for the flights. Seriously. Seems that some of the pilots who fly all the time are getting tired of the same meals, poor darlings. Hell of a logical use for a physics Ph.D., isn't it? That was nice work you did, by the way."

I said thanks and asked him if he had any hints about when he could go again.

"I thought there was a chance on a spacelab flight that's scheduled for a year and a half from now, but the last I heard was that they're getting pressure to put more Europeans on it, so I don't know. My problem is that I complain far too loudly for my own good. I'm surprised you're not still on vacation."

"Figured I'd save some of it. You know me; can't get enough of this place."

"That reminds me. I hate to be the bearer of bad tidings, but I think John Young is going to crawl your butt when he sees you."

"Me?"

"At the Monday morning pilots' meeting he had an article from one of the Denver papers that some muckety-muck from downtown had sent him along with a nasty letter. The guy saw the article in the Denver airport or something. I guess that when this reporter asked you how you liked living in Houston, you said it was like living in a Calcutta full of Cadillacs."

"Oh, Jesus."

"So John told everybody that he didn't want to have to get

any more nasty letters from the Chamber of Commerce. Said we only have one option when we get asked questions about Houston. *Lie.*"

"I'm afraid I did say it. But . . . what the hell. Maybe it'll help keep me off the PR circuit."

"Yeah, but it also might have knocked you back about six missions. You never know what little indiscretions they're locking away for future reference. If I thought I had a decent alternative, I might just bail out of here before long. I mean, what are my chances? Maybe two, three missions over the next ten years? At best."

"What else would you like to do?"

"That's the hard part. Not college. Absolutely not. There is zero money in that bullshit. Maybe go into business. I've talked with a couple of the telecommunications companies, but it hasn't gone anywhere."

"I got an offer from an outfit that makes machine guns. I'll pass it on to you if you want it."

"Machine guns? For Christ's sake. They think we're all fucking soldiers, don't they? What about you?"

"I suppose I'll sit tight for a while. I might be willing to teach if I could do it in Colorado. But I'm pretty sure I'm not much of a teacher. My credentials are way too weak to get me a job doing major research. What I'd like to do is fly space missions for a living, but that looks like the toughest prospect of all, doesn't it?"

Steve methodically set his fork and spoon on his empty plate. He leaned back in his chair, then forward, speaking quietly, as if he might be heard above the din in the dining room. "This is none of my business, Jack, but it's pretty obvious to me that you're one of the lads that they've got pegged for the sexy stuff. It was no accident that you got to fly that retrieval. And you didn't fuck it up. You did a hell of a good job with it. You, Sally Ride, Crippen, Young till he's so old he can't see—they need to have a few high-profile hotshots. Otherwise, if it looks like any Joe Blow can do it, it loses its mystique and the public loses interest. You'd be a crazy butthole to up and quit."

•

A sullen and drenching storm had swept inland from the Gulf on Saturday morning, but by the time I reached Brenham, the torrents were simply showers. The clouds were broken and unenthusiastic in Giddings, and by Austin the sky was a hot blue haze. The house that Peggy had rented on Blanco Street was shielded by sycamores, and the kids' bikes lay on their sides on the lawn. Mark MacArthur's silver Saab was parked in the driveway behind our old Chevy station wagon, and he came out the front door as I walked up the cracked concrete steps. It seemed fairly obvious that Peggy had tried to hustle him on his way before I arrived, but either I was early, or he had stayed a minute or two too long.

Peggy asked me if I remembered Mark; I said yes, and we shook hands. He seemed assured of himself, relaxed and friendly—a little too friendly for my taste, as if he were a politician trying to look cordial for the cameras in the moments before a debate began. He asked me some silly question about a fuel-cell problem on *Columbia*—writers always think they are such insiders—and Peggy was noticeably nonplussed when I told him I didn't know what he was talking about. He left in a roar of engine noise, his amiable expression gone as soon as he got inside his car.

Peggy had cut her hair, and I said yes, I liked it very much, as we went inside the house. She held my hands when we stopped in the living room and told me she was happy everything had gone so well. "I tore my nails to shreds while I watched TV," she said. "Without the kids, I was about to go nuts by the time you got back into *Challenger*. I called the motel in Cocoa Beach and got your dad. I don't know if it was the fact that you were okay, or maybe it was talking to me, but he sounded so tearful. When Sarah got on, she didn't really seem to be able to connect you with what she had seen. I was so happy for you, Jack, but boy, that was a bad day. Being alone, and in Austin, of all places . . ."

Peggy squeezed my hands before she let go and turned to walk into the kitchen. I watched her pour iced tea into two tumblers and thought about what partners we once had been, aware of how calm and secure she still could make me feel, and aware of the maddening ways in which we forever gnawed at each other's frailties. She looked pretty—poised and healthy and very happy, I presumed—in the bright kitchen light, and I ached in the instant that she handed me the tea, offering it in a way that reminded me I was just a guest.

The kids were in the neighbors' backyard, she said, and we went out to the deck to see if we could spot them. I told her that if she didn't have plans, I thought maybe we could have an early dinner before I drove home—nothing elaborate, just El Rancho or something, if she was comfortable leaving the kids for a couple of hours. I caught her slightly off guard with the invitation, but she said okay, sure, before Matt came bounding into the big backyard.

Except for Sarah's missing teeth, I was surprised that neither of the kids seemed to have changed in the weeks since I had seen them; I guess I always expected my absence to make their spurts of growth seem shocking. At eleven, Matt was still young enough to be able to hug me without any of that odd adolescent self-consciousness, and Sarah, who had a small Band-Aid taped to the bridge of her nose, let me carry her back through the house and out the front door. Peggy waved good-bye from the porch, and the kids insisted that they share the front passenger seat. I buckled them in, pleased that Peggy would see me being so conscientious, and I gave the horn a silly little honk as we started off.

Our first stop was at Hut's for a hamburger, and while we
waited for a chubby blond waitress in a tight VIVA TERLINGUA
T-shirt to take our order, Matt said, "Hey, Dad, you know
while you were in space, could you see cars and houses and
stuff?"

"We could see a few highways, and airport runways, but not
houses."

"I said I bet you could see something like that, but Mark said
all you could see would be clouds and oceans."

"Do you guys get along with Mark?" I asked, aware that I
probably shouldn't be asking.

"He's okay," Matt said.

"He's nice," said Sarah, "but he always wants you to ride
piggyback and stuff."

Sarah asked about Gus while she was eating, and I told her
he still purred as loud as ever, and that I assumed that meant
everything was fine. She wanted to know if he could come live
at their house. I told her it was okay with me, but explained
that cats don't like to travel. "Cats like Gus like to stay home
where everything is real familiar."

"But it's not familiar if me and Matt and Mom aren't there,"
she said, stumbling over the word "familiar," and I wished I
could tell her how correct she was.

Although they both seemed comfortable and were happy to
see me—the father who had been on TV and *everything*—it
was strange to see the kids without Peggy. Except for the three
days that I had kept them when Peggy went to a college
friend's wedding a few years before, and the four or five afternoons we had been together since they had come to Austin, I
had never spent time with either of them without their mother.
It was as if I knew them only as extensions of her, as the two
terrific undertakings we had accomplished together. And who
knew what they thought about me? I suppose I was the guy
they didn't really know that well, but around whom every-

thing had always been shaped—late dinners and short vacations, weekends spent wondering when I would call, too many bedtimes spent hearing me shout.

We went to Zilker Park after lunch and watched hundreds of people swimming and splashing in Barton Springs. We debated whether we ought to go back to the house to get their suits, but Sarah was plainly intimidated by the crowd and Matt was noncommittal. When I suggested that we could rent a canoe, both were immediately game, and soon we set off intrepidly from the shores of Barton Creek, Matt paddling in the bow and Sarah sitting on the hard aluminum hull, her hands clutching the thwart more than a little timidly, the orange yokes of their life jackets tied under their chins. The surface of the water was smooth and murky green, and the thick tangle of trees at the banks helped us pretend we were out in the wilds of territorial Texas, but we could see the tops of the buildings downtown when the creek met the quiet Colorado—not *the* Colorado, of course, but the lovely, impounded Hill Country impostor. There was virtually no current—the river languished between a series of low dams as it angled through the city— and we slowly paddled upstream toward the big, shaded island at City Park. I asked Sarah if she would like to try to paddle, but she firmly declined the offer.

"This is neat, Dad," Matt said, turning to catch my eye. "Papa said we could canoe up there sometime, too."

"We should definitely do that. Next summer. I can think of lots of rivers I should show you guys."

"Can Mom come?" Sarah asked.

"Sure. She can if she wants to. But..." When I spoke again, quietly and haltingly, my words sounded as if I were listening to someone else. "I guess you guys already know that Mom and I think maybe we shouldn't live together anymore."

"You're never going to live with us again?" Matt asked. This time he didn't turn around.

"I don't know, Matt. Your Mom likes her new job here, and

this is a nice town. You both told me you like it. But I have to
be in Houston. Lots of families run into these kinds of problems, don't they?" I wanted him to tell me he understood, but
he was too honest to do so.

"If you quit being an astronaut, would you move over
here?" he wanted to know.

"I'm not planning to quit," I said, "but if I did, it would be
because I had another job, and I would have to go wherever
that job was."

"I think there're lots of jobs here," Matt said. And Sarah said
she was sure they had room for me and Gus before the bow of
the canoe slid into the soft mud at the shore of the island. I told
them to take off their shoes and socks before they got out, and
Matt was the first to step into the dark muck that sloped up to
the grass.

"Dad," Sarah said, a little apprehensive about how she was
going to get out of the boat, "I don't think maybe you should
ride that shuttle anymore."

•

Peggy had met Mark MacArthur a year before when *Texas
Monthly* sent him down to do a story on the lives of the con-
temporary astronauts' spouses, an article spawned by the film
version of *The Right Stuff.* Peggy's morning interview had
evolved into a long lunch and a late-afternoon drive to Galveston. As I recall, both the kids were off at Astro World with the
Grimes clan when she finally got home that evening, giddy and
slightly drunk, telling me some strange story about hunting all
over the city for a part for the writer's Saab. Peggy had never
had to fabricate explanations before, and her first attempt was
terribly transparent. I reacted not with anger, but with a surprising kind of interest; I could guess that she had had an enjoy-
able afternoon, and I had been party to too many short-lived
liaisons over the years to feign any sort of shock or sense of

betrayal. It wasn't until Peggy began to make weekly trips downtown, on the pretext of planning a drive for the local MS chapter, that I began to suspect that the two of them were staying in touch, and I finally confronted her when I found a packet of shampoo from the Four Seasons Hotel in the back of a bathroom drawer.

In the cold and rainy weeks after Christmas we seemed to fight incessantly, arguing about how I was ignoring my obligations at home, about how Matt's attitude was beginning to reflect my inattention, about NASA's meager salaries and its demands for total devotion, and of course, about the fact that Peggy was fucking some handsome and sensitive English major. Mark MacArthur was only the second person she had ever slept with, probably only the fifth or sixth she had ever kissed. She told me, amid my sarcasm and sorrow and a deepening sense of emptiness, that they brought out the best in each other. She told me he made her feel vital and intelligent and important; and then one miserable Sunday night in March, she returned from Austin and haughtily announced that she had rented a house.

"The kids have never gotten up in the morning and found Mark at the house," Peggy said, sitting across a small table from me at El Rancho. She had on a teal skirt and those old Navajo hammered-silver earrings we had bought in Ganado a dozen years before. She looked lovely, and as we drove to the restaurant I felt strangely as if the dinner had become a bona fide date. "I guess I wanted you to know that. It's important to me that that isn't one more thing to confuse them. Mark seems to understand."

"Listen," I said, "I really wasn't trying to get his goat about *Columbia* this morning. I really hadn't heard about any problem."

"That's okay. But I know he'd like to think you two could talk whenever you saw each other. It would be too bad if you had to be enemies."

"You can't expect us to become fishing buddies, Peg. You know, there is a fundamental deal here that he and I look at real differently." I smiled at her. "I just wish you didn't seem so goddamn happy."

"I guess I am happy. Not just with Mark. I feel... I don't know, capable, I guess. And it's a nice feeling. I hope I don't have to work in a university admissions office for the rest of my life, but I could do it if I had to. Don't take this the wrong way, Jack, but what I mean is... I like being *me* and not just Mrs. you." She glanced at the table, then took a sip of her margarita, her tongue touching the salt at the rim of the glass.

"So," I said, twirling a bottle of Bohemia between my fingers. "So what's to be done? Is it time for the D word?"

"Maybe," she said, touching my hand for a second. "I think I'm pretty clear on it now, but I don't have any sense of urgency about it. Being married or not married isn't really the issue, is it?"

"Do you and Mark want to get married?"

"He was married for a couple of years, just out of college, so he's not one of those guys who is desperately curious about it. But I think he would like to marry me. One time he made some comment about having children and I just about fainted. Then I made it very clear that I was not about to start that business all over again."

"The kids asked me this afternoon if we were ever going to get back together."

Peggy's eyes were wet when she looked at me. "What did you say?"

"What *could* I say?"

"Oh, Jack..." she said, and then she was briefly silent. "It's their questions that I can't handle. They're my weak spot, I'm afraid." She bit her lip. "My other weak spot is that I do miss you dearly sometimes."

"Me?" I said, trying to muster a comic smile.

"How are you doing?" she asked as the waitress brought our

dinners. I studied my plate and took a bite before I answered.

"Let's see. I took a big trip recently, but you know about that. Then I went to Colorado, saw the folks, pissed them off, saw Michael, pissed him off, saw your mom and dad, but I wasn't with them long enough to piss them off."

"How'd you upset your folks?"

"Oh, God. I don't even want to admit it. I was supposed to talk about my flight after the service last Sunday. But I had gone up in the mountains with Jane Bergen on Saturday. I ended up forgetting to go, totally forgetting."

"Jane Bergen. Very interesting. She had always been a major fantasy of yours, hadn't she?"

"Peggy."

"Just curious. I wasn't going to ask about all the sordid details."

"Her dad died last week. Cancer. We went up to his cabin to get some things."

"Oh. Gosh, Jack. I'm very sorry," she said. "Did you get to see him?"

"No. But Dad said Hal got to watch the flight and everything on TV from the hospital. I was happy to hear that, I don't know why."

Peggy nodded and smiled faintly, and her eyes assured me that she understood what I meant. They told me too that she could still be proud of me. "It must have really been something."

"Everything just went so beautifully," I said, "and my God, being in orbit...Dad and I sat up late one night talking about it and I think for a minute, the way I talked, he thought I had got religion again."

"Maybe you did."

"No. No, I didn't see God. But seeing everything else really did do something to me. It really did. On our last sleep cycle before we landed, Bill and I decided not to bother to go to bed. We were just passengers on the ride home, so it didn't matter if we were bleary-eyed. We went up to the flight deck and floated by the cockpit windows and listened to tapes on a Walkman we'd brought along. It was amazing. There we were, the lights off and everybody else quiet, listening to Marvin Gaye, the earth absolutely dazzling, going from day to night. It seemed as if *Challenger* was totally motionless and the earth was doing this elegant spin beside us."

"It made it all worth it, didn't it?"

I stopped. "You mean you and the kids were a fair price? I don't—"

"No, I just meant..."

"I'm not sure I hold the mission completely responsible for our calamities."

"I don't," she said, speaking softly now, her voice edged with a certain sadness. "Oh, that's not true; I suppose I do. I hold NASA responsible—that whole Big Brother mess over there. But..." She sighed. "That's the business you're in, isn't it?"

"It's a fucking crazy business sometimes. I can't argue with you about that."

"Well, it's definitely crazy, but it's what you want to do. I can't—couldn't—deliver an ultimatum. NASA or me. That wouldn't be fair."

"It's pretty hard not to believe that's what you did when you moved over here, you know."

She reached across the table; her fingers clutched my wrist. "Jack, something terminal happened to us, didn't it? Maybe it was because you were so busy. Maybe it was because I was just a selfish bitch. I don't know. But there we were in the middle of it. We were sinking in it, and we were scared, I was scared. Sometimes I think we lashed out at each other just because we were frightened."

"What were you afraid of?" I asked.

"Oh... afraid of being nothing more than your goddamn associate, I suppose. Going from what we had, what we really

shared once upon a time, to just being business partners or
something. That felt like death."

"That house sure feels dead," I said when I finally responded.
"But then I think about living in some singles complex in Sea-
brook or something and that sounds hideous. When I go places
by myself, see people who know us, I feel . . . embarrassed, like
I went bankrupt or something. And everybody's too polite to
bring the subject up."

"The easy thing was to get out of town," she said. "I just cut
and ran, didn't I?"

When we left the restaurant we walked down Brazos Street,
then angled our way across the steep, grassy slope on the north
bank of the river. The sun had set behind the wooded hills, and
the sky's high haze had turned orange. We passed two women
with fishing poles who sat in lawn chairs at the water's edge,
but the cindered path was empty. I wanted to put my arm
around Peggy, or to hold her hand, but I was afraid she might
think it was some sort of signal, some sort of wordless plea, so
I buried my hands in my pockets. I didn't want to talk about us
anymore; that conversation was too bleak, too predictable. I
just wanted to walk, to savor the strong, inexpressible things
that still connected us to each other. She asked about Michael
and Mary and my mother and father, and I said something
vague about Jane, probably not so much to make Peggy jealous
as to convince her I wasn't the emotionless drone she had often
accused me of being.

"Do you think there's a chance?" she asked, sounding mad-
deningly disinterested, as if my answer would certainly have no
effect on her. "For the two of you?"

"Do you care?"

"Well, I want you to be happy."

"I don't want to be alone for the rest of my life. I know that
much."

"Is that reason enough?"

"Peg. I . . . I don't think you're the proper counselor for me on this."

She laughed. "I'm sorry," she said as she took my arm. "God. I am my mother's daughter."

Walking at the edge of the still water, its wet, musty odor somehow full of emotion, it was easy to remember why I had fallen in love with Peggy so long ago. Yet now there was a new distance between us, a kind of estranged civility that kept us from tearing into each other and reopening all the wounds. But it was a distance that also prevented us from drawing too close, from daring to seem vulnerable or dependent. Even during my most desperate nights, I had never imagined begging Peggy to come back, promising that things would be different. And that night in Austin, I wasn't tempted to tell her we should try again, starting from seasoned scratch. But neither did I want to simply shake her hand and tell her to stay in touch. I still cared for her more than I could imagine, more than I could confess, but that fact had become merely melodrama.

A narrow finger of water cut into the slope ahead of us, and the path curled into the cove. We stopped at the spot where a thin sandbar separated a stand of trees, and I bent down to put my hand in the water.

"Let's go swimming," I said.

"You're crazy."

"No, really. Come on." I unbuttoned my shirt and tossed it onto the grass.

"Jack!" Peggy said, her voice a loud whisper. "This is the middle of the city, for heaven's sake. Somebody's going to come along."

"No they won't. And what if they do? Come on; it's warm." I was quickly out of my clothes and I waded in a few steps before I glanced back, then dived. I swam three strokes underwater, and when I came up I was surprised at how far I already was from the shore. I waved at Peggy in the dim light; she shook her head. I could hear the traffic on the Congress Avenue bridge as I started to swim, and soon I was far enough out of the cove that I could see the headlights of the cars as they roared overhead, the vibration from the big bridge echoing off the water. When I began to swim back, I could see Peggy across the rippled surface, and she was stepping gingerly into the water. She wore only her panties; she held her arms across her breasts, and I was suddenly numbed by a terrible sense of loss.

"Come swim," I called when I got closer to the shore. She shook her head again and smiled, and I could barely see the tears that now streamed down her cheeks. The water rose above her knees and she stood motionless for a long time. I treaded water, watching her stand there in the disappearing light like an aloof and lovely stranger.

"God damn you, Jack," she said at last, and then she dived.

•

Peggy promised she would kiss both of the kids goodnight for me when we sat in the car in front of her house. Her hair was wet and smelled wonderful when she leaned over to kiss my cheek. I told her I would call and that I would send a check in the middle of the week, and she kindly said good-bye when she could see I was starting to cry. I drove home without stopping, the radio off, the windows open to the the steaming Texas night. I parked in the dark driveway beside our house, then rolled back the seat and slept until daylight made it easier to go inside.

four

Jane's plane was more than an hour late, but the Orlando airport was an easy place to wait in. I checked in at the rental desk and got the keys to the car, then browsed through a long magazine rack, where I found Henry Cooper's latest book-length account of the space program in *The New Yorker*—the story of our retrieval mission, in fact, an article so long and surely sleep-inducing that I wasn't confident even I could get through it. But kind and patient Mr. Cooper had written flatteringly about my retrieval, it appeared, so I took a copy of it up to the jaded, gum-chewing cashier, her red fingernails as long as the little scoring pencils they give away at golf courses.

With my magazine inside my garment bag, I rode the monorail out to the concourse where the United flight from Denver would arrive, and found a table in a little bar done in trendy neon and wicker and blond wood, a bar with a lovely view of the lush, landscaped flatlands that flanked the runways, a bar that demanded a near ransom for a simple gin and tonic. I could do this, I thought. I could be one of those Monday-through-Friday guys whose expense accounts are geared for business suites in downtown hotels, twelve-dollar breakfasts, and lunches that last until three. I could live with the bus rides to the rent-a-car lots and the rude receptionists who would tell me to please be patient, Mr. Jones was a busy man; I could live with the long and liquored waits for an endless succession of airplanes. As I dropped the slice of lime onto the ice, I tried to convince myself that I could do anything I had to.

The weeks at home had been predictably boring—as flat and shapeless as any I could remember. My hours at the space center were boring, very nearly a complete waste of time; and the evenings at the house were so vacant, so slow, that I finally had gone alone to a couple of Astros games, and had even spent one night getting stupidly drunk in a singles bar for the cresting-forty crowd over near the Galleria, far enough away from home, I thought, that no one could possibly know me, the kind of place where the deejays always play "Yesterday" when asked for a slow song, where the men always manage to bring up the subject of their vasectomies in the first few minutes of conversation. I danced with two women, but neither of them seemed interested in the issue of my sterility—or my virility, for that matter—and I spent most of the evening bent over a highball glass, awkwardly out of place.

Peggy and Mark dropped the kids off the following Friday evening on their way to Corpus Christi; I asked them to come in, but they declined, waiting in the car with the motor running while the kids took their bags out of the back. Peggy didn't admit it, but I knew she wouldn't—that she couldn't—go into the house. Both Matt and Sarah had friends stay over on Saturday night, and on Sunday we went to Kemah and ate shrimp at Joe Lee's, watching the small square-rigged yachts and white cabin cruisers with names like *Texas Miss* and *The Kids' Inheritance* sail out into the salty bay. They were both asleep on Sunday night when Peggy and Mark returned, two hours late. I'm sure I was a little icy, and when Mark offered to help carry Sarah out to the car I told him I thought I could remember how to do it. Peggy said she was sorry they were so late, and I had the feeling she wished she could somehow make Mark disappear for a minute. "I'll call," she said when Mark mentioned that it would be two in the morning before they got to Austin. I said sure, but I didn't return her wave as they backed out into the street.

On Monday I called Shirley Stockton, a realtor and the wife of a shuttle pilot, a woman who had a reputation for being charming enough and crafty enough to sell oil to the Saudi Arabians. We met for lunch, and before I went back to work she had me so convinced that she could get a great price for the house—despite the sorry shape that Houston's housing market was in—that I agreed, on the spot, to list it. But by Wednesday, when she called to say that she already had a couple who would like to see it, I said something about how I knew I couldn't really proceed without Peggy's approval—which was true—hoping I could stall for a week or two, realizing that once I started to show people the closet space it would be difficult to change my mind. Shirley seemed a little irked at my indecision, but said she understood, the sweet South Texas lilt in her voice going sour as she spoke. When I hung up the phone, George Abbey, the director of crew operations and my immediate boss, came into the office with the news that somebody at NASA headquarters had decided I ought to speak at a VIP reception at Kennedy on the evening prior to *Discovery*'s launch—nothing elaborate, he said, just a dramatic tale or two from the dark unknown.

"God, George," I said. "You know how I hate that kind of stuff."

"Sounds like a personal problem to me," he said. "We'll send you commercial; I'll have Sandy take care of the tickets."

So a week later, I sat in the Orlando airport on a sunny, suffocating July afternoon, wondering what in the world I would actually say to the assembled Very Importants, wondering how it would be to be with Jane again. It hadn't been hard to convince her to meet me; I told her on the phone that since she was the great space skeptic, I wanted to see whether the spectacle of a launch could capture a bit of her callous cowwoman's attention. She asked if a trip to Disney World was part of the package, and I said absolutely not. She said she'd settle for a dip in the deep Atlantic, and called back an hour later to tell me she'd gotten a flight.

•

I watched a stream of passengers walk off the Denver plane. Many of them wore Martin Marietta name tags and must have been en route to watch the launch; I was terrified for an instant that the woman who had written me, who was still among my most pleasant fantasies, would be among them, walking a step or two ahead of Jane. But she did not appear, of course, and at last Jane walked through the narrow door, spotting me immediately, her dark eyes shining from across the open room. She was certainly no ranch hand, in her sandals and cotton skirt, a black shoulder bag, and a pale blue T-shirt that hugged her handsome breasts, but she kissed me like a brash cowgirl, and we held each other for a long moment before we turned to get out of the way.

"So this is Florida?" she said. "Florida becomes you. You look great. Sorry I'm late."

"So do you. But I guess I was expecting Annie Oakley."

"Disappointed?"

"Not yet."

While we waited for the monorail, she told me my dad had

sent his love. She said she thought she had found a buyer for her cattle—a rancher near Mancos who had come from California with money stuffed in the trunk of his Mercedes, no doubt; and Pegasus the colt was already racing across her pastures. "It's a good summer," she said. "I feel almost optimistic again, like I've really got some sort of a chance."

The Beeline Expressway cut a straight swath through the cypresses and coastal pines, the land so flat that the horizon seemed to hang no more than a quarter-mile away. Stout, slick-hided cattle lay in the shade of the trees; a few grazed belly-deep in the tall and tawny grasses. "It's funny to think that this is the real cattle country," Jane said. "We may play Wild West, but places like Florida are where they get serious about growing cows." Then she told me she hadn't been farther away from home than Albuquerque in almost two years, not since she and Kenny had gone to Rochester, Minnesota, where a Mayo urologist told him he was certain Kenny couldn't have children.

"Did you ever talk about adopting?" I asked.

"Just long enough to know it was out of the question. That wasn't the point, really. Kenny didn't really want a baby, I don't think. He just wanted to see what his genes could produce—especially in the way of a son."

The highway shot straight off the lip of the mainland and a causeway carried us to Merritt Island, the bridge's arch climbing high enough that I could point out the space center's Vehicle Assembly Building in the hazy distance, a building so big, I told Jane like a tour director, that it has its own weather system, clouds clustering against its flat metal ceiling. We crossed the Banana River and turned south at the Air Force station onto A1A, a two-lane beachfront road flanked by gas stations and T-shirt shops and small cinder-block houses, the town of Cape Canaveral giving way to Cocoa Beach without an identifiable break between them. Neither town would have ever been much more than a supply stop for scattered citrus growers, or a

frowsy weekend haunt for families from Orlando, I don't suppose, had not the Army begun testing its V-2 rockets on bare
nearby beaches in 1950. The towns boomed in tandem with the
burgeoning federal missile programs, then turned into tin cities
as the tentative space age dawned. A quarter-century later, the
two towns sprawled along a ten-mile strip, filling the thin barrier island with places like the Satellite Lodge, the Rocket
Drive-In, and restaurants with bright Naugahyde booths that
advertised "shuttle lunches." Yet Jane and I agreed there was a
kind of gimcrack appeal to Cocoa Beach; it was a town that
looked simple and shoddy and already a little old, its aluminum
siding and painted cinder-blocks battered by wind and salt-
water and sand. "If you traded the palm trees for junipers, I'd
feel right at home," Jane said. I told her that if she liked the
rat-ass approach to community planning, she definitely had to
come to Texas, as we pulled into the Holiday Inn—the room
arranged by NASA—a large antenna dish mounted on a four-
tired trailer in the parking lot, and letters reading GOOD LUCK
DISCOVERY mounted on the tall marquee.

I leaned against the pillows and headboard of the square,
king-size bed while I called to find out when I could pick up
our passes, and Jane stepped out of the shower as I was about
to hang up the phone. Her hair was wet, her face flushed and
shining, and she struggled with one hand to secure the towel
that was wrapped around her.

"Now that's a job you ought to let me help you with," I
said. "I'm good at that kind of work."

"No doubt. I bet you spend lots of time in motel rooms,
ministering to energetic young groupies."

"In my dreams, I do."

"Do you know how old I've gotten, Jack?"

"Well, you're a year older than me, and I'm pretty damn old,
I'm afraid."

"Darla Hightower and I were in the same class in high
school. Now her daughter's ready to graduate, and her son

pumps gas at the Chevron station, and Darla sleeps with a fifty-year-old mortician."

"Is she married?"

"Yeah. I don't know who Paul sleeps with. I really don't try to keep track of that kind of crap."

"You just sneak off to Florida to rendezvous with dashing strangers."

"You are something of a stranger, aren't you? But I didn't sneak. Donny, my irrigator, has got the motel's number, in case that rancher comes through with the money, or the place burns down or something. And your dad drove me to the airport, for heaven's sake."

"Did he know any more about Mike?" I asked. I had spoken with my parents just before leaving for Orlando and had heard there was some new trouble. Michael somehow had become terrified of one of those men who sleep at the church and had tried to strangle him. Now a decision had to be made about whether Mike could continue to live there.

"Your dad said he talked to Father Long, who feels pretty strongly that Mike ought to stay, but your dad's afraid that maybe it just won't work."

"I'm not sure it will," I said before I let it drop, making an effort to push my brother out of my mind. I propped a pillow beneath my head as I watched Jane get dressed; she knew I was paying shameless and rapt attention, but she didn't seem to mind. She dried her hair while I shaved; it seemed odd—but very pleasant—to be in that kind of casual proximity with someone again.

We ate dinner in a ramshackle restaurant built on a small pier perched above the Banana River. A screen held the mosquitoes at bay but did not block the slow breeze that carried the pungent smell of sluggish water. We drank Mexican beer, ate scallops and hush puppies, and watched comical brown pelicans jockey for position on a series of waterlogged posts, waiting for the kitchen door to swing open and for scraps to sail into the water. We watched three children who had been sitting at a table next to us walk to the deck on the outer side of the screen and begin to throw crumbled saltine crackers into the water. Following each toss, the water seemed to boil as dozens of crazed catfish fought for the meager prize. The kids squealed with delight, their parents casting them smiling glances as they spoke, but there was something so strangely maniacal about the fighting catfish that Jane was plainly uncomfortable.

"They shouldn't let them do that," she said. "Those stupid catfish probably never leave this pier. I bet they just eat crackers and chew each other's whiskers off."

"What about the pelicans?"

"Well, at least they've got a little style. A little self-respect."

Jane told me she had begun to wonder whether she should stay in Durango, as the kids came back to get more crackers. "I don't know," she said, "Maybe I need some shaking up." Then the sun sank below the low line of trees on the opposite side of the river, and I paid the bill and we left, leaving the car where it was, walking the three hundred yards to the seaward side of the island, past a house where two shirtless, muscular men sat drinking beer on the hood of an Oldsmobile, past a house where we could hear a woman singing in Spanish, over the wooden footbridge the city had built to span the grassy dunes, and onto the hard sand beach.

The distant yellow lights of fishing trawlers seemed to hang in the darkness, and dim orange runners of light flashed momentarily as cresting waves crashed into the shore—a lyrical kind of light emitted as the pounding waves excited bioluminescent plankton, the light fading almost as suddenly as it appeared. Flat, foaming water rushed up the sloping sand and reached our feet; Jane slipped off her sandals and carried them in her hand as we walked northward toward the checkered lights in the condominiums, toward the faint lights suspended on towers at the space center.

"So where would you go?" I asked, reminding Jane about what she had said at the restaurant.

"Oh... I'm not going anywhere. I really don't think I am. Sometimes I just feel myself turning into someone so staid it's kind of scary. I don't want to end up being one of those tight-assed old widows who yell at kids when they write in the dust on their cars. I just want to try to keep a little life in me."

"Have you gone out with anybody?"

"No, not really. This stockbroker that Kenny used to deal with took me to dinner one night a couple of weeks ago. Then we went to his house and he showed me this album, all nicely arranged, with pictures of his ex-girlfriends, most of them crotch shots, the girls spread-eagled on his water bed. I couldn't believe it."

"Sounds like a real charmer."

"I had my car, so I produced a sudden headache and got the hell out of there. Jesus. Doubt I'll try that kind of thing again for a while. It's funny, I don't really want to be alone, but the thought of having to work at a new relationship just sounds impossible."

"I know."

"Sometimes I could just kill Kenny for dying on me like that."

I laughed, then wasn't sure whether I should have. "Something else I've been curious about," I asked, speaking tentatively, making the question sound more portentous than it was. "Do you go to church? Regularly, I mean. I guess I was a little surprised that you and Dad seemed so close these days."

She didn't say anything for a moment. "When I was in the hospital after the accident, about the only people I saw for weeks were your dad and my dad. I was in pretty bad shape, terrible shape really, suicidal, and I guess they kind of screened people out. For some reason, I couldn't ask my dad to help me out, so one morning—I remember it was a lovely day—I asked

your dad if he could get me a couple of dozen Seconals. That's
all I asked. I had thought it all over and it seemed like such a
simple and logical kind of decision. Anyway, your dad didn't
respond for a bit. Then he finally said that he wanted me to
know that he could imagine situations—desperate situations, I
think he said—in which he would very willingly agree. But in
my case, he said he was sure it wasn't the right decision. I
suppose I have to agree now that he was right, but ever since
then, he has been incredibly kind to me—I mean, fatherly, to
be sure, like he's looking after me, but also like he was flattered
in a way that I had asked him for that kind of help." She had
spoken to the sand and the sheeting water, but now she turned
to me. "So, yes. Yes, I've gone to church almost every Sunday
since I got out of the hospital. I'm sure all the devout ladies on
the Altar Guild assume the accident shook some sense into me,
but it's just your dad, really. It's the only way I can think of to
show him I appreciate him sticking by me. Besides, it gets me
out of the house."

"I don't think he'd ever bring up the issue of the church with
me," I told her. "Not anymore. I know it would mean an enormous amount to both of them—Mom as much as Dad—if I
were to—what's the word?—practice the faith again. But...
well. What I ought to do is bring it up myself sometime. Tell
them it really isn't a major rejection of him or the church or
anything. It's just that there's something, something in me that
. . . I don't know."

"Was it ever important to you?" Jane asked.

"Oh, God. There were a few years there, at the end of high
school, when I was your basic junior monk. There wasn't ever
a dramatic change, but somehow the passion subsided. I don't
know what took its place. Maybe science. Not that physics or
cosmology made Christianity seem stupid. At least they didn't
pose great conflicts with it in my mind. It was just that the
more I studied astronomy, the more enticing it was—like the

cosmos itself had a kind of, well, spirituality, that made it all the more compelling."

"Sort of the Carl Sagan school of theology," Jane said. I could see her grin in the dim light that reflected off the water.

"Well, yeah, except that makes it sound every bit as maudlin as he can be. I'm definitely not the cosmic evangelist he is. And I'm sure I'll always be a sucker for the liturgies—what Dad calls the bells and smells, and the chants. They certainly aren't out of my system. I had to make a quick trip to see people at British Aerospace last year. I was in London on a Sunday morning and I went to mass at St. Paul's—just seemed like something I wanted to do, for some reason. And it turned out to be this very emotional experience. I was a little shocked at myself. I mean, I did not see the divine light or anything, but I felt like I sure as hell knew what my roots were."

"You should tell your dad sometime," Jane said.

"But then he'd get his hopes up."

"He deserves more credit than that, Jack. You know, it's too bad you had to be his son. I bet you two could have been good friends."

I knew what she meant, but, for some reason, I didn't tell her so. I did tell her about my trip to Austin, trying to explain how finding Peggy so confident, so vibrant, made me feel proud and jealous and angry all in the same instant, trying to tell Jane—without having to speak the words—that I was still wrapped in Peggy's emotional web. If I had control of Michael's mind, then surely Peggy was the person in possession of mine.

"Why don't you swallow hard and try to make it work?" Jane asked.

"Well, because for one thing, I think she's in love with somebody else. And we couldn't just pick things up again. Peggy really hates the NASA life. And as long as I'm there, I'm going to be committed to it in a way that she finds unacceptable. Ten years ago or so, I think we really had something. I mean, our relationship had a kind of substance to it. We dealt with our lives in tandem, as a family. We really did. But that kind of dissolved over time—probably more my fault than hers—and I don't think you can just wish that . . . that substance back. I guess I suppose it really should be over. Honestly. But there are days when I sure don't want it to be."

"How did Peggy feel about it when you first applied?"

"Matt was just a toddler. Sarah wasn't born yet. Peggy had given up a job that she really liked at IBM in Boulder to have Matt and to be at home with him, and I think, well, I'm sure she was happy with that decision. When I told her I wanted to apply, she was so enthusiastic, maybe because the odds seemed so slim. Then when I got word that I was a finalist, we both had to begin to seriously consider the possibility. When I got home from my interview at the space center, I told her to relax. I was sure I had totally fucked things up, and that was that. Then one day—it was in late May of that year—I had been out getting drunk on a Friday afternoon with my dissertation chairman and I got home and there was Peggy looking like somebody had died. She said John Young had called and I was supposed to return his call as soon as I could. John was appropriately cagey with her, but she knew. She was sure he was offering me a spot, and she was crying like it was all over. After I got off the phone with John, I held her for a long time, trying to console her. Poor little Matt couldn't figure out what was going on. I had just gotten a job that thousands of people would die for—an incredible opportunity—and there I was trying to tell Peg that it wouldn't be so bad."

"She wasn't the one who got the job, Jack. All she got was to tag along."

"I know. No, I understand why she had very mixed feelings about it all. But what was I supposed to do? Call Young back and tell him the deal was off?"

"And so that was the point at which things started to change?"

"Yes. Yeah, I'm sure that if you want to isolate it down to a specific point, that was it. We had some good years when we first went to Texas. It was fun to be someplace new, and we got to travel more than we ever had, but . . . well, you know how the story ends."

We had a drink in the motel bar before we went to bed, and Jane wondered aloud about whether she and Kenny would have endured the years together. "I think I'm basically one of those through-thick-and-thin types," she said. "But I'd hate to think that I would have put up with something second-rate forever."

"Was it second-rate?"

"It seemed like it had gotten to be. But then he died and for a long time all I could remember was true love."

Jane and I made love on the motel's king-size bed the way we had on that small, cold mattress in the La Plata Mountains. Neither of us spoke, our attentions to each other necessarily silent and serious, our kisses and thrusts so determined, so strong they were a kind of combat, until I found the stump at her right wrist and began to lick it, nibbling it, putting it between my teeth, and she started to laugh. Her laughter brought mine—it was uproariously funny somehow—and we rolled laughing across the big bed, Jane on top of me when we stopped, her nipples near my mouth, still laughing, joking, the two of us at last able to surrender our strange solemnity, fucking for almost an hour, our stern passion mercifully replaced by play.

In the still hours of the night, Jane shouted in her sleep, yelling, "No, no, you can't, no, he won't make it," until I put my arm across her shoulders, her hard breath subsiding, her fingers clutching my forearm. We slept late in the morning. I got up, took a shower and went out. When I came back with the paper and a pot of coffee, she was awake, smiling sleepily, looking lovely with the white sheet draped across her waist, and I decided I wouldn't ask her if she remembered why she had shouted.

•

We drove the little rental car to the space center in the middle of the afternoon, showing our passes to an officious guard at the south gate who studied them as if they contained a secret code, then driving between rows of orange trees and alongside deep lagoons. Lazy alligators sunned themselves on smooth rocks and hordes of gulls squawked as they swung out over the water. Hundreds of cars were parked at the visitors' center, and tourists jammed the exhibition areas and the gigantic gift shop that sold Gemini capsule earrings, NASA caps, jackets, and mission patches, antigravity pens and Apollo playing cards. While Jane and I browsed through the long rack of launch postcards, a voice on a loudspeaker announced that because of special events surrounding the launch, the visitors' center would close in ten minutes. People packing cameras with long lenses and people towing two-year-olds on leashes began to leave immediately, and soon the place seemed deserted, empty except for the plump men in plaid sport coats and women in Izod dresses, all wearing badges, who were congregating in the covered courtyard that had been filled with folding chairs.

Five hundred people must have seated themselves by the time Richard Smith, Kennedy's director, stepped to the podium and welcomed everyone to "America's Spaceport" and to *Discovery*'s maiden launch. He said a few words about the history of launch operations at the Cape, something optimistic about the future of the shuttle program, and acknowledged the crew —now sequestered in a nearby building—before introducing a tall, wiry woman on the White House staff who conveyed President Reagan's best wishes and then started a jingoistic spiel about how space was America's destiny. She didn't mention the crew, or the fine new ship in which they were about to sail, but she did say, "God bless the shuttle; God bless America," before she sat down to polite applause.

There were noticeable gasps and the collective craning of necks when Smith introduced John Denver—a towheaded boy from Texas named Deutschendorf, who had moved to Aspen and changed his name, a singer who had become a staple at shuttle launches—presumably free of charge—in hopes of improving his chances of becoming the first pop musician to fly in space. And the NASA brass had always seemed thrilled with his interest, assuming, I'm sure, that if he could turn a song about Jacques Cousteau into a hit, he could do the same for the shuttle. Denver's trademark bangs were brushed back, his wire-rim glasses replaced by contacts, and because Judy Resnik, only the second American woman to fly in space, was part of *Discovery*'s crew, he said, he sang "Annie's Song," its sentimental lyrics a tribute to his estranged wife. Then he sang "Rocky Mountain High," supposedly for my benefit, but probably just because everyone expected him to, the song a popular paean to Colorado that had become something of an embarrassment to many of the state's residents—and I counted myself among them.

It had been too hot to wear my coat, but it was time to put it on. I tightened the knot on my tie, straightened its tails, and asked Jane to wish me luck. She whispered back, wanting to know if I knew what I would say. I grimaced, shaking my head. "I'm just going to let the Lord speak," I said, and Jane laughed so loudly that the couple in front of us turned around and glared. John Denver was still on the little stage when I walked up following Mr. Smith's introduction; I had met him briefly once before, but he greeted me like an old crony, taking my hand in both of his, pumping it, saying, "Great to see you." I shook Smith's hand as well, then went to the podium.

"You're looking at a lucky guy," I said in a thin voice that surely betrayed my nervousness. "Two months ago, as Mr. Smith mentioned, I got to take quite a trip. Ever since I was a kid, looking at the moon through a small telescope with my friend Hal, seeing it from a mesa in Colorado, I've known I wanted to travel, to see as much of the earth as I could see, and also to see what lies beyond the earth. Since that time, I have seen, through much larger telescopes, planets with exquisite ring systems, dying white dwarf stars, and the stupendous explosions of supernovae, places millions and billions of miles away from home. Our recent trip, taken in the orbiter *Challenger*, took us only about two hundred miles away from home, less than the distance from here to Miami, but instead of traveling via the lenses of telescopes, we actually left the earth, something that is rather astonishing when you stop to think about it.

"Any type of travel is a form of exploration, I guess, whether it's a mission to the moon or a trip on horseback up the side of a mountain. Travel tells us about things that are new or unknown to us, and—just as important, really—gives us new ways of looking at the place we started from, at *home*. While we orbited two hundred miles above the earth, and especially while I flew alone in the MMU away from *Challenger*, I think I truly realized for the first time that the earth isn't separate from space. It is as much a part of space as the moon or meteors or the Milky Way; it is part of the everything astronomers call the cosmos. Even though without the aid of rockets we cannot push through the thin envelope of the atmosphere and leave this planet, we're still truly connected to the solar system, to our inconsequential little galaxy, to our local supercluster of stars, and to the *everything*. And when we fly in our rocket machines, ships like *Columbia, Challenger*, and now *Discovery*, we aren't really going to places that are frighteningly foreign, we're simply going a little bit beyond the places we know to the places that remain unknown. Our journeys to space seem similar to me to the search for the passage to the Far East that led to the discovery of this continent, and they seem similar to my son's brave explorations of the swampy woods behind our house in Texas.

"Regardless of what some people may tell you, this isn't just another way to waste the government's money. Tomorrow, *Discovery* and its crew will go to space not just to explore, but to go to work, work that benefits us all. But I can assure you that in the course of doing their work, those six people will have a whale of a lot of fun. They'll be able to see the earth and the rest of space from a startlingly new vantage point, one that's really overwhelming, and if they aren't changed just a little by that experience, well, it will be because they just weren't paying attention. Thanks very much. I sure hope you all enjoy the launch."

It was short—and a little schmaltzy—but there wasn't much else I wanted to say or could think of. I stood at the podium, grinning stupidly while people applauded, then waited while Mr. Smith made an announcement about cocktails out in the "rocket garden" and the dinner in the cafeteria. I signed my name to the backs of a few postcards and to the jackets of a paperback book called *The Kennedy Space Center Story*, and was chatting with people clustered around the stage when Jane reached me, kissed me on the ear, and whispered, "That was sweet of you to mention Dad."

"You were supposed to catch the reference to trips on horseback."

"I caught it," she said, then waited until I found a way to excuse myself, and we walked out of the courtyard to the grassy field crosshatched by sidewalks, where several launch vehicles, supported by a web of guy-wires, stood like a collection of space-age candles—an early, unmanned Jupiter and a Juno, an Atlas-Agena, and a stout Titan II with a black Gemini capsule mounted atop it. "Trifle phallic out here, isn't it?" Jane said.

"You love it."

"Yes, but we don't want to scare the children."

Young women in black skirts and white blouses served wine at tables covered with linen cloths, and the guests milled about the bases of the rockets as if they were attending some sort of NASA fund-raiser. "Did one of these things send them to the moon?" she asked.

"No. The Saturn vehicles were like eight or ten times the size of that Titan over there." I pointed it out. "We're talking big firecracker."

"Must have been fun," she said.

"Oh, Jesus, can you imagine! I know I'm a real geek about this kind of stuff, but just think what it was like for those guys in lunar orbit, crossing the terminator from the dark side, seeing the earth rise above the moon's horizon, this planet looking like a goddamned *planet*. I think it's a wonder they didn't all just wig out."

Jane laughed, amused by my earnestness, I suppose. "I think there's some evidence that that's what happened to you. But I shouldn't—" She was interrupted when Mr. Smith walked up with the woman from the White House and the Indonesian ambassador—whose country's satellite we had deployed on my mission. He introduced them and I introduced Jane; she put out her left hand and each of them made an awkward attempt to shake it. Then she excused herself. While I made small talk, I could see her reading the plaques on the base of each of the rockets.

Following a quick dinner of barbecued pork, served up by the jolly, beer-bellied Florida crackers who cooked it, we drove away from the visitors' center in the dying light, past another checkpoint where I had to do a little creative storytelling in addition to showing our passes, past the Vehicle Assembly Building, which looked in the floodlight like the world's largest filing cabinet, and alongside the crawler-transporter track to a bare field in front of a final checkpoint, security at that spot taken so seriously that the guards wielded machine guns. We got out of the car and sat on its hood, the damp air still sticky and hot, the launch vehicle brilliantly lit, Jane silent, her eyes fixed on the imposing, enormous machine, the orbiter erect and ready, looking sleek in the white light, looking impatient. I started to explain how they would begin to fill the external tank with the cryogenics in just a couple of hours, and how the catwalks and the vent arm would be swung away from the tank and the orbiter in the final minutes before the launch, but instead I just let her look.

A few other cars were parked nearby, and a bus filled with people who were at the reception rolled to a stop, its passengers spilling out, filling the quiet night with excited conversation. Jane curled her hand beneath my arm and pulled me close to her, then finally spoke. "So you rode that outfit, did you? I had planned, for your benefit, to remain rather unimpressed."

"I'll pretend I didn't notice," I said as I saw a station wagon stop in the dim distance. Its six silhouetted passengers got out, then did nothing for several minutes except stare at *Discovery*, leaning against the car's fenders, draping their arms over its open doors. "See that car over there?" I said, pointing into the night. "That's Hank Hartsfield and J.R. and the rest of the crew. They're supposed to be in their jammies by now, but almost all the crews try to sneak out so they can see this thing at night, like this. I remember that looking at it here, lit up like some sort of cathedral, was when it really hit me. God, I was psyched. Now those poor bastards are supposed to go back and try to sleep."

•

Neither Jane nor I slept much either; we didn't get back to the motel until after midnight, and the wake-up call came at four. We drank coffee from Styrofoam cups as the long line of buses, filled with the crew's families and NASA's invited guests, rolled in the darkness across the Banana River causeway and north toward the space center. Hundreds of cars had already pulled off the roads on Merritt Island—people gathering in clearings at the water's edge to wait for the coming launch. In the clusters of cars, vendors hawked hot breakfasts, shuttle T-shirts, and cheap binoculars from the beds of pickup trucks. "Must be quite a show," Jane said, and I admitted to her that I couldn't honestly say. This would be the first time I had seen a launch in person. I had *felt* a launch, to be sure; my launch shot through my spinal cord and shook me to life as nothing before had ever done, but all I could see through my visor were the compartmented walls of the mid-deck and the sudden change through the hatch porthole from bright daylight to blackness. Except for dozens of video replays, today would be the first time I had actually watched a launch vehicle lift off the ground, then leave the ground suddenly and spectacularly behind.

But ninety minutes later, standing in the tall, damp grass at the viewing site, the fiery ball of the sun rising above the sloughs, I knew my wait would continue. Launch Control announced an unscheduled hold in the countdown to check on a glitch in the onboard computers, and then, following a failed fifty-minute attempt to get the five computers to synchronize, came word that the launch had been scrubbed. The crowd surrounding us moaned in sudden disappointment; people began to whisper their disbelief, and then we all slowly made our way back to the buses.

Jane and I ate a weary breakfast in a diner on A1A, neither of us saying much, both a little at loose ends, I suppose, both of us listening to the three men at the counter banter with a gray-haired, gravel-voiced waitress about which of them would make the best catch. "If you three was my only damn choice," she said as she filled their coffee cups, "I think I'd just keep buying batteries and keep to myself." The men, two of them balding in the back, each wearing a T-shirt out over his trousers, hooted at her remark, and Jane gave me a quick wink. "Smart decision," she whispered, and she nodded affirmatively when I asked her if she felt like a little illegal sightseeing. "Where?"

"The Air Force station. The old launch pads. They'll probably shoot us or audit our taxes or something if they catch us in there, but—"

"Let's go," she said. "That's what I meant the other night. I'm looking for a little intrigue."

At the guard station, near the docks where the shuttle's solid-fuel rocket casings are brought back to shore and where, that day, a dark Trident sub floated passively in the morning sun, I showed every piece of JSC identification I owned, explaining that I was on NASA's VIP detail, explaining that Jane was a congresswoman from Colorado who was hoping, since the launch had been delayed, to get a better sense of what had preceded the shuttle. "I'd just like to show her the Navajos and Redstones and everything there by the museum," I said, "if we won't be causing any problems." On a Thursday that was to have been a launch day, the serious young guard with the sunburned nose surely had instructions to keep the station secured.

"Sir, I . . . ah, I guess I could let you pass if you're just going to the museum. But all the restricted areas are totally off limits. You understand, sir." He handed my cards back to me, then bent into the open window to see Jane. "I'm from Helper, Utah, ma'am," he said, just as earnestly as he had spoken to me, "southeast of Provo. Got some family in Colorado, over by Fairplay."

"What is their name?" she asked, sliding her hand under my knee as she leaned over to speak to the young man.

"They're all Dodsons."

"Dodson. Well, I believe I've met some Dodsons from Fairplay. It's a big family, isn't it? They seemed like awfully nice people."

"That's them," he said, his face breaking into a grin. "Son of a gun. You have a nice day, ma'am. Sir."

The guard saluted as he stepped back, and I tried to muster a civilian salute in reply before I drove slowly ahead, through the thick stands of scrub pines and eucalyptus, past the turnoff to the museum, along the narrow, empty road that skirted the shrouded launch pads, their rusted gantries rising above the trees like ramshackle steel skeletons. A sign said that Complex 14, hidden somewhere in the short distance between the road and the rising surf, was the site of the launch of John Glenn's first orbital flight and of the remaining Mercury missions, but it read NO ADMITTANCE in big block letters.

"Yeah, this is a good one to show you," I said, and I turned onto the asphalt spur that ran through the trees to the cement-and-sandbag bunker that had once protected launch observers, its low dome—looking a little like a minor Mayan temple—now sprouting clumps of grass. A hundred yards away, the gantry that once loomed high above the pad had been dismantled, and the concrete ramp on which launch vehicles had been rolled into place was buckled and badly cracked. Signs that read ABANDON IN PLACE had been bolted to the few metal walls that still stood, leaning away from the ocean wind, their thick coats of marine paint peeling away in twisting strips.

Jane and I climbed the rickety stairway that curled around the base of the bunker and that led to a padlocked metal door; then we stepped over a rusted railing and scrambled to the top of the mound, our feet slipping on the bright green moss that clung to the concrete on the seaward side of the bunker. "I'm surprised they let it get like this," Jane said when she sat down, her head turned toward the pad and the thin line of sandy beach we could now see beyond it.

"They weren't the sort of guys who would have ever thought about making this a shrine," I said. "This pad was probably built in a matter of weeks and its only job was to get the Mercury capsules into the air. It was cheaper and quicker to build new pads, on up the beach, than to keep retooling this one. It must have been a wild time; Kennedy had already made his man-on-the-moon speech by the time Glenn was shot out of here."

"It looks so little," Jane said. "The pad. I remember watching John Glenn's launch in Mr. Peterson's class. He was so excited I thought he was going to wet his pants; and listening to Walter Cronkite, it seemed like it was probably the size of the Empire State Building or something. Wesley Weston made some crack about Glenn singeing his ass off, and old Peterson just looked crushed that everybody wasn't taking it as seriously as he was. You weren't in that class, were you?"

"I talked my mom into letting me stay home to watch it. I'm afraid I was probably even a little more gung ho about it than Mr. Peterson was." I gave her a sheepish grin, confessing what she already knew, that I had been a bit of a nerd. I didn't go so far as to wear a row of pens in a plastic pocket protector, but I'm afraid I was pretty weird. I think I comprised fully one-third of the science club.

"The main thing I remember about you is that you were about a foot shorter than me. I spent a lot of time in those years feeling like an Amazon, some sort of giraffe with big boobs. Whenever we had to walk down the aisle together in our choir robes, I just wanted to melt." I laughed, and I lied, telling her I didn't remember noticing her breasts. "Jack," she said softly, pausing as she said it to change the subject, "isn't it a shame that now we're almost old enough to know what we're doing we can't spend a little more time together?"

"Then why have you dodged all my invitations to come to Texas?"

"Oh, I'd come to Texas for a while," she said, looking away from me. "It'd be fun. But you'd worry about keeping me entertained, and you'd have to explain me to your friends. And after so many nights of me having a drink ready for you when you walked in the door, you'd start to get scared."

"Maybe I'd love it. Maybe it's what I need."

"What you need is to sort things out. You're going to need some time."

"But it doesn't have to be spent in solitary confinement."

She glanced at me. "I guess I haven't told you that Kenny was having an affair when he got killed. A woman who worked at the Strater, some twenty-year-old tart who worked at the front desk and could usually sneak them a room. He knew I knew, but we never talked about it. I guess I had a hunch that it wasn't something that would last long. It made me feel like I'd had the breath knocked out of me, sort of weak and stupid, but I never confronted him. I guess I just wasn't up to it, and I really did love the son of a bitch." She pulled pebbles of concrete out of cracks in the bunker and tossed them to the ground. "There's something similar with you. This has been terrific, seeing you at home, and down here. It's been exactly what I needed, but you won't know what you think about me until you and Peggy are really settled."

"You haven't been listening to me. Peggy and I are done. I'm sure of that. And you are a lot more than a convenient hotel clerk."

"Am I?" She turned to look at me. "I hope I am. But listen. You may know everything there is to know about spaceships and whether the moon is made of green cheese, but you don't know what you want yet. What you want for yourself. I don't want to be alone either, but . . . oh shit, I don't know." Jane got to her feet, brushed the dust from the seat of her pants, and pulled her hair back with her fingers. She made her way slowly down the bunker's slope, then walked across the expanse of concrete, avoiding the small flowers that grew out of its cracks, and climbed the ramp to the pad, its exposed I-beams still charred by heat and rocket smoke. While I watched her, I wondered why, in some subtle way or other, I chronically crossed signals with the people I cared most about—the kids not understanding why I couldn't be with them, Peggy only flourishing without me, my parents too supportive for my own good, and poor Michael too tormented to know whether he could count on me, me too selfish to truly lend him support. Now here was Jane, dear Jane who had swept away my silly doldrums, telling me I didn't know what she meant to me. She called from her perch on a massive sheet-metal wall that was pierced by threaded bolts, standing on a rusting ruin of the space age, waving her arms to get my attention, her hair whipped by the wind that washed in off the water. "Hey, here I am," she shouted. "Ready when you are." She hung her arms close to her sides and stood at attention, mimicking a small and slender rocket. "Come on, Jack, blast me off," she called, and I pushed the imaginary button on the top of the crumbling bunker that sent her shooting into the sky.

•

Dad was depressed, grimly afraid that Michael might have to return to the hospital, when I called from Cocoa Beach. Jane sat on the edge of the bed, watching me pace, twisting at the end of the phone's short tether, hearing me suggest to my father that I stop in Denver on my way back from the Cape.

"Jack, I'm not sure you should," he told me. "I don't think it ought to look like we're rushing up to rescue him." When I asked how Father Long felt, he said he was sure he was worried, but that he thought it would be a mistake to move Mike back to Pueblo. "John's the one we ought to trust on this," Dad said. But when my mother got on the phone she told me that Dad had called the hospital early in the afternoon to see whether they had room to readmit him. "Thanks so much for calling, Jack," she said, "You two take care of yourselves." I smiled at Jane when I said we would, mindful that when Mom was worried about one of us, she always insisted that the rest of the clan be careful.

Jane's liftoff from the Mercury ruins, her rocket flight of

fancy, was the only successful launch at Canaveral that week. At dawn on the following morning, a main-engine fuel valve stuck momentarily and the onboard computers aborted the launch at $T-4$ seconds, shutting the engines down just two seconds before the solid boosters would have fired and pitched *Discovery* into the drink, the orbiter certainly sinking, the crew conceivably lost. The radio reports immediately began harping on how the shuttle program was plagued with problems, and I'm sure I argued the point endlessly, and rather needlessly, with Jane on the bus back into town.

We checked out of the motel and drove up A1A toward the Beeline, past the auto-parts stores and surfboard stands, past the entrance to the Air Force station and the turnoff to the pads at Kennedy where *Discovery* still stood on its tail. I tried to tell Jane how sorry I was that she hadn't been able to see it sail up and out of the sky, but she wouldn't listen. "Next time," she said, patting my thigh, running her fingernails along the seam of my jeans. "I'll come watch you lift off inside it sometime."

"So, how much time has to elapse before I can see you again?" I asked over coffee in an airport cafeteria.

"Just a while," she said. "Just long enough for you to snap back to your senses." She showed me her handless arm. "I'm old, Jack, and I'm lame... and I'm not sure I ought to be at auction."

I tried to tell her she was wrong, before she laughed and said she too needed time, time to wear out her mourning clothes. "If there's anything to it, it'll keep," she said as her smile flattened, her eyes looking bright and wet and probably wise.

She held me tight, telling me to cheer up, for heaven's sake, then turned and walked away before I finally had to head down the jetway to board my Houston flight. I realized I had forgotten to tell her to let me know how her land deal turned out as the L-1011 lumbered down the runway. I could see the shuttle landing strip and the string of concrete pads along the coast as the plane climbed up out of the sluggish haze and the Florida disappointments. I wrote Mike a postcard, telling him I hoped everything was going fine, at about 33,000 feet.

five

August is only a humid haze by now, and all I really remember about September is that it was the time when my life
in Houston began to seem like a kind of lonesome suffocation,
akin to what I supposed Michael continued to feel. I was more
isolated than I had ever been—solitary in the sense that I had
no one to look out for other than Gus the cat, no one to tear
away that self-absorption that can cover you like a clammy
sheet when you're responsible only for yourself. Yes, I put a
check in the mail to Peggy each week; I called the kids on
Saturdays, and during the week I suppose I was amiable
enough with the people in the astronaut office. But I was in
desperate need of a deep breath of compassion, some measure
of care and concern for someone else. I needed somehow to be

drawn outside myself, to be rid of this John Richard Healy character whom I couldn't manage to escape. I was tired of his smooth maintenance of the status quo, tired of the compulsive way in which he kept a tidy house and an unruffled facade, sick to death of the way he pretended to coast—like an object in perpetual orbit—without wobble or drag or destination.

I did stay in touch with my parents and abreast of Michael's condition—he was still at St. Andrew's, but it now seemed unlikely that he would remain there for very long—and I talked to Jane on the phone frequently, often calling her after midnight, Texas time, finding her sleepy but sweet, willing to hear my vague complaints, too willing, really, to let me indulge in my sullen brand of self-pity. I tried repeatedly to convince her to come down for a while—for a week, at least, sometime—but she repeatedly told me she could not. Lawyers were laboring over the details of the land sale, she said; her horses had to be attended to; she finally had agreed to be fitted for a prosthesis; and besides, she told me on a night when she said she could hear coyote pups howling beyond the house, I didn't sound like I would be very good company. "I'm no good at playing nurse, Jack," she said. "I've got enough to do to look after myself. I don't want to have to take care of the rest of the sick and wounded."

I had finished the last of my flight reports shortly after I returned from Cape Canaveral, then spent the next six weeks on a selection-committee assignment, interviewing an earnest batch of astronaut-candidates—tall and strapping fighter pilots with tiny American flags pinned to the lapels of their civilian suits, physicians and astrophysicists who, to a person, said they wanted to go to space because space was the new frontier. Over the course of the weeks of interviews, I asked each candidate whether he or she would be willing to wait seven or eight years for a flight. Each one said yes, certainly, but I saw more than a few faces betray surprise and a degree of dismay at the suggestion that a long wait would be likely.

It remained to be seen when, and if, I would fly again. Secretive military missions were interrupting current crew assignments; faulty payload-assist motors on several shuttle-deployed satellites had slowed the scheduling of missions I might be assigned to; and, of course, a couple of dozen people with longer tenures than mine were still waiting to fly for the first time. My best guess was that I would be able to fly again someday, but in the meantime, I had to assume I would spend two or three years on languid long-term policy-review committees, on teams evaluating issues like inflight crew efficiency and fatigue, and out on the public relations circuit—awarding productivity pins to employees of the private contractors, telling boozy, disinterested conventioneers that the space program had already improved their lives.

But on a Sunday morning in early October, a day when the heat had finally begun its autumn fade, George Abbey stopped by the house as I was barbering the backyard hedge with a pair of long electric shears. "Had something on my mind, so I thought I'd stop by," he said, as I wiped the dust from the patio chairs. He declined a beer, but I got one for myself before I sat down to listen. "I think it's about time we put you back to work. If you're ready. I guess I want to know how things look for you these days. I take it you're still a bachelor?"

"I'm... well, I think I'm pretty permanently separated, George. There isn't a divorce in process yet, but there probably will be before too long." I grinned at him. "You mean you wanted to find out if I was too strung out to do decent work for you?"

"The University of Colorado is going to have a couple of Halley's experiments on a *Challenger* mission in January. We got word last summer that Headquarters had gotten some pressure for somebody who'd been to school there to be on the flight, which I didn't have any problem with. I thought about you, but I didn't think it was fair for you to have to start training again immediately, and, to be honest, I had heard some scuttle-

butt that this business with you and Peggy had been pretty
hard on you. So, anyway. We gave the mission to El Onizuka,
and he's going to do a hell of a good job for us, but that leaves
me wondering what I can do with you."

"If you want me to fly, George, I'll fly in a minute." I tried
to choose my words before I spoke again. "Yes, it's . . . it's been
an adjustment for me, but I'm okay. A little at loose ends
sometimes, but frankly, you'd be doing me a favor if you put
me back in training."

George seemed to be studying the quality of the hedge trim I
had in process. "We're going to deploy the telescope a year
from now. Looks like October. Crippen's going to command
the mission. It'll probably be *Discovery*. No pilot set yet. It
looks like Gina Rinaldi will operate the arm. You and Ron
McFarlin would be in charge of the power-up of the telescope;
no EVA unless we have a glitch of some sort. The mission'll be
short—three, four days. But from a five-hundred-mile orbit,
there ought to be a hell of a view. What do you think?"

What I thought immediately was that this couldn't possibly
be true. Yes, I had hoped I could be involved in support for the
deployment of the telescope, but I had never dreamed that I
might be part of the crew. The telescope, big enough that it
would fill *Discovery*'s entire cargo bay, the most powerful telescope ever constructed, was expected to expand the perceivable
volume of the universe by something like 350 times. It would
be able to detect light sources so distant, their light emitted so
long ago, that astronomers would very nearly be able to ob-
serve the beginning of time. I was no longer an astronomer—I
had really never been one—but the thought that I might be
able to help deploy this remarkable new instrument was one
that I instantly relished. Yes, absolutely, of course, I wanted the
mission, I told George before he said he was off to get his car
washed.

I walked out to the street with him, and he explained that if
the crew selection was finalized and approved quickly, we

would begin training in about three weeks. I wanted to tell George how much I appreciated the assignment, the trust, but my words were muddled, and he waved them off as he drove away.

Inside the house, giddy, anxious, and still a little unbelieving, pacing the floor by the kitchen phone, I tried to call Jane, letting the line ring for a long time before I gave up. Then I began to dial my parents' number, but I stopped when I realized that they would be at St. Mark's.

I did talk to Jane on Sunday evening; she seemed pleased for me, but she was unmistakably distant. The telescope held no particular fascination for her, and the mission simply meant that the two of us would grow more separate. "I'll be thinking about you," she said as we hung up, as if I were a sailor who was ready to put to sea.

I called my parents a few minutes later, but I got no answer, and I still had not reached them with my great good news late on Tuesday night when Dad called me to say that Michael had hung himself.

•

According to Father Long, Lucy Coleman—the woman I had met who ran the kitchen at St. Andrew's—had returned home from a movie with her son at about ten o'clock that night. When she walked into her bedroom, she found Michael standing beside her dresser, its drawers open, his jeans pulled down to his thighs. He was holding a silk camisole in his hands, rubbing its smooth fabric against his penis. Lucy had told Father Long that surely Michael must have heard her and Simon come into the house, but he evidently was oblivious until he saw Lucy standing at the bedroom door. He looked shocked, then terrified for a second, she said, before he pushed her out of the doorway and ran from the house.

Lucy reached Father Long by phone and told him what had happened. He checked Michael's room, but it was empty. He looked in the kitchen, in the rooms where the street people slept, and he searched the grounds of the church and the alley behind it. A few minutes later, when he turned on the lights in the nave of the church, he heared a bumping sound that seemed to come from the sacristy. The light inside was on when he opened the sacristy door, and he saw Michael hanging from the high hinge of a tall vestment cabinet, hanging by the white cotton rope called the girdle, the long waist sash that Father Long wore at mass. A footstool lay on its side near Michael's feet.

John Long told my father that by grasping Michael at the hips, lifting him and pressing him against the cabinet, he was able to slacken the rope and, finally, to untie the knot around his neck. Michael was breathing, but unconscious. His eyes were open and seemed fixed in place when Father Long laid him on the wooden floor. His heart seemed strong when Father Long ran to call an ambulance.

●

My parents could not get a flight to Denver until seven in the morning; Dad said he thought they would be at the hospital by about eight-thirty. I got his call at two, then dressed, packed a bag, and drove across town to Intercontinental. But the first Denver flight wasn't scheduled until six-thirty, and I had to wait for three hours in the hushed and deserted terminal. The bars were closed; the morning papers had not yet been delivered. Soldiers slept in TV lounges; a few impatient businessmen paced the floors near scattered gates waiting for red-eye flights that would take them to the East, and black men in brown uniforms, their eyes red with fatigue, rode buffing machines as big as lawn tractors through the quiet corridors.

Michael had hung himself. I still could barely comprehend what that meant. He was alive, at least, but I—as Dad had seemed to be—was surely in the buoyant, nearly emotionless throes of shock. From a bank of phones beyond the security check, I tried to get hold of Father Long at Denver General—I didn't understand why they hadn't taken Michael to one of the hospitals nearer St. Andrew's—but I couldn't locate him. Someone in the family lounge near the eighth-floor intensive care unit said she had seen a priest earlier, but he did not seem to be there now.

I didn't know how long Michael had hung before John Long found him, and I wasn't sure what happened when you hung yourself. Did you suffocate? Would you snap your spine and tear your fragile spinal cord? Would you be aware of what you had done, suspended by your neck and surely choking, in the seconds before you blacked out? If Michael was alive, then it must mean that he would survive, I decided while a few passengers began to board my flight. I remember that I was surprised that morning that I wasn't already wracked with guilt—convinced that I was responsible, at least in part, for whatever it was that sent him to the sacristy in search of a bleak solution. Mike was embarrassed, surely horribly ashamed when Lucy saw him pressing his hard penis into her lingerie, and that was the only reason he went looking for the rope. It didn't have anything to do with me, I assured myself in the numbing, noisy drone of the plane's engines. The seats beside me were empty; I leaned back, closed my eyes and tried to sleep, but by the time we had started to descend to Denver, I knew there weren't any easy explanations. Michael's attempt to kill himself wasn't Lucy's fault; it wasn't Father Long's or my father's or mine. Yet if Michael could not be held entirely responsible for his actions, if he was ill, if his brain was beset by a haywire of bizarre connections, then didn't we all have some responsibility to see that he didn't harm himself? I got off the plane, tired and perplexed and somehow very scared.

•

When I first saw her, my mother was standing in a hospital corridor cluttered with empty beds and laundry carts. The Colorado weather was still warm, but she was wearing a wool suit; somehow, these strange circumstances had warranted dressing up. She began to cry when she hugged me, and I tucked a strand of graying hair behind her ear as she blotted her cheeks with a tissue. "How is he?" I asked.

"I'm so glad you're here," she replied. "Mary said she could come out right away, but with the little one, we told her to wait until we got here. Till we knew how he is."

"Have you seen him?"

"He's in intensive care. They only let us in for five minutes every hour. Dad and I both have been in twice. Dad went down to the chapel for a minute, but I thought I'd stay nearby."

"Have you talked to a doctor?"

"The one they have in charge of him is a neurologist. They're most worried that he went without oxygen for too long. She's young, but she's very nice, and we think she's quite capable. She said there's a chance there's some brain damage, but they won't know how bad it is for a while."

"Is there anything that . . . should we be doing anything?" For some reason, I wanted to get busy, to take charge, to hustle around a bit, as if all we had to do to get Michael back on his feet was to expend nervous energy.

"Father Long should be back in an hour and a half or so. He met us at the airport. I know he just feels terrible. Dick walked down to his car with him when he left and tried to talk to him. But, my Lord . . . he saved Michael's life." Her voice broke as she spoke, and tears stained her cheeks. "I called Marge. Buddy had already gone to work. I think she's going to come up sometime after lunch. She's so dear. I guess Dad and I will stay with them . . . if we don't just stay here at the hospital."

"You'll need to get away."

"She told me to be sure to tell you that you're welcome as well."

"Thanks," I said, certain that I wouldn't actually accept my in-laws' hospitality. "I want to see Mike. Why don't you come in with me?"

"I think we'd better wait. They'll let us in on the half hour. It won't be long."

"Just for a minute," I said. Mom shook her head, but waved me on.

The intensive care unit beyond the two heavy swinging doors was a large, high-ceilinged room with curtained beds spaced against three walls. A long desk, a series of illumined monitors, and video screens that pictured each patient lined the wall beneath the eastern windows. I saw four other patients, people with tubes in their noses and needles in the veins of their arms, whom I presumed must be in desperate shape, before I found Mike, looking frighteningly like the people in beds beside him. A two-pronged oxygen tube had been pressed into his nostrils and strapped to his head; intravenous drips were inserted into both forearms. His neck was swollen and a purple bruise already showed where the rope had ringed his neck. His dark hair was untied and it draped across his pillow. His eyes were open, but they were blank. They saw nothing, I was sure, and they registered no sentiment, no knowledge.

"Hello, brother," I said in a whisper. "What a place to find you." I held his hand while I watched him; his hand was warm and strong, and I had never noticed before how much bigger than mine it was. I spoke out loud for some reason, telling Mike to hang in there, telling him he was sure to be okay, telling him that as soon as he was well he had to come to Texas. Hell, I had a house in Houston that was surely big enough for both of us. He could fish in the bay, or play softball on some Clear Creek contractor's team, or—I didn't care—read Arthur

Clarke books all day long out on the backyard lounger. "I need some company, Miguel," I told him, my voice faltering, failing me just as I needed to sound strong. "So get well, goddamnit. Maybe we can even get to know each other again."

A nurse in a sea-green uniform had noticed me standing beside my brother's bed, but evidently she had not been too concerned by my rule-breaking. She acknowledged me with a faint smile, and Michael and I were alone until a woman with lovely olive skin and dark hair as long as his walked up to the foot of the bed. Pinned to her white coat was a plastic name tag that I couldn't read; a pair of glasses sat on her head. "I'm Michael's brother," I said before she spoke.

She smiled, then spoke in a soft voice. "I'm Dr. Parkman. I'm a neurology resident and I'm looking after him."

"How's he doing?"

"Have you talked to anyone yet?"

"My mother told me that you're concerned about brain damage." I stepped away from the bed with her and we walked toward the windows.

While she spoke, she took a stethoscope from the pocket of her coat and ran it through her fingers like a rosary. "He definitely traumatized his neck, but there are no broken vertebrae, and his spinal cord appears okay. The major concern, though, is that the pressure from the hanging effectively clamped his carotid arteries, blocking a lot of the blood flow to his brain for a period. We don't know for how long. We've done an EEG and he's had a CAT scan and they show that he's definitely had a major anoxic episode which—" She caught herself, then offered me a simpler explanation. "He definitely was without oxygen for long enough that much of his brain is very swollen. With as much edema, swelling, as he has, we can't tell yet how much brain tissue was destroyed. The swelling itself can also pose real problems, so he's on heavy doses of a steroid to try to minimize it. He's also on a barbiturate that will slow his brain metabolism and, hopefully, also help with the swelling."

Finally, the gravity of Michael's condition began to confront me. "You . . . make it sound like it doesn't look too good."

"He's a very sick fellow," she said matter-of-factly. "The EEG shows that he has little normal brain function right now. If we can get the edema down quickly, well, that's what we hope we can do. If the swelling remains severe, then no, his chances aren't good." She looked at me as if to say she was sorry I would lose my brother, but she said nothing more before she went back to Michael's bed. I watched her examine his vacant eyes, and I saw her squeeze his fingers and toes and press hard on the sockets of his eyes to test whether he could respond to pain. But for Michael at that moment, pain did not exist. It was far more illusory than the voices he had often heard from space.

●

I found my father in the hospital's huge first-floor atrium, making his way back from the chapel through the peopled rows of plastic chairs that made the room resemble a bus station—young mothers changing children's diapers; old men slumped in their seats, snoring; Hispanic punks in sleeveless shirts and headbands, laughing, shouting, calling each other *cabrones*. I hadn't seen my father since the day in June when I had failed to make it to church. He looked healthy, slimmer and tanned, but his eyes were red and swollen. He hugged me and held me fast for a moment, until one of the *cholos* said, "Hey, Father, are you into boys or something?"

I told the kid to fuck off; he and his friends just laughed at my challenge, and Dad led me away to the elevator. "How are you, Jack?" he asked in that manner of his that always implied that—for that moment at least—that was all he was interested in.

"I've already been upstairs for a bit. Found Mom. I saw Michael for a minute and got to talk to his doctor."

"Is there any change?"

Several people had joined us to wait for the elevator; I took him by the arm and we moved away. "I wanted to come find you before I talked to Mom again. Does she know how serious this is?"

"What did the doctor say?"

"Well... I guess the fundamental thing is that unless they can reduce the swelling in his head fairly soon he... his chances won't be good if the swelling doesn't come down."

He was suddenly ashen; like my mother, he had not heard this grim prognosis, and my words seemed to strike him like a blow. He pursed his lips and blew out a long breath before he said, "Dear God, Jack. I guess I was only afraid of paralysis or something. Are you sure it's that certain?"

"I don't think anything's certain, but she made it clear that things look pretty grave. I just...."

Dad's eyes were wet now, and they exhibited an aching kind of sorrow I had never seen in them before. I wanted to take hold of him, to try to shore him up, but his hands were pressed into his pockets and I was somehow hesitant. "Didn't... didn't Michael deserve just a little bit of good fortune by now?" he asked me. I couldn't respond, my words blocked by sadness for him as well as for Michael, before he said he wanted to find my mother.

We waited for the rest of the morning in the sparse, carpeted eighth-floor family lounge. I made instant coffee for the three of us and sat in an upholstered chair across from my anguished parents. My father held my mother's hand. She, too, was shaken by what she had learned, what the doctor had hesitated to tell her, but she sat erect and straight, a tear sometimes spilling from her eyes as she took a sip from the Styrofoam cup. It seemed strange, strangely uncomfortable, to be waiting there with them. The circumstances of our wait were unique to each of us, to be sure, but there was something else. I had spent little enough time with them outside the familiar environment of their house over the last years that to be sitting silently with them here—in this dank, depressing Denver hospital—made me feel young and anxious and somehow foolish again. The situation reminded me very certainly that I was their son, and that once I had depended utterly on them. In more ways than I understood, surely I was still dependent.

"The only thing we can do is to wait," my mother said, speaking into the cup she held at her chin. She had been beside Michael's bed when we found her, and when the visiting period ended, my father had walked to the lounge with her while I tried to telephone Mary.

I was leaving a message on Robert and Mary's answering machine, saying I would call back at about noon, when Mary got on the line. "Jack, Jack, I'm here," she said. "Sorry. I thought you were somebody I didn't want to talk to. How is he?"

"He's not good. I don't know. From what I can find out, I guess the next ten or twelve hours will be pretty critical. Mom said—"

"I found somebody who can take Adrian. I think I should just come on out, don't you?"

"Maybe you should. But just whatever you think. I don't know what to tell you."

"Is Mike conscious at all?"

"No."

"But you sound like he... Listen. If I get organized here I can get a flight by early this evening. Yes. I'll definitely come out tonight, Jack. Okay?"

I gave her the number of the telephone in the lounge so she could call when she knew her arrival time, then I went back to join my parents' vigil. Dad had spoken to Mom while they were alone, I was sure, telling her what I had told him downstairs, trying to tell her to have hope but not to hope too much, and now they were saying little. She was right. All we really could do was to wait—wait until the swelling subsided and

Michael's brain miraculously began to function again. Or, only to wait the long and hollow hours until he gave up the ghost, his much-besieged brain finally still.

"Well, how have you been, honey?" my mother asked me out of the midst of a long silence; she mustered a wan smile.

"I've been fine, Mom." I returned a grin, and I think I really meant what I said. The self-obsessed stupor I had been in for the past weeks now seemed of little consequence.

"Did you meet Lucy Coleman when you were here before?" my father asked; I told him I had. "Mother and I have known her for several years. She's a wonderful gal. I sure hope this isn't too hard on her."

"It's bound to be," my mother said. "She probably knows Michael as well as any of us do these days."

"I mean feeling responsible. Finding him in her house. That must have..." Dad decided he didn't really want to consider out loud what had happened at Lucy's house.

●

Father Long was waiting in the lounge when we returned from our twelve-thirty watch at Michael's bedside. He rose to greet us, squeezing my hand inside both of his, telling me I looked good, saying he was very sorry these were the circumstances under which we were meeting again. His black cassock and ruddy beard made him appear monastic, and something about him was immediately likable in a way I hadn't remembered; perhaps I was simply glad to have someone else share the awkward waiting with us. "Any change since this morning?" he asked.

"No," my father told him. "Jack talked to his doctor after we had talked to her, and she was a good bit less optimistic with him."

"Saying...?"

"She isn't expecting a good outcome," I said.

Father Long sat on the edge of the sofa and took my
mother's hand. "That was my fear right from the start, of
course. But when he was still with us when the ambulance
arrived, I thought maybe..." My mother patted the back of
his hand. "Had I found him a minute or two sooner...I'll
wonder for a long time why I didn't check the church first."

"John, we're thankful that Mike's alive at all," my father told
him. "If it weren't for you..."

"Have you talked to Lucy today?" my mother asked.

"Yes. She's at work. I had a chance to talk with her. Lucy has
seen a lot. She's very, very sad about Michael, about last night,
but I don't think she'll blame herself. I'm sure she'll stop by
here this afternoon. You know, Lucy and Michael work very
well together, and like each other. His...his eccentricities
don't seem to trouble her."

"We owe all of you a real debt," Dad said. "Michael hasn't
been an easy person to be with."

"Dick and I really would have loved to have him live with
us," my mother said, "but that just didn't work for him. It
didn't seem right, I guess. You've given him the best home he's
had in a long time."

"Mike talks a lot about you, about growing up," John Long
said, sounding now like a clergyman making a house call. "He
has very warm memories about camping out of the end of an
old station wagon with the whole family, of hiking in the high
country with Jack and his dad. He often tells us about a miner's
shack he's going to move to one of these days, way up above
Silverton somewhere, a place he's known about since he was
young. He says it's reserved for him and that no one else can go
there. When I ask him what he'll do there, he says he'll climb
the peaks, a different one every day. He likes the image of just
sitting on the summits. There's nothing there, everything just
drops away, no turmoil, nothing. Just silence, he says."

"I bet I know the cabin. It's up in Ice Lake Basin; it really is
there. It's a beautiful place." I smiled at them. "And we think

he's crazy, don't we? It makes perfect sense to want to be there."

"Jack," my mother said, meaning to admonish me for calling my brother crazy.

None of us had eaten yet that day, and when Father Long asked whether we had, then suggested we get some lunch, Dad and I agreed. But my mother did not want to be away. "Just bring me back a little something," she told my father. "I'm fine right here."

In the elevator, Dad said he would rather not go to the cafeteria if there was another option nearby. "I could use a block or two of fresh air," he added.

"There's that place called Racine's on the other side of Speer," Father Long said. "Let's do that. They may be busy, but let's see."

The October air was warm at midday, yet it carried the crisp and emotive cast of autumn; the leaves of the deciduous trees had begun their lovely yellow transformation. As we waited to cross Speer, I was surprised for a moment to note that this day seemed to be indistinguishable from any other for the people passing in a long succession of cars. None of them seemed to be facing family crises; no one whose face I briefly saw seemed to be confronting the prospect of death. They were fine, all of them. Everything was splendid, or at least it was benignly ordinary, and for an instant, I wanted to wave them down to tell them how wrong they were.

I drank a beer while we waited for a table at the restaurant, but neither Dad nor John Long joined me. As we followed the hostess to the back, weaving through a sea of tables where jovial business lunches were in process, I imagined that people noticing us would wonder why a seemingly normal fellow had brought these two clerics in celluloid collars to this place that was so clearly outside their milieu. But the glances that I noticed did not sustain any interest. Years ago, I had always followed my father into public places with a sinking kind of embarrassment, and I had spent much of my life assuming that priests necessarily caught people's attention. But the truth is, I suppose, that most people watch themselves in mirrors and check on themselves in window reflections much more readily than they ever concern themselves with anyone else.

My father said grace in a quiet voice when our lunches arrived; the two priests made the sign of the cross, but my hands stayed in my lap. Then, perhaps because my mother wasn't with us, Dad asked Father Long if Michael had done anything else that he called sexually inappropriate.

John Long waited before he answered. "Well. I guess I'd have to say that Michael has a fairly juvenile concept of sex. Presumably, he has the same sexual urges of other men his age, but I get the impression that he isn't at all comfortable with them. Out of the blue he'll ask me if I ever masturbate or if I've ever slept with someone, some parishioner he's curious about. I don't get the impression he's interested in me so much as he's trying to figure himself out. For some reason, he seems to have a very guilty attitude about the whole issue."

"Did that come from us?" my father asked, turning to me.

I tried to grin. "No. No, I don't think you are to blame for that. But I know what you mean," I said to Father Long. "Last time I was here, he brought up something similar with me. I don't know. I don't think Mike's ever had a real girlfriend, a normal sort of relationship. The whole business probably seems a little bizarre to him."

"Has Mike ever bothered Lucy before?" Dad wanted to know.

"Not that I know of, no, I don't think he has. At least she hasn't said anything to me. He was aggressive toward me one time, soon after he came here, and well, you know about him trying to choke one of the men downstairs. But I guess I haven't answered your question. One night, probably six weeks ago, we found Michael standing in the doorway of the women's sleeping room. Two of the three women who were there slept right through it, but the one who woke up was pretty scared. He was wearing a T-shirt, but otherwise he was naked. He didn't have an erection, and he wasn't acting aggressive or anything. She said he just stood there and watched before she started to shout. And her shouting didn't scare him away. He was still standing there, kind of catatonic, when I got there. I asked him what he was doing and he said the women downstairs had been calling for him every night to come down and have sex with them, but he said he really didn't want to."

Dad ran his fingers through the hair at the sides of his head, but he didn't say anything. And I, too, was silent. It wasn't easy to hear. We had long heard Michael's fantastic stories; we were very familiar with his hallucinations, with the screaming voices that beset him, but somehow these sexual episodes—the one we had just heard about and the one at Lucy's house that had triggered his suicide attempt—signaled something new. In neither situation did Michael seem to be contemplating rape, yet I couldn't help but wonder whether there was something depraved, something perverse and potentially very serious in his actions. But the other possibility seemed to be that his condition wasn't worsening. Perhaps Michael, like his brother, like everyone else whose brain was supposedly healthy, was only reaching out for someone to love and to make love with. Maybe Michael wanted nothing more than what we all want. Perhaps he simply knew even less than the rest of us know about how to try to find it.

I left the restaurant before Dad and Father Long did, taking half a sandwich wrapped in a paper napkin back to my mother, and as I looked at the high walls of the hospital from across the street, trying to determine behind which tinted window my brother lay, I was reminded that questions about Michael's schizophrenia or about his sexuality, for now at least, were beside the point. The issue of whether his psyche would ever function normally, of whether he would ever fall in love or know the sublime pleasures of sex, were subordinate to the question of whether he would survive.

Buddy and Marge were sitting in the lounge with my mother when I returned. Buddy's tweed cap was in his lap; Marge wore a sweater and pants that demonstrated she still had a handsome figure, and I thought of Peggy for the first time since I had arrived. I should call her, I thought; she would want to know.

"Hello, dear Jack," Marge said when she recognized me; she stood and gave me a warm and sympathetic embrace without saying anything more. I shook Buddy's hand. "Damn, Jack," he said, "I sure was sorry to hear about this."

"Yes," I said. "Gee, it was nice of you to come up. I hope you didn't take the afternoon off on our account, Buddy."

"My girl, Louise, is looking after the shop for an hour or two. It wasn't any problem. She's good help. How's your dad?"

"He'll be along in a minute. He's okay. I think we're all hanging in there pretty well, aren't we, Mom?"

She gave the three of us a smile that said this was not the first time that she had ever suffered. "Yes, we'll all be fine. We're just praying and waiting . . . and hoping. The prayers come easily at a time like this, but the waiting . . . the waiting isn't easy for me." Marge sat down beside her. I motioned for Buddy to join them on the sofa, and I sat across from the three of them. I gave my mother her sandwich and she set it on the end table as if she would attend to it another time.

"I got hold of Peggy after your mother called this morning," Marge told me. "She said she hadn't heard from you yet. I told her Dorothy said you were already on your way up here. She sure was sorry to hear about Mike."

"Thanks for calling. I didn't want to wake them up in the middle of the night, and I haven't tried yet since I've been here. I can catch her once she gets home this evening."

"I'm sure she'd appreciate hearing how things are. Said everything's fine with the kiddos."

"I talked with them on Friday night, I guess it was. Matt's on a soccer team, which he seems to be getting a bang out of. I was going to try to get over to see his game this next week-end."

"All the kids are playing soccer these days," Buddy said. "And all the British and Mexicans and Brazilians kill each other over it, but I don't know. Just seems like a lot of running around to me."

"It's a good sport for the little ones, Frank, that's the main thing," Marge said. "Isn't it, Jack?"

"Seems to be," I said, assuming sports was as good a topic for us as any.

"But then where's our next crop of football players going to come from?" Buddy's rhetorical question was meant to bring us all to our senses.

"You kids didn't play many team sports, did you?" my mother said. "Jack was on the ski team for a couple of years, and Mary . . . was Mary on any teams? Michael was the swim-mer in the family. Always a little water dog. We've got his medals framed and put away in one of the closets. I'm sure he's still a beautiful swimmer," she said wistfully, and her brief re-membrance of the time, long ago now, when Michael's life was full of accomplishment was enough to end that conversation. We sat in silence for a moment, but I had a sudden, sharp image of Michael slicing through dark water.

"How did he look the last time you went in?" Marge asked.

"You're welcome to come in with us when they let us in again," I said.

"No, no, I'm sure the less commotion the better," she said.

"He looks kind of absent, doesn't he, Jack?" my mother said. "He looks as if he's far away from here. His eyes are open, but they don't blink."

"These brain things," Buddy said, clutching his cap, "I guess they can sure be touch and go." I nodded.

"What he looks like," my mother said, still attempting to describe her son, "is like some of those Renaissance paintings of the crucified Christ. You can see the pain, the sadness, but maybe because of it, there's something beatific there too, something almost serene."

•

Michael's condition did not change during the course of the afternoon, nor did his absent expression. When we saw him at three-thirty, just after Buddy and Marge had left, Dad told Michael in a soft and weary voice that all of us were with him. He held my mother's hand to Michael's face, then mine, then his own, naming each of us, telling him that Mary was on her way. He told Michael that Father Long had been nearby, and that soon he would be saying a eucharist for him at St. Andrew's, but he did not mention Lucy or say that she, too, would soon be there to see him.

At five-thirty, my mother told Michael not to worry; her face was streaked with tears, but her voice still had its steady timbre. She told him the Holy Spirit was with him, with us as well. Then, her arm pressed across his chest, she told him she would take good care of him. I saw Dr. Parkman come into the ICU, and I walked away to talk to her while my mother still cradled her son.

Dr. Parkman scanned Michael's chart before she spoke to me. "We'll be doing another EEG here in a minute, but there's some deterioration. His urine output is dropping, which, with the amount of fluid he's getting, means his kidneys are beginning to fail. And his blood gases don't look good; his oxygen uptake is pretty poor. His heart's still strong, but..."

"What about the swelling in his brain?"

"We scanned him again about forty-five minutes ago. Still

massive edema. We'll keep him on the steroids and the pento-
barb, but . . . well, I have to be honest. I'm not encouraged by
any sort of improvement."

"If he continues to deteriorate, how long could he hang on?"

"I'm going to be here at the hospital most of the evening.
Maybe sometime after dinner, you and your parents and I
should talk about the sorts of things that often happen at this
stage. There are some things to consider, and I'd be glad to try
to explain everything as best I can."

By eight o'clock, we had not seen Dr. Parkman again; Lucy
had called the waiting room a few minutes before to inquire
about Michael, saying hesitantly that she had hoped to come
by, before her voice trailed away. Dad called Buddy and Marge
to say yes, they would come and sleep for a few hours, but he
wasn't sure what time they'd arrive, and when he hung up, he
convinced my mother that it would do her good to get away
for bit. The three of us drove to the airport to meet Mary, and
as we parked in an upper-deck lot, I told them I thought it
made sense to rent a second car. "You're going to need a way
to get to Buddy and Marge's later on, and now with Mary
here . . ." I handed my father the keys. "Here. Why don't you
pick up Mary; I'll get another car and meet you back at the
hospital. Tell her I'm glad she's here. I'm going to stop by
Lucy's for a minute on the way back. I'd like to. Just to say
hello. I don't know, I just think maybe one of us should."

"Yes, fine," Dad said. "And tell her . . ."

"Tell her we're thinking about her," my mother said, her
gray hair whipping in the steady wind, her eyes so very tired in
the amber light of the parking lot.

The phone book listed an L.A. Coleman at 1810 Clarkson. I
knew she lived near St. Andrew's, so I presumed it was her
address, but I didn't try to call. Bright street lights lit the grassy
medians on Martin Luther King, and as I drove away from the
airport, I hoped she wouldn't mind the intrusion. I didn't really
know what I wanted to say, but I thought I should try to say

something, to tell her that Michael cared about her, to thank her for being so kind to him, to apologize, perhaps, for his intrusion the prior night.

•

I'm sure Lucy didn't recognize me at first as she peered onto the porch through the thin crack in the door. But as I began to tell her my name, her expression changed and she said, "Jack Healy," before I did. She closed the door to unlatch the chain, then opened it and invited me in. She wore a long terry-cloth robe, her feet were bare, and in the soft light of the foyer her round and lovely eyes looked black as jet. "Is everything...?" Her face completed the question.

"No, there's no change," I said when I realized she presumed there was now something final to say. "I just wanted to come chat for a bit. I hope I didn't catch you at a bad—"

"No. No, come sit down. I just put Simon to bed. He'll be sorry he missed you." I followed her into the living room; she turned off the television and said, "please," as she motioned me toward an overstuffed chair. "I was planning to come by the hospital when I finished work, but I... oh, I've spent too much time in hospitals, sitting waiting like you all are doing. I knew I couldn't be any kind of help to Mike, so... Father said a mass for Mike late this afternoon. Several of us from the church were there. At least we could do that." She sat on the edge of the sofa and pulled the fabric of her robe securely around her knees. "But he's not any better?"

"He's worse, if anything. He... well, I guess we just have to wait, but the doctor is pretty pessimistic."

"Oh," she said. She bit her lip.

"I, I don't know how this has hit you—and maybe I shouldn't even say this—but I sure hope you don't feel responsible at all."

She started to say something, then was silent. Finally, she asked if I would like something to drink. "I've got beer, and there's scotch and there should be some bourbon, too."

I told her scotch sounded perfect, and when Lucy returned with our drinks, she knew what she wanted to say. She sat at the end of the sofa nearest my chair this time, and she stared at me for a moment before she started to speak. "I haven't told Father this, I guess because I don't want him to think it's been a bigger problem than it has. Mike and I have been working together every day for several months now. Since late spring. He was so shy at first. Hardly said a word. I made some attempts to get him to come have supper with Simon and me, or to go do something with us, just to get him away from there for a bit, but he never would agree to come. Then, I don't know, maybe in August or so, I started to wonder if he was kind of getting a crush on me. It wasn't anything big or anything, but he just started to say things in a different way. He would ask me funny questions, like if I ever dreamed about him. Or if he'd see me talking to someone, a man, he'd want to know if I was going to marry him. I'd tell him no, of course, but he'd always start sulking. Wouldn't say anything for the rest of the afternoon. And he started making me things, giving me things." She pointed toward the dining room, which was lit only by the light angling into it from the room where we sat. "He made that cross that's above the table. It's beautiful, probably took him forever to make. But then there were things like boxes of candy, and an atrocious silk scarf one time." She smiled. "It was very sweet, but it was starting to get awkward. I had been trying to figure out a way to talk with him about it, but you know Mike. I was afraid I'd hurt him if I said the wrong thing."

"Had he ever come over here before?"

Lucy put her drink on the coffee table. "Once before. A couple of weeks ago. Simon and I had been over at my mother's house. It was dark when we got back, and Mike was sitting on the porch, in the dark, just waiting, I guess. I said hello, but all he said was 'You weren't here,' like he was a little angry about it, and kind of nervous. He was acting strange enough that I wasn't sure I wanted to invite him in—you know, he'd gone after that old man not too long before—so I sent Simon inside and I sat on the porch rail and talked to him for a minute. He wanted to make sure that I wasn't out with anyone, out on a date, and he pestered me about it long enough that I finally kind of snapped at him. I told him it really wasn't any of his business where we'd been. He got this horrible look on his face, hurt and kind of outraged, really. He stood up and called me a name and threw this cardboard box at me, then ran off down the street. Boy, I did not want whatever was in that box." She shook her head. "I finally opened it before I went to bed. It had this creepy, cheap kind of negligee inside. Oh, I just wanted to burn it, I felt weird, so awkward. I decided what I had to do was to give it back to Mike and to have a talk with him. The next day, though, he seemed perfectly normal, saying nothing about the night before, of course, and I just let it go. It just seemed easier than to risk upsetting him again."

"Sure," I said.

"But damn it." She was angry with herself. "If I had talked to him, maybe I could have put an end to it. Maybe he wouldn't have come back last night."

"You shouldn't feel like you're the only person who's had trouble talking to him," I told her. "My God, that's the whole basis of my relationship with Michael. Him thinking I mess with his mind, and me feeling guilty as hell that I don't know what to say. Or that I don't try hard enough to say it. I'm just sorry that . . . you must have been pretty frightened when you found him here in the house."

"It would have been a lot more scary if I hadn't recognized him, but I did right away and I . . . I wasn't afraid for me or for

Simon, really. I just had that same sinking feeling, like I just
wanted to run away. I didn't want to have to deal with it."
Lucy sat back against the sofa, her drink in her hand again.
"I've been alone for five years now. I know exactly how it feels
not to have somebody you can hold onto tight, somebody you
can wrap around you. Sometimes you just ache to have somebody love you and smother you. But you just have to ache,
because he isn't there, and all you've got is yourself. Mike's just
like other people in that way. He has that ache too. Course he
does. It's just that he's disturbed in a way he can't understand,
so when he does something crazy like last night, it seems so
weird or sick to everybody else. But don't you suppose Mike
just wanted to stop that ache? I think that's all it was."

Lucy got up to get me another drink; she took my glass, and
this time I followed her into the kitchen. Simon's drawings
were taped to the tall refrigerator; the dinner dishes were
washed and stacked in a drying rack. As she bent to take the
bottle of scotch out of a bottom cabinet, her robe parted
enough for me to see her small brown breast, and I thought my
knees would buckle. Of course, Michael had to be in love with
this woman, I thought; he would be crazy not to be. I wanted
to tell her so, to make a joke of Mike's infatuation—and my
own—but, probably wisely, I refrained. We sat down again at
a small kitchen table that was flanked by only two chairs. Lucy
pulled herself close to the table and rested both elbows on its
surface, the sleeves of her robe as wide as those of a nun's habit.

"How long have you been separated?" she asked.

"You know I'm separated?"

"When you're standing peeling vegetables, you have lots of
time to hear about all kinds of things."

"So you've heard about how I scream at Mike from long
distances," I said.

"Yes indeed. And about how you were really the first man
on the moon, and how you've been to Mars as well."

"I see. All the family secrets." I looked down at my drink.
"Yes, we've been apart for about a year. I've assumed . . . that
you're a widow."

"Yes. My husband, Richard, Simon Richard, was a pharmacist. He worked in a small drugstore–liquor store combination
over on Colorado Boulevard. One February night five years
ago, two kids held it up. They had the liquor clerk on the floor
when Richard came out of the back. The clerk said she didn't
think he knew anything was going on. He surprised the kids
and one of them turned and shot him. Three times. He lived
for fifty-seven hours. I sat and waited just like you're doing."

"I'm sorry," I said, sounding stupid in response, "you must
. . . I'm really sorry. You've had to deal with an awful lot by
yourself." Why was I always so inarticulate, my comments so
inane?

"I grew up here. Got lots of family—a sister, two brothers,
my mom's still alive. And I've got a few friends like you
wouldn't believe." She smiled. "That's what gets you through
it. Finally. For a couple of years, I felt like nobody on this earth
knew how bad I hurt. Nobody could say the right thing. I
thought everybody I loved had become so cruel, so insensitive.
Everything was great for all of them, and they just didn't give a
damn about me, I thought. I put up this steel barrier around
me, just like to hell with them, I'm tough and I can manage
and I'm doing fine. I was so proud of myself 'cause I could
handle anything, but everybody else thought I was cracking
up."

"How did things get better?"

"I don't know. Just time, I guess. Time enough that I
couldn't help but realize I wasn't the only person who'd ever
gotten a raw deal. That and loneliness. You get real lonely after
so long of convincing yourself you don't need anybody."

"I bet you had a good marriage," I told her.

"Yes, I think it was good, at least it's good as I remember it.
But it wasn't something out of a romance novel." Lucy

laughed. "I wanted to kill that son of a gun a time or two. The thing about being married—I guess you think about this when you're on your own—is that, when it works, you've got an ally, you know, a partner. The tough things, the hard things, the things that eat you up, you face them with somebody else and that's one great big advantage. Course, I've got Simon and the rest of my family, and I've got Father Long and the people at the church who're as good as family—better some ways— but it's not the same. Maybe that's why Mike got to me so quick when he came here. I'd never seen anybody so alone, so isolated, in all my life. I really tried to reach him, to let him know I was there and that I sort of knew what he felt like sometimes. But..."

"You did reach him," I said. "You reached him in whatever way he could be reached. I think Mike must have sort of fallen in love with you. He was very strange about it, I know, but I bet that's what happened."

Lucy looked at the table. "I'm not sure that—"

"This is a strange thing to say, probably, but I kind of hope that's what happened. I mean, at least maybe he got to fall in love with someone. He hasn't had a lot of good things happen to him. I hope least that did." Lucy started to speak, but I interrupted her. "Of course, it was at your expense, and you're the one who's had to put up with it, but I hope you know what I mean."

"I know what you mean," she said.

It was late before I left Lucy's house. We continued to sit at her kitchen table, talking about Peggy, about the perplexities of parenthood and the strange solemnity of living without a mate. We talked about Father Long, about his commitment to the people at society's desperate fringes that so inspired Lucy and that somehow seemed to threaten me. We talked about Michael again, about how, despite his clumsy gestures and the rage that sometimes engulfed him, he had so often seemed serene.

At the front door, Lucy gave me a long embrace, holding on

to Michael as much as me, I'm sure, then she pulled away enough so I could see her eyes. They seemed to say that, yes, I was welcome to kiss her, and I wanted to terribly, but somehow the risk seemed too great. If I misread her, I thought in the second that her dark eyes held my gaze, my kiss would be a crueler trespass than Michael's erotic rummage through her lingerie had been. So I simply thanked her and told her that I would call with any news, and then I said goodnight.

•

Mary was asleep on the waiting room sofa when I got back to the hospital. She opened her eyes as I closed the door behind me and sleepily said, "Hello, stranger." I sat on the edge of the sofa and bent to kiss her cheek, then I took hold of her hand, but I didn't say anything until I asked her if there was any change.

"Last we heard is that his urine has stopped. Which means kidney failure. I guess they can't do anything about it." She gave me a drowsy smile. "How are you? It's good to see you."

"I think we're going to lose him, Marie." For some strange reason, I had always called her Marie.

"Didn't we lose him a long time ago?" she asked. Her eyes widened; her face was pale but she seemed robust despite the demands of motherhood. Mary was one of those women who would grow to be very good-looking in middle age.

"Maybe we did," I said, "but I hope we didn't. That would make me feel even worse. Where are Mom and Dad?"

"They went to Buddy and Marge's. Marge called and kind of insisted about an hour ago. I'm glad she did. Mom was just exhausted. I promised I'd call if there was any reason to. Dad said to tell you that the doctor wants to talk to everybody at eight in the morning."

"She was supposed to stop by tonight."

"She did, just for a second. I guess there was some emergency."

"You've seen Mike, haven't you?"

"I've been in twice. It makes me feel so odd. I haven't seen him since the summer before last. It's kind of like looking at a photograph, isn't it? He looks just like himself, but it's not really him, I don't think. They said you went to see the woman who found him in her house."

"So you've heard the whole story?"

"Basically." Mary twisted herself upright on the sofa and I moved to sit beside her. "How is she doing? I don't remember her name."

"Lucy. She's okay; she's fine. She's been a real friend to Michael. Unlike me, for instance, he felt like he could trust her. He never heard Lucy's voice screaming at him."

"What do you mean?"

"You do live a long way away, don't you?" I turned to face her. Mary pulled her feet onto the sofa, tucking her knees beneath her chin. She was wearing socks with rainbow stripes. "Evidently, I've been one of the voices he hears, that drive him crazy. During my mission, I guess it was particularly bad for him. The idea of me being in orbit made me seem all the more menacing to him, like I was watching over him or something."

"Like you were God."

"A pretty scary kind of God, maybe."

"Jesus." The word was a slow exclamation; she was surprised by what I had told her. "I ... thought he had been doing a lot better."

"He had. At least he was managing to stay out of the hospital."

Mary was quiet for a moment. She burrowed her feet in the crack between the cushions. "I realized a year or two ago that there's a reason why I live in California, and it doesn't have a hell of a lot to do with California. There's this feeling that I get

around Mom and Dad, and Mike too—not you so much—
that feels like claustrophobia. Like being in these categories
called daughter and sister just boxes me in. The only safe thing
is to be a long way away."

"What does being a mother feel like?"

"It's different. Adrian's a big responsibility, sure, but in her
case, I'm the one in control. The scary thing is that as soon as
she gets older, she's going to feel the same way, like I'm some
kind of millstone. She's going to have to get away from me.
Not for a few years, I hope, but I already have to tell myself
it'll happen."

"How did Mom seem to you?"

"You know. Saint Dorothy. Handling even this. Dad's a little
shakier, but he's okay. God, Jack, sometimes I think I must
have been left on the doorstep."

"Why?"

"If it was my son in there, I'd be wailing like one of those
Palestinian women. I'd be destroyed."

"It's your brother in there and you're not wailing."

"I guess that's what I was trying to say." She stared across
the room at the darkened television.

"You're wrong if you think Mom's just taking this in stride.
Mike . . . Mike's her baby. You know how she's always felt
about him."

"Then why this sea of calm, the sniffles and the tear or two,
then steady as she goes?"

"Well, I wasn't left on the doorstep, evidently. I'm like her in
that respect, I suppose. I have such an even-keel facade that it
disgusts me sometimes. But it's just a facade. Some sort of
defense, maybe. And Mom has her faith—whatever that word
means. She believes there'll be something more for Mike; she
believes it and feels it as truly as . . . as you love your daughter,
and that . . ." My attempt to explain my mother was complicated by the fact that she often confounded me as much as she
did Mary.

Mary tossed her head back. "You know, the concept of heaven or whatever, of eternal life, there was a time—God, a long time, wasn't there?—when that made an intellectual kind of sense to me. Sort of like all these otherwise intelligent people in Berkeley, or Shirley MacLaine, for God's sake, who think it's perfectly reasonable to assume you'll come back to life as a cow. But even when I was into the idea of heaven, I could never personalize it. I could never truly imagine Grandpa or somebody going someplace, or continuing somehow. I would try to think of myself in some spirit world, and I'd just draw this huge blank."

"But it isn't blank for Mom; it must be a vision, a sense or something, that's vivid and wonderful and ... It's funny, Mom's the one who seems really religious, isn't she?"

"They must feel like total failures to have such agnostic children."

"Mike certainly isn't agnostic."

"What about you?" It was more a challenge than a question.

"Sometimes," I said, "I'd love to feel like ... I don't know. Maybe people like you and me are making a big mistake."

"And we'll go to hell to pay for it."

"No, I don't mean that. I mean, maybe we think we know too much. It's pretty egocentric to think that if something isn't obvious to you, then it necessarily doesn't exist, or doesn't have any meaning. Sometimes I wonder if I'm like the people in Kepler's era who could plainly see with their own two eyes that the sun rotated round the earth. You know what I mean? Einstein said he wanted to be considered religious in the sense that he knew that some things that would always be impenetrable to him nonetheless truly existed. That's the context in which I really do want to have something in common with Mom and Dad, with Mike."

"But what if we're more like Kepler than like the people who scoffed at him?"

"God, Marie," I said. "Don't give us that much credit." We

were too sleepy to say anything more, each of us using an arm of the long sofa for a pillow, our legs twisted together as we dozed.

•

Michael died a few minutes before five that morning. Out the window, I could see faint light on the horizon when the nurse came into the waiting room to wake us and tell us. I tried to reach my parents, but on the phone Buddy said they had just left to return to the hospital. Buddy called me "son," and said he was very sorry, and he told me my mother had awakened with a sense that Michael needed her.

In the intensive care unit, someone had closed Michael's eyes and the tubes were removed from his arms and nose. His hair had been gathered and folded behind his head. I asked the nurse if it would be all right to leave him there until my parents arrived. Of course it would, she said, and Mary and I sat on the mattress on either side of him, this third partner of ours in the complex business of being siblings, our little brother who now seemed to sleep. We watched Michael, saying nothing, and I remember that I had a sudden sense of what seemed like pleasure to find that I could note no drastic change in him. I had seen three dead grandparents and two friends who had died, embalmed on their burial days, and each had seemed foreign to me, waxy and otherworldly, but Mike, Mike's body, still seemed familiar, hinting to me somehow that death was not so strange. I rubbed his warm arm with my palm and turned to see tears streaking Mary's face. "Take care of yourself, Mikey," she said. I wanted to say something too, but a stony sorrow seemed to lodge in my throat and wouldn't let me speak.

My mother and father found us at Michael's bed. Mary and I moved to let them near him. "I called, but you were already on your way." Dad nodded. He pressed the sign of the cross into Michael's forehead with his thumb and began to pray, commending into His hands His servant. "Receive Michael into the arms of your mercy," my father said in a faltering voice, "into the blessed rest of everlasting peace, and into the glorious company of the saints in light." While my father prayed for his son, my mother cupped Michael's head in her hands, and for the first time, she began to sob, her grief finally spilling in a way in which Mary thought it could not.

•

A few hours later we stood in the blustery air outside the hospital, loitering there at nine o'clock on that vacant Thursday morning because there was little else to do and nowhere in particular to go. We no longer belonged in the hospital; Michael's body had been taken to the morgue, then on to a mortuary. I had assumed that my parents would want his body to be cremated, his fragments of bone and gristle scattered near that miner's shack, perhaps. But they had decided what would be done sometime while he was still tenuously alive. He would be buried in the cemetery in Durango, on the benchland above the river.

My father had dealt with many deaths during his ministry; he had said requiems and funeral masses for both his parents, for a stillborn son who would have been my older brother, and, only recently, for his best friend, Hal. It probably wasn't surprising, then, that he seemed so businesslike that morning, making arrangements for Michael with that same kind of detached compassion that I had so often seen in him years ago when, as his acolyte, I had helped him bury his parishioners. When Dad said he would need to call the Durango mortuary to arrange for shipping Michael's body, I suggested that perhaps it made sense for me to drive him down. He and Mom and Mary could catch a flight in an hour or two; I could exchange my rented sedan for a van and could be there by eight or nine that night. Dad wanted to be sure I was willing; Mom, composed again and, like him, buoyed by the need to make these few decisions, said yes, that would be a wonderful way for Michael's body to make the journey. Mary said she wanted to ride with Mike and me.

After a while, after we had stood like somnambulists at the hospital entrance for what must have been twenty minutes, the strange inertia that had kept us there seemed to dissolve, and my parents drove to Buddy and Marge's to get their things, then met Mary and me at St. Andrew's on our way to the airport. Inside the rectory, John Long embraced each of us and told us he had scheduled a requiem for five that evening. "It was a privilege to get to know him," he said as we stood in the empty dining room downstairs, drinking coffee, and I think he meant it. I liked him even more, hearing him say he was going to miss Mike instead of assuring us his soul was safe with the Holy Spirit. I went into the kitchen to look for Lucy, but the lights were off and it appeared she had not yet arrived. I wrote her a note on a wide white sheet of butcher paper, thanking her for the conversation the night before and wishing her good fortune.

At the Hertz lot near the airport, we turned in one car, exchanged the second for a Ford van, then Mom and Dad got on the shuttle bus that took them to their plane. Mary waited while I called the astronaut office. I had completely forgotten to do so the day before and surely a couple of people were wondering why I was AWOL. George Abbey was out, but his secretary said she would relay my message. I said I would call again as soon as I knew when I could get back to Houston, then hung up and dialed Buddy and Marge. I told Marge I still had not phoned Peggy, but she said she had reached her before she left for work. "She asked me about the funeral, but I didn't know the details. She said if a friend can look after the kids, she's going to try to come up. She'll stop through here and spend a night with us. The fares are really good right now." I told Marge that I hoped she could come; Peggy was still the best person to be with when there was little to say but much to try to communicate.

At the mortuary, we drove the van to a loading dock in the alley and waited for two men to roll Michael's coffin out on a long aluminum dolly. We had to angle the dark, dome-lidded coffin in the back of the van in order to get the doors closed, and I used the spare tire as a wedge to try to keep it from sliding on the hundreds of highway curves we were about to encounter. Michael would appreciate this prosaic journey, it seemed to me.

A hard wind blew eastward off the Mosquito summits and battered the boxy van as we crested Kenosha Pass and drove into the broad short-grass expanse of South Park. We met the first spitting drops of rain at Antero Junction and by Buena Vista, the clouds were dark and sinister and the rain was steady. Mary and I were often silent as we drove; there was much we could have heard about each other's lives, a lot of time that could have been caught up on, but there was an aspect of our trip that was unmistakably ceremonial and that seemed to deserve a bit of decorum. When we did talk, we skirted the subject that consumed our thoughts, saying nothing about Michael's too-short life or the death that he chose for himself. Although his body was already embalmed and sealed inside a coffin, I'm sure we both had a sense that we shouldn't speak within his earshot.

We had dinner in Del Norte, then drove west in the last of the stormy light. "I've already got that feeling," Mary said, staring straight ahead, her voice interrupting the dolorous whine of the wind and the monotonous roar of the motor.

"What feeling?"

"Like I'm about to get on a roller coaster. How do you suppose I ever got so afraid of going home?"

"Is it home or is it you?"

"What do you mean?"

"I don't know. But it's just a place. You've lived in California as long as you lived in Durango."

"The Bay Area is just a place. Good and bad. But this . . . this is where all my ghosts are, all the idiotic things I did. This is where I had to be fifteen years old, thinking God had singled me out as a particularly bad joke."

I laughed. "You were quite a sight back then. Your hair. Mike and I called you Hive-Head. He had this great imitation of the way you talked to boys on the phone."

"Don't," she said.

"We used to try to find your—"

"No, Jack. Don't." The cab was dark, but I could see she was wincing, as though the memories actually induced pain. I let the subject drop and we were silent again until she said, "Don't you wonder what would have happened to him if he hadn't gotten sick?"

"I think the reason he was so special to Mom always was that she knew he was the one of us who could really do something. There was something there that . . ."

"Don't say he was better than us just because he's dead," Mary said sadly.

"I'm not saying anything, Marie," I told her in a hollow voice.

A yellow light was flashing at the Wolf Creek chain station west of South Fork and a man in an orange parka that was soaked by the rain flagged us to a stop. "It's snowing like sixty up on the pass," he said in a loud spurt of words when I rolled down my window. "Checking for chains or adequate snow tires."

I told the man the van was a rental but that the people at Hertz had mentioned it had its winter tires. He walked around the van to check them, then stopped at my window again. "Should be okay," he said, "long as you've got some weight. What are you hauling?"

"My brother," I said.

He looked across at Mary and grinned. "She doesn't look like no brother to me."

"No, in the back," I said, motioning over my shoulder.

He peered in beyond me, and I saw his expression change in the instant he recognized the coffin. He backed away a step, but he wasn't flustered when he spoke. "Shoot, I'm real sorry. You wouldn't believe all the kind of things you see people carrying in cars."

The man waved us on and we drove slowly as we began to climb, hauling our brother in a blue utility van, carrying the quiet cargo that had once had such vibrant possibilities, the rain giving way to snow a couple of miles below the ski area, the snow a kind of absolution somehow, the early storm powdering the trees and blanketing the road bed, the weight of Michael's coffin over the axle.

six

You understand in a very visceral way that one day you too will die, when you bury a brother or sister. The deaths of your grandparents are often only strange abstractions, vaguely explained departures if they occur when you're a child. When your parents die, I presume that amidst the sadness and the regret of things unsaid, you finally enter adulthood—your progenitors forevermore absent, your children now your only family. But when your brother dies—when my younger brother died, I realized in a way that was at once rueful and oddly chilling that I was as mortal as Michael was. Although I had never been able to truly imagine it, my brain, too, would lose its circuitry, my blood someday would cease to course. On a superficial level, I had long understood that certainty, but never before had I felt it absolutely.

From the time I was seven or so, I had witnessed my father on Ash Wednesday of each year, dipping his thumb into the powdery ashes of palm fronds, then pressing his thumb onto many bowed foreheads, marking a gray cross on the solemn face of each person who knelt at St. Mark's communion rail. As he shaped each cross, he said in a throaty whisper, "Remember, old man, that dust thou art, and unto dust shalt thou return." It is a phrase I have heard surely a thousand times, one with a certain enduring appeal to a cosmologist, an exhortation from the Ash Wednesday liturgy that wound repeatedly through my thoughts on the day we buried Michael. Yes, everything that exists on this planet is composed of nothing more than the cosmic dust that began to scatter at the beginning of time. And the ancient churchman who composed those words must have known that matter is never destroyed, offering a very real kind of immortality to everyone and everything, to Michael, and to me. But although my father would have strongly disagreed, it seemed to me that returning to dust meant that you had to surrender cognizance, you had to lose the nascent awareness, the fragments of knowledge that separate us from the rest of the matter that swims in unfathomable space. That was what I began to truly grasp for the first time as I stood beside Michael's grave, and that was what frightened me. I wanted to remain aware, sighted somehow, forever.

Father Hinrichs from St. Barnabas in Cortez had driven over on that Saturday morning to say the funeral mass; my father had sat silently, passively, in the first pew with my mother, Mary, and me. Michael's closed coffin, covered with a violet pall and again riding on a mortician's dolly, had been beside us in the aisle. There had been many mourners behind us. Most of the pews had seemed full when we walked to the front of the church before the service began, escorted by men from the mortuary, but the pews were filled by parishioners—people who remembered Mike only vaguely and who had come to his funeral principally out of regard and concern for my parents, some of them surely out of a sense of obligation. Peggy had declined my invitation to join us in the front pew, and I wasn't sure where she sat during the service. As we walked in, I had noticed two high school chums of Michael's whose names I could not remember, dozens of familiar faces who had long been part of the parish, and Jane had been alone in a pew near the back. I had caught her eyes and had smiled in a way that was meant to convey something somehow ineffable when she walked back to her seat after she took communion.

The storm had cleared. The day was bright and cold, and there were only a handful of us at the cemetery. Green carpets covered the mound of dirt that had been taken from the grave; three wreaths of flowers lay on its smooth-napped slope. The four of us, each wearing sunglasses, stood on a similar carpet near the grave, at the spot where the officious mortician placed us, everyone else behind us, and we watched while the pall-bearers, all members of the St. Mark's vestry, carried the coffin from the waxed black hearse to the framework that spanned the grave. Beyond the polished dome of the coffin, beyond the hidden hill of dirt, the bluff dropped away to the river. Beyond the river, the flat roofs of the buildings downtown were vivid in the morning sun. Away to the north and east, yellow and ocher treetops hid the houses and the busy streets.

At the head of the grave, Father Hinrichs read from his missal:

"Man, that is born of a woman, hath but a short time to live, and is full of misery. He cometh up, and is cut down, like a flower; he fleeth as it were a shadow, and never continueth in one stay . . ."

The young priest from Cortez had never met Michael, and the prayer that he continued to recite had long been offered at

every graveside, yet the words seemed to describe Michael
with sad precision. His short life was all too full of torment,
full of a cerebral kind of misery that he battled with constant
movement, with continual flights from himself. But now, I
wondered, if there were indeed some kind of conscious eternal
life, would his soul, his consciousness, be well? Would we bury
the voices, the inexplicable anger, with his body? Perhaps it
was better, safer, to hope for nothingness.

There were only a few prayers to be recited before Father
Hinrichs scooped a handful of dirt from beneath the carpet
and with it sketched a cross on top of the coffin—two thin,
intersecting lines of soil above the spot where I imagined
Michael's face would be. He said a final prayer, committing
Michael's spirit to God's gracious mercy and protection, then
he stepped away. With a gesture meant to bespeak great sorrow, the mortician motioned us toward the limousine and we
obediently walked away from the grave, none of us crying
bitterly, but each of us shielding errant tears behind our
glasses. Before I got inside the car, I went over to Jane and
asked her in a whisper to please come by my parents' house;
there was to be a meal of some sort, and I wanted her to be
with us. I had spoken briefly with her on the phone the night
before, but I hadn't seen her. She said she would see us there,
and she began to hug me, but hesitated, and only clutched
my hand.

Inside the limousine, looking out through its smoked-glass
windows, I could see the coffin still suspended above the hole
where it would rest. Cemetery protocol evidently insisted that
the bereaved family and friends leave before the coffin was
lowered into the fiberglass vault that resembled a septic tank,
the vault's lid was fitted, the carpets were pulled away, and the
dirt was replaced by a backhoe. But that was work *we* should
be doing, it seemed to me for a moment. He belonged to us
and we should see him safely into the ground. Yet I didn't get

out of the car, didn't take off my coat and roll up my sleeves. I sat compliantly, quietly, as we pulled away, the coffin still in the autumn air. After all, I reconsidered, it wasn't really Michael inside the box. It was only his remnant body. And despite being injected with formalin and exotic preserving fluids, it wouldn't be long, in the larger scheme of things, before his body would just be dust.

•

In the two days that she had been home, my mother's grief seemed to have been mitigated, or perhaps simply postponed, by some maternal resolve, a latent and still very strong instinct to look after us. Mary and I were under her roof again, together there for the first time in a long time, and we seemed to offer her the kind of domestic purpose that had always seemed to bring her pleasure. She was a nurturer, a protector, and her attention to herself had always been subordinate to her concern for us. In the strange, slow-motion days that preceded and followed Michael's funeral, it seemed as if my mother's private anguish was set aside simply because her two remaining children briefly were back at home.

My father, on the other hand, had lost the ministerial calm he displayed in Denver. At home, he wasn't forced to play the role of the cleric offering comfort and reassurance. At home, with little that specifically had to be accomplished, he was a parent who had lost a child, and he seemed beside himself—flighty, anxious, walking nervously from room to room as if he needed to check on the furniture, turning the television on, then off again in flurries of indecision. He and I drank together late on the night Mary and I arrived—me drinking away the strange, callous sensation of having delivered Michael's body to Hood Mortuary instead of bringing him the final six blocks to the house—Dad telling me as he got drunk that he dreaded having to say the funeral eucharist. His anxiety seemed to be relieved a

bit on Friday morning when Father Hinrichs called and offered
to take his place, but soon he was pacing again, remembering
chores that needed doing, then forgetting them as he went
from one room into the next.

When we got back to the house after the funeral, Mom
was much the same, coordinating in the kitchen the casse-
roles and salads that friends brought to the back door, her
suit jacket off and an apron over her blouse, Mary working
comfortably with my mother in a way she probably could
not have on any other occasion. But Dad seemed very nearly
relaxed now, sitting in the living room with Peggy and me
and Father Hinrichs—talking a kind of ecclesiastical shop
with him about the finalizing aspects of ritual and about families' responses to death, telling all of us he was touched that
so many people had come, hugging Jane when she came to
the front door.

Peggy had flown in late on Friday afternoon. I went alone to
the airport to meet her, and we drove slowly back through the
farmland that now supported treeless subdivisions, with me
describing the sad and pallid events of the past days, hearing
about how the kids were, and the two of us talking in that
relaxed and easy way in which we used to share each other's
news when we had been apart for a while. Peggy had agreed to
stay at my parents' house. She slept on the bed in my former
bedroom—where we had made love in delightful secrecy the
summer before we were married—I in Michael's room, now
my father's study. We had had dinner with Mary and my parents on Friday night, the conversation devoted almost exclu-
sively to children, to Matthew, Sarah, and Adrian in particular,
surely three of the most remarkable youngsters ever sired, to
judge by what was said, my mom and dad anxious to hear
about the grandchildren they saw too seldom, happy to talk
about a subject full of hope. By the time we got back to the
house following the funeral, I hadn't been alone with Peggy
again, hadn't asked her about the magazine writer, hadn't told

her that Jane seemed to know me too well to let herself get
carried away. I hadn't told her Jane would be stopping by.

Dad introduced Jane to Father Hinrichs. He shook her left
hand without hesitating, in the straightforward way I knew
she appreciated. Peggy kept her hands in her lap when Dad
asked, a little awkwardly, if she and Jane remembered each
other. They both said yes, then Jane, quickly aware that she
had encountered a situation she wasn't expecting, said she
could only stay a minute. She added something that seemed
obviously untrue about having to meet a man who was sell-
ing a horse. "I just wanted to say hello," she said, directing
her words to Dad, "and... to let you know I'm thinking
about you all. Is there anything at all I could do for you? Get
for you?"

He shook his head and put his arm around her shoulder.
"We're fine," he told her. "But thank you."

"Well..." she said with a kind of obvious finality as she
sidled toward the door. "I'm... sure I'll see you all soon
then. It was nice to meet you," she called across to Father
Hinrichs.

I followed Jane out the door and walked her to her car. "I'm
sorry you can't stay," I said.

"Thanks, but this guy is... everybody seems to be doing
okay. You do." Her voice seemed to say she had known me
well once, but it was a very long time ago.

"I'm sorry you didn't know Peggy would be here. But you
must have assumed that she'd be staying—"

"No, sure. Sure. It's just... it's a family time. Really. I'll see
you again before you go."

"You're family, for heaven's sake. Jane, she came up for
Mike. She knew him pretty well once. Not for me. She hasn't
come up to rescue me."

"No. No, I know. I... I'd better run, Jack," she said, getting
into the car.

"Are you going to be home in the morning?" I asked. She nodded affirmatively. "I'll drive out. But I wish you wouldn't go."

"I just wanted to tell you all I was very sorry," she said, stifling tears, her barrier finally breaking down. "It's not just Peggy. Really. I hope she doesn't think so. It's just . . . I guess I've been to too many funerals lately. I mean, people die, of course, but then you just . . . I'll see you, Jack," she said.

•

I had presumed that it was Mark MacArthur, Peggy's beloved English major, who was looking after the kids while she was away, and I'm sure she noted my pleasure when she told me a friend from the university named Anette was staying at the house with them. Peggy was flying to Denver to see her folks on Sunday morning and we had gone out after dinner on Saturday night. We had invited Mary to join us, but although she seemed anxious to get out of the house for a bit, she hesitated, then declined, telling us she wanted to help Mom sort through some of Michael's things, assuming, I'm sure, that we had sensitive marital issues to discuss.

We still were married, weren't we? Neither of us had even so much as found a lawyer's phone number, nor had we ever discussed how we might split our meager estate. I think perhaps we were so slow to move toward divorce not because either of us harbored hopes that we could somehow make things work, but because each of us saw divorce as a sign of failure, as evidence that our lives together had ended in collapse. Yet if we shied away from formalizing our estrangement, so did we shy away from making new and meaningful connections with each other. We sat in deep-backed chairs at the Solid Muldoon—the bar surprisingly quiet on that Saturday night, the skiers from Texas and Arizona still two months away from descending on the town—and we spoke to each other like friends from long ago, buoyed by the emotional residue of the old days, but bereft of any real intimacy.

"So how are the two of you doing?" I asked her. "You and Mark?"

"You still think Mark was what started all this, don't you?"

"I guess I think if he hadn't come along, my mission would have been over before too long, and then who knows what might have happened? Maybe, miraculously, I might have stopped being an asshole."

"Utterly impossible," she said, entrapping me as always with her smile.

"I haven't mentioned this to anyone yet—I just found out a day or so before Michael—I'm ... getting assigned to a new mission. We'll be deploying the telescope. It's funny. I was thrilled to get it. It's going to be a great mission, and I wasn't sure I could stand two or three more years of nothing but committee bullshit. But now, I just feel kind of blank about it." I glanced at her, my eyes shifting up from the cocktail table.

It was the first time I had ever seen Peggy respond to news about my career at NASA without a mixture of pleasure and resentment. Gone was the familiar expression that always before had told me it was news she would rather not have heard —still further proof that the breach between us was more than merely geographical. "That's great, Jack. It is. I know everybody will be so happy for you—whenever you decide to tell them. I'm happy for you."

"It seemed like you should be aware. Once I'm back, we'll start training before long. I probably won't get over to Austin as much as I'd like."

"We'll work something out," she said. "Do you know yet when you'll go back to Houston?"

"In a few days. There's really nothing to do. Not really. But ... I don't want just to rush right off. Dad said something about maybe the two of us hiking up to Ice Lake Basin. Mike had told the priest at St. Andrew's that he was going to move up there. He had this idea of living up above timberline in an old miner's shack. I mean, it was just a fantasy, but..."

"Won't it be snowed in?"

"I doubt there're more than two or three inches up there. I'm sure we can make it. Might even be melted off by Monday."

"Jack," she said, pausing to decide how she would ask the question, "was it really a suicide?"

"What do you mean?"

"It's been a long time since I really knew Mike. He was already sick by the time I met him. But... even knowing what he was like when he was having his worst times, I can't imagine him deciding that was the solution. I wonder if he wasn't just terribly scared, or embarrassed, and that was the catalyst. Do you know what I mean?"

"Don't you suppose those impulses are involved with most suicides?"

"I don't know. I guess I assumed people decided to kill themselves when things just looked too desperate. No solutions. No way out. Embarrassed seems different to me."

I asked her the question I'd been asking myself. "Do you suppose it's ultimately okay for people to kill themselves? I mean, is it basically your own business, your choice whether you want to be alive? Or is staying alive the one real responsibility you have? Other animals don't kill themselves."

"Old cats go crawl under sheds when they're ready to die."

"Yeah, but they wait nineteen years before they do it. They do it because they can tell their heart is about to stop or something."

"Maybe that's what Mike felt like. Maybe he had just had enough, too long being driven crazy by his own head. But it's the suicide, not just his death, that's hardest on you, isn't it?"

"Mike had effectively told me to fuck off for the last fifteen

years," I told her, "along with telling other people how proud
he was of me. He told a woman who works at St. Andrew's
that I was actually the first person on the moon." Peggy
grinned at that suggestion. "I guess there are basically two
Mikes in my mind. One is a kid who lived to be sixteen or so.
In my memory, it's hard to know where that kid stopped and
where I began. The other Mike is somebody I never really got
to know, never was comfortable with, but who I've been trying to make something up to—I don't know what—for an
awful long time."

"Now you can quit trying." Peggy put her hand on my forearm.

"Now that I've totally failed to."

"No. Now that there's no way you can even try."

"Oh, both Mikes are gone all right. That's the part I'm sure
of."

●

Mary knocked on the door of my room, Michael's room, early
on Sunday morning. Her hair was wrapped in a towel and she
wore a robe she had borrowed from my mother. From the bed,
I told her Peggy's plane left at eight and that we'd go in about
half an hour.

"Then you'll be back in time to go to church," she said.

"I was planning to drive out to Jane Bergen's."

"Oh, yes. Mom intimated something about you two.
Couldn't you wait for a couple of hours? It's not going to be
easy for him at the church today. I think it'd help if we all were
there."

"I'm glad you'll be there," I told her, hiking myself onto my
elbow. "It's . . . important for me to see Jane. I'm sorry, Marie.
If I really thought it would make a difference I would, but—"

"No, please don't do anything for anybody else, Jack. God
forbid. Sometimes I forget what a star you are these days. Cer-

tainly can't expect too much of you, can we?"

"Cool it, Marie. I don't need a lecture from you this morning."

"It's not a lecture. It's a simple request for you to think about somebody else. But it's my mistake. I didn't realize what an impossibility that is."

"Listen. This is pretty ridiculous coming from someone who hasn't set foot in this house in two years, and who hasn't talked to Mike or seen Mom and Dad in all that time. How is it that you're so sainted all of a sudden?"

"Fuck you," she said, her voice carrying a cold and intense anger. She started to go out the door, then stopped. "The reasons I've kept my distance are my reasons. They have to do with me and not with anybody else. And they don't mean that I don't care about this family or that I can't try to be helpful when I'm here. I've got a life in Berkeley that you don't know a damn thing about. You think you've got the world all figured out, but you don't know a thing about me."

"You, on the other hand, know me incredibly well and you've decided that I'm a selfish asshole, I see."

"Just go to Jane's," she said as she left the room. "I don't care what you do."

I took a shower, feeling leaden, not so much angry as uncomprehending, wondering why in the world Mary had needed to make that onslaught on me—wondering if she was right. Her perceptions were certainly incorrect if she assumed I thought I understood myself, the family, or—my God—much of anything. And no, I knew all too well that I was not selfless, but I wasn't sure that selflessness was something I aspired to. I wanted to be a decent son, whatever that meant—perhaps simply trying to live my life in a way that my parents could see was approached with a certain... consciousness—but the evidence suggested that I couldn't be a decent brother. Not to Michael—I was the one, after all, who had been his imagined nemesis—and evidently not to this sister I barely knew.

Mom and Dad, already dressed for church, embraced Peggy as we stood in the driveway, each of them holding her like a daughter-in-law in good standing, thanking her for coming, asking her to thank her parents for their kindnesses, telling her to be sure to hug the kids for them. Peggy cried as she said good-bye, shedding tears, I'm sure, for the certainty that her relationship with them, despite the evidence that morning, would become rather perfunctory. They would always be Papa and Gram to the children, but to her, inevitably, sadly, they would be people she used to know.

Mary came out of the house before we drove away. She leaned in the open window on Peggy's side of the car and told her it had been good to see her again. Peggy asked her to give her regards to Robert, and she said she hoped she could meet Adrian someday. "I'm not sure when that'll be," Peggy said, drying her eyes. "Don't let her grow up too much in the meantime." Mary nodded, smiling sadly, aware that she might not see Peggy again, and missing her daughter, no doubt. She held Peggy's hand, and she was careful not to look at me.

At the airport, I told Peggy I would come to Austin soon after I got home. "We'll go out to Lake Travis or somewhere, have a picnic," she said cordially.

"The four of us? That sounds a lot like the happy family."

"It's legal. It's allowed when the dad's a pretty good guy. You're a pretty good guy." She paused, considering what to say. "But I'm worried about you."

"Why?"

"Last night. I know you can't help but think a lot about what your relationship with Mike was like, but it wasn't your relationship that caused anything."

"I think I'm okay, Peg. Really. I'll be all right." My eyes always water when I assure someone of the great shape I'm in. "Thanks for coming. You know, you're still the one I feel like I'm related to. Will you be sure to tell those knotheads that I love them?"

She nodded; she bit her lip, and I held her as tightly as I could, trying to squeeze away our stupid separation.

●

"I hope I'm not keeping you away from St. Mark's," I said to Jane, sitting on the picketed rail of her porch, keeping the kind of physical space between us that should have followed a fight. But there had been no harsh words between us, no sudden changes of heart, no betrayal. I had believed Jane the day before when she said she was not upset by Peggy's presence, yet something unmistakable, something unnameable, now distanced us from each other. Perhaps it was simply that for the third time in little more than a year, there had been a death in the family, this time in my family instead of hers. Both Jane and I knew better now than to think that death brought a sense of community to its survivors. No, all death brought was an end of things.

"I don't go as often as I used to," she said. "I still go, but... How're your folks?"

"Okay. Mom's either a rock or a remarkable actress. Dad's better, calmer since the funeral. Mary gave me hell this morning because I wasn't going with them. I don't know, maybe I should have. I realize that this won't be an easy Sunday, but I don't see how I could help. I'm going to stay for a few days. Dad and I are going to go up to the mountains tomorrow."

"When's Mary going to leave?"

"I don't know. Probably in a day or two."

"Once everyone's gone, I'll stop by as regularly as I can. Just to check in."

"That would be nice. They'd appreciate it."

"It's my turn, I guess. This is getting kind of common around here, isn't it? When we were at the cemetery yesterday, afterward, I went to Kenny's grave, and to Dad's. They say some people really find comfort in visiting graves, having chats

or whatever, maybe just tidying things up and leaving flowers.
But I don't know. All I can do is imagine the satiny insides of
the box down under there and think about the bodies, how
much they've broken down so far. It's kind of sick."

"I should probably try to have a chat with Michael now. We
might finally be able to get things across to each other."

Jane smiled. "At least what he has to say shouldn't hurt you
anymore."

I considered what she said. "God, I hope that wasn't it. I
mean, I never really thought he was trying to hurt me. I honestly don't think I took it that personally."

"You're one of those people who want everything to look
like it's perfect—not that that's terrible. You'd like to think that
there are no awkward relationships, no resentment that lingers
forever, nobody staying in any pain. I think you always
thought that if you and Mike just had the right conversation, if
things were said in the right way, the voices would be quiet and
you'd never feel guilty again. But those right conversations . . .
they're pretty rare, if they ever happen at all."

"You've made quite a study of me," I said, probably sounding defensive.

"No. Not really. I've just gotten to know you a little. And I
also know this astronaut who seems to think that if I'd just
come to Houston—and do God knows what with myself—we
could live happily ever after. He's the same kind of person you
are, always assumes there's some handy, tidy solution to
things."

"And he probably keeps trying to have the right conversation with you, doesn't he?"

"You must have met this character," Jane said, smiling again.
"Let's go take a walk." I followed her down the porch steps,
and she let me take her hand when we closed a wire gate behind us and headed across a hay field toward the creek. The
autumn air was full of that scent, that sentiment that suggests,
inexorably, that soon everything will be cold and dormant,

covered with the fatal weight of snow. It was the kind of
weather that seemed to presage the end of giddy romance,
of hopes fed by wild infatuation. As we approached the row of
tall old cottonwoods along the creek, their yellow leaves rus-
tling in a kind of low, oceanic roar, it seemed to me that I was
about to be told that whatever it was between us had also had
its season, and was done. I said nothing as we walked, hoping
Jane, too, would be silent until this ominous weather cleared.

"I used to be damn near happy-go-lucky," Jane said finally,
sitting on the leaf-strewn slope that dropped to the little creek.
"Life looked like a succession of good times, interrupted by
occasional irritations. I admit that I didn't think much, didn't
pay a whole lot of attention to anything, but who needs to
think when you're having fun? You know what I mean? If I
went to see a shrink, he'd probably tell me that the change is
just a depression, something that happens when you lose people. But I don't know. I think it's really a different way of
looking at the world. It's like back then I expected bliss, I really
did. Now, I don't think I expect anything. Or if I do, I probably expect the worst."

"When I saw you in Florida, you seemed so optimistic."

"I thought I was falling in love. That'll do that to you."

"But it didn't happen . . . ?"

"No, I think it sort of did."

"I don't understand what you're saying," I told her. I sat
with my knees pulled up, my hands tearing the fallen leaves
that weren't yet brittle, dropping the pieces at my feet, watching my work instead of Jane. "I don't understand this sense of
doom. It seemed like we had just gotten to the point where we
both thought we wanted to try to sustain something. I still feel
that way. But it seems like you've decided it's impossible, or
that you're not interested, even if it is possible."

"Oh God, I'm interested, Jack." There was a new emotion in
her voice now; I turned to look at her. "I'm still lured by the
fairy tales, sure I am. But every time I've talked to you lately,

it's like the only thing you can imagine is this simplified picture
of us being together. You refuse to consider little issues like the
fact that we live a thousand miles apart, or that for the next
year or so you're not going to have a spare minute for me. I'm
too old to pretend. That's all it is, Jack. If we were going to
sustain something, it had to be based on reality, not on some
crazy come-to-Texas, we'll-be-happy dream."

It took me a while to know what I wanted to say. "I can't
help but think you're searching for proof that it can't work—as
if when something starts to seem positive you have to make
sure it actually isn't. I didn't mean to be a Pollyanna. Jesus, no,
there aren't any guarantees. I know that. But why give up now,
why should we run and hide just because it looks a little complicated?"

Jane threw a rock into the moving water. "I should show
you my new toys," she said. "Up at the house. They're
loaners—like driving a demonstrator before you order the car
in the color you want. One of them is your classic hook, and
you really can do a surprising amount with it, it's pretty amazing. The other is this rubbery thing that's kind of like a manne-
quin's hand. It's operable too. It's harder to use, and it doesn't
have the dexterity, but it looks like a *hand*. It appeals to your
vanity. But my problem with both of them is that when I've
got either of them on, I feel like I'm kidding myself. I look at
myself in the mirror and I think, Jesus, Bergen, who are you
trying to fool? It's the same sort of thing with us, isn't it? We
could fool ourselves for a while, and, damn it, we might even
fall in love, but eventually we'd have to face the facts. I want to
live in one place; you have to live in another. You have a career
that you're committed to; I'd want you just for myself. You're
still married to somebody, for God's sake; I'm still married too,
but the situation's a little different."

"I'm not sure you and I have a lot to do with your wearing a
prosthesis," I said, sounding defensive again. "But who's to say
you're fooling yourself when you wear one? It's not pretend-

ing, it's doing something specific, something for a purpose. If it helps you, then you wear it."

"It's that simple, is it?"

"I'm not saying it's simple. But, God...if it looks like something's out there, something maybe good, something better, you don't just give up on it. Not just because it doesn't look easy."

"This is your islands speech again, isn't it?"

"It isn't a speech at all. It's just me not understanding why the only alternative is to give up."

She threw her head back, looked up at the fluttering leaves, blew out a long breath. "No, I don't want to give up. Not on you; not on me, for that matter. It's just that...as long as you imagine us in these naïve, rosy terms, my instinct is going to be to argue just the opposite, to tell you you're full of it. Maybe it's just to protect myself. Naïve is something I'm determined not to be anymore. There's a big, basic difference between being a widow and some girl on her wedding day, isn't there?"

"I doubt there's as big a difference as you think there is."

"I'll make a proposition," she said, reaching for my hand. "If you'll stop trying to convince me of how perfect this is, or how it could be, I'll shut up about how the world's falling in around us—although it probably is."

"Here's my deal," I told her. "If you'll make love with me, I'll promise never to mention Texas again."

"Don't blame this on Texas. You mean now?"

"Right now."

"I've got a bed over in the house that hasn't seen that kind of action in a long time."

"Do you suppose it can handle it?" I stood up and pulled Jane to her feet. She brushed the dirt from the seat of her jeans.

"If you're any good at all, I might even show you my hook."

"God, what pressure," I said, laughing, and we turned toward the house. The brooding weather I had imagined earlier was somehow gone on the short return from the creek. The day was merely crisp and blustery, a brief reprieve from winter. And I didn't understand this reprieve of Jane's, this decision of hers that things were not so bleak that she couldn't have sex with me again—and I didn't want to try too hard to figure it out. I simply wanted to hold her again, to give up these fumbling words in favor of flesh, or sweat and straining muscles and aching physical emotion. For God's sake, sex was the antidote to death, wasn't it? What better way to defy it, to hold it at distant bay, than to thrash wildly in a widow's bed?

•

Late that Sunday afternoon, I found Mary and my mother at the kitchen table. Dad was in the garage, they said, looking for a backpack and the hiking boots he hadn't worn in several summers. I heard enough to know I'd interrupted a conversation about Mary's family, and I meant to exit quickly to let them continue their talk. But Mary pulled a chair away from the table for me, a gesture that said I was welcome to join them, and that also seemed to tell me I was forgiven. Except that Mary was the kind of person who found it nearly impossible to say she was sorry, her gesture also might have been an unspoken apology.

"How was your day?" my mother asked. She looked tired, but there was no longer any anguish in her eyes. She seemed relaxed, sedate at the end of this several-day siege of difficult encounters and drowning emotions, buoyed at the moment, it seemed to me, by her daughter's stories and confidences. I was glad to see her out of a dress or a dark suit for the first time since I had seen her in Denver. Her casual pants and a sweater now seemed to certify that the ritual days of grief, if not the grief itself, were done.

"It was good," I said, sitting down. "Jane's got such a nice place. So quiet out there."

"I wonder if it isn't a little too isolated for her by herself," Mom said.

"She said one time that she had given some thought to moving into town, here or in Mancos, but I guess she decided that was really home. And she's got a satellite dish, for heaven's sake. You can't claim you're too isolated when you've got a dish out behind the house."

"God, those things are ugly," Mary said. "They sure seem to be all the rage around here, though."

"Watch it," I said. "Those ugly things are helping to keep your brother in business. I mean, I don't *want* to deploy those satellites, but somebody's got to do it."

"I'll remember that," Mary said, grinning. "Every time I see one of those hideous things, I'll remember that at least they're putting food on your table."

"Exactly. We can only take this aesthetics business so far, after all."

"Listen," she said, her good mood surprising me, "I have to live with a scientist who's an aesthetic cripple. Don't you start in on me too."

"Mary was telling me about Robert's sabbatical in the spring." Mom joined the conversation. "They're going to be in Ecuador all summer. Did you know about that? Doesn't it sound great?"

"Robert's going to be there. Adrian and I are staying only as long as we can put up with him. You ought to see him when he's out in the field. I call it his Darwin complex. He gets absolutely obsessed."

"What's he going to be doing?"

"Oh, it's this mammoth project he's had going for a long time, long before I came into the picture. It involves a couple of other people at Berkeley. It has to do with moth habitats, but honestly, that's about as much as I know."

"I've always wondered," I said, "how you, of all people, ever ended up with a scientist. I mean, *I* know that they're the only people worth hanging around with, but I'm surprised that you had that much insight."

"Artists scare you all that much, do they?"

"They don't scare me—they give me the willies, maybe, but..."

"At least neither of you ended up with a theologian," my mother said, with a wink at the two of us. "They, my dears, make for interesting companions."

"Too much heaven and not enough earth?" I asked.

"No, that's your profession, Jack. No, it's more a question of expectations. Seriously, I don't envy men in the clergy at all. There's a pressure to be exemplary, to be seen as rather saintly, that can be very stifling. In my experience, it seems as though what happens with most priests is that their frailties and short-comings end up becoming all that much more glaring than other people's. But somehow, with a few of them, they actually do manage to lead lives that are... well, remarkable. But it isn't easy."

"What group is Dad in?" Mary asked.

"Oh dear, well, your dad, I would like to think, does fall into the latter group—I'm biased, of course—but he's kind of a special case. Dad's a very secular person, I'm sure you know. His strengths as a priest are that his passions and angers, and his foibles, are so up-front, so obviously like everyone else's. I guess you could say that instead of being someone who is consumed by the spiritual side of things, Dad is the sort of person who's truly enthralled by the secular world, but who tries to bring something deeper to it. Does that make any sense?"

"Sure," I said. "It also sounds like the preferable approach."

"It is for some," my mother said. "But there are people—plenty of them around this diocese, I have to tell you—who see people like Dick as the worst kinds of impostors."

"To hell with them," Mary said, drawing a reluctant smile out of my mother. Mary turned to me. "This hike sounds like a good idea, Jack. I'm glad you can stay and go with him."

"You want to join us?"

"I'm going to leave tomorrow afternoon. You couldn't get back to town that soon, I don't think."

"Got to get home?"

"I really should. I miss my daughter like crazy, and I wouldn't mind sleeping with my husband."

"Mary..." my mother said, enjoying the comment but chiding her nonetheless.

"Hey, Mom, come on," I said. "Marie's a healthy girl."

"I suppose she is," my mother said, blushing.

Mary leaned back in her chair, unabashed by this brief attention to her sex life, but she was still thinking about our hike. "I wish there was something you could take up there with you, some sort of memorial. I mean, if it was Mike's favorite place."

"He had several special places," Mom said. "Lots, really. I think he talked about Ice Lake Basin chiefly because it seemed so safe, so empty. No people—and people were what made life so frightening, weren't they? Just rock and snow and weather. I think he must have thought that nothing could scare him up there."

"I'll build a cairn," I said. "Somewhere where it seems appropriate, up on a ridge or someplace."

"What's a cairn?" Mary asked.

"You've seen them, those piles of rocks that people build as markers."

"You two build it together," my mother said.

"Yes," said Mary, seeming connected to the Healy clan at the end of her stay—the sister I liked so much when I liked her. "Do."

•

I hadn't known that elk season was under way; Dad had known, but forgotten. When we stopped at the Hermosa Store for coffee just before dawn on Monday morning, the little grocery was busy with men in blaze orange caps and jackets, giant gutting knives strapped to their belts, most of them speaking in loud, out-of-state accents, buying long loaves of bread, canned beans, and cases of beer.

"Oh damn," Dad said as we walked in the door. "I completely forgot. Do you suppose we ought to be up there with all these guys on the loose?"

"Not unless we look the part, we shouldn't. But they probably have orange vests for sale in here. I don't mind a bit as long as we stand out from about ten miles away."

"It won't be nearly as quiet."

"The hunters mostly stay down in the timber, don't they? Once we get up into the basin, we ought to be out of their way."

"All right," he said, "let's see what we can find."

We found the vests, bought two of the last three left in the store, and I insisted that we buy two orange stocking caps as well; they seemed like a poor investment for a single day's use, but I wasn't taking any chances. The last thing either of us needed was to be blown off a mountainside by some drunk parts salesman from Beaumont or Corpus Christi.

Mary and Mom had gotten up to see us off, and the four of us had had coffee in the kitchen—Dad and I at the table eating breakfast, the two of them in robes and slippers, leaning against the tiled counters. I told Mary I hoped I could meet Adrian before long and asked her to give my regards to Robert.

"I will," she said. "Why don't you come visit us? You're not in the midst of another mission, are you?"

"Oh, you never know. It's like being a bomber pilot. You've always got to be ready."

"Sounds entirely too much like being a bomber pilot for my taste," she said, smiling, "but, well, I hope everything goes well for you, whatever it is you do down there."

"You too, Marie," I said, hugging her, saying nothing more.

Dad held Mary for a long time—while Mom implored us

both to be careful, while Mary told him she loved him.

"I love you too, sugar," he said, teary-eyed, flustered by what he had not expected her to say.

The car was climbing Coal Bank Hill when Dad first mentioned Mary to me. "Doesn't she seem to be doing well?" he asked.

"I think she is," I said. "Motherhood seems to suit her."

"Is that what it is? I don't know. There is a change somehow, more noticeable to me down here than when we saw her in Denver. Your mother said they sat and talked for nearly two hours yesterday—just general things. That's something Mary wouldn't have wanted to do not too long ago."

"I don't think she wants to be as distant as she used to be— not that she ever wanted to be necessarily. When we were driving down, she tried to explain why home was so difficult for her. She doesn't understand why herself, really."

"Maybe it's your mother and me. First children have it kind of hard in some ways. They get the brunt of the parents' trial and error. Their silly mistakes. By the time you and Mike came along, maybe Mom and I had learned something. I think we certainly gave you more freedom than Mary got. I've kind of assumed that that's why it was so important for her to strike out on her own."

"I'm not sure I totally buy this business of parents shaping their children's personalities. Maybe now that I'm a father I just don't want to believe it. In six or seven years, is Matt going to be who he is basically because of my relationship with him? That puts a kind of pressure on me that's pretty scary. My God, my role these days is like playing the fun uncle who shows up every now and again with goodies under his arm."

"No, it's not the ideal situation, certainly."

"No . . ." I said, letting it go at that.

The sky was clear in the diffuse morning light. The recent snow still looked fresh on the summits of the Needles and the Grenadiers, but it had melted from the flanks of the mountains.

Dad stopped to let me pee at the top of Molas Pass, then we wound down to Silverton, the old mining camp that first looked abandoned as we glimpsed it from above, then looked inhabited but forlorn as the highway skirted the edge of town.

We passed several hunters' trailers on the dirt road that paralleled Mineral Creek, and the campground at the end of the main road looked like a migrant camp. Pickup campers and boxy pull-behinds and several big canvas cowmen's tents had overtaken the place. Fire rings smoldered beside each rig, and the lawn chairs that encircled them were empty, abandoned after sleepy breakfasts, to be filled again by early afternoon, no doubt. We encountered two orange-outfitted, broad-girthed men—also a father and son, perhaps—after we had parked the car, debated who would carry the small pack that contained our lunch, a faded topo map and assorted supplies, and started up the trail. Dad looked absolutely foolish in his orange vest and his stocking cap pulled low over his ears, and surely I looked no more debonair, but we must have resembled brothers in the hunting bonds as we approached the men.

"Just heading out?" the younger man asked, his rifle slung in the bend of his elbow.

"Just hiking," Dad told them.

"We been out—what?—two hours now," the older one informed us. "Ain't seen nothing but pretty pictures. I got to go sack out for a little bit. This rare air up here like to suffocate me. Where you headed?"

"Ice Lake Basin."

"There elk up there?"

"Probably not with this new snow," I said.

"You keep your eyes peeled anyway," the older one said, giving us definite instructions, "case we see you again. Son and me's going to have at it again here after while." Son nodded, so did we, then we headed up the trail.

I hadn't been in the mountains in this brief, icy interlude between fall and winter in many years—a brooding, emotive

bridge between the seasons that was given over too much to
the hunters, it seemed to me. The sunlight was dappled in the
thick growth of evergreens; the air still and cold and fragrant.
Dad walked ahead of me, keeping a pace that my sea-level
lungs could manage, carrying the pack, he said, on the easy
part. We crossed Clear Creek, then continued the steep climb
to the small tree-encircled lake in the lower basin, neither of us
talking, but offering each other faint smiles when we stopped
occasionally to catch our breath. The final mile up out of the
timber and into the tundra in the wide alpine bowl was slow,
the trail still good but very steep, switching back on itself as it
climbed through the short, delicate grass and exposed rock that
now were spotted with snow.

Ice Lake, befitting its name, was blanketed by a thin, snow-
caked layer of ice, but in patches near the shore its clear aqua-
marine water was visible, stubbornly liquid still despite the
freezing weather. Dad pulled the pack from his back and we sat
down near the water's edge on a boulder that had been dried by
the sun. I was sweating beneath my cap and I pulled it off.

"You suppose it's safe to unmask yet?" I asked.

"Let's be brave," he said, joining me, the bald top of his head
wet and shiny in the sunlight. "My Lord, it is glorious up here,
isn't it?"

"I don't think I've ever been up here this late before. It's . . .
yeah, it's beautiful. It's a different world."

"One of the regrets at the end of my life will be that I didn't
spend more time up in this country, didn't take enough advantage of the place I was fortunate enough to live in."

"You don't think you've got a few years left to rectify the
situation?"

"Oh, I probably have a few years. But one of the things that
happens to you when you get older is that you bolster your
misgivings about yourself, your fear of becoming useless, by
convincing yourself of all the heavy responsibilities you have.
If you're a parish priest you have this large extended family that

surely needs you—and it feels good to think you're needed. But the vagabond pleasures—the kinds of leisure that get you more than a few feet away from a telephone—sadly take a backseat."

"What about all the retirees out jaunting around in their RVs? They don't seem burdened by responsibilities."

"Oh, they're pathetic, aren't they? Suddenly they've got way too much time on their hands and they realize exactly what I'm talking about—these guys realize they haven't really *wanted* to take a walk, go for a drive with their wives in twenty years. So off they go—not seeking adventure, just a change of scenery that will make things seems a little new—trying to make up for the lost time. No, if that was the only other option, I think I'd just work till a coronary took me."

"That's beginning to look like the route you're going to take."

"Heavens, Jack, I'm only sixty-seven. Don't start packing me away quite yet."

"No. I don't want you to retire. Not at all. What I mean is that I can't imagine you retired, really."

"Hal and I used to chat about being retired, about how it sounded like a fine life. But, shoot, all Hal needed to keep him happy was a fishing pole. I told you I took him fishing the day before he died, didn't I?"

"You did."

"It's funny. Hal enjoyed it. Sure, it meant something to him. But the person it really did something for was me. I couldn't talk. I couldn't sit beside his damn hospital bed and tell him what a friend he'd been to me. But sneaking him out of that place was—remember how the catechism defines a sacrament? An outward and visible sign of an inward and spiritual grace. That little fishing trip of ours was sacramental, I suppose—an outward sign." Dad was looking away from me, toward the craggy line of peaks that bounded the basin on the west. From below us came the echoing reports of rifle shots, three or four of them, doubling, tripling, quadrupling in number as their echoes caromed off the ridges, the first shots we had heard since we started out. He listened until it was quiet. "I'll be continually sorry, I'm sure, that we didn't get to give Michael some kind of sign. Surely we should have found some . . . an equivalent of taking him fishing."

"There had to be some evidence, a sign maybe, in his acceptance by everyone at St. Andrew's. They didn't just put up with him. They put him to work. That means something when somebody has work that you can do. I think that's why he was happy there."

"But not so happy that . . . oh, I don't know, Jack. A child killing himself is such a terrible message to a parent. Regardless of the circumstances or the mental illness or what have you, it's a goddamn indictment, isn't it? My job is to be pastoral, to care for people, and I let my own son get so desperate that he . . . I ought to be ashamed of myself."

I didn't know what to say, so I said nothing for a while. Sitting motionless, I felt the cold air begin to draw in on me, and I zipped my parka up to my neck, trying to think of a way to tell him that my guilt was as sharp as his, a way to lessen his sense of culpability by telling him that the fault was really mine, that I was the one who had tormented Mike, yet who had done so little to persuade him that I was his ally. More rifle shots thundered off the mountains before I finally said, "None of us probably is ever going to feel at ease about how we were with Mike, what we did for him. I'm not. When I think about how seldom I . . . I don't know, Dad. Every night since it happened, I've been awake for a long time with this weird paralyzing sense that somehow I'm finally going to be held accountable, that now it's obvious that I'm the cause. The sick part is that the feeling isn't one of concern for Mike. It's totally selfish—like now my ass is in real trouble."

"I always tell people that the guilt will give way with time. It's what I ought to tell them, because it's true, for the most part. But telling myself that now, or to try to tell it to you, would seem like the worst kind of charade." He got to his feet, seemingly ready to climb again, the guilt too palpable at that moment to let him simply sit. "At least I can spare us both the platitudes. Are you cold?"

I nodded, watched him close his coat, and I took the pack this time. "Shall we trudge on?"

"Where's that shack you talked about?"

"See this bench right above us?" I pointed to the flat lip of rock at the top of the snow-swept talus field just beyond us. "As I remember, you can see it from there. It's between there and the summit of Pilot Knob. Thirteen thousand feet or so. But it might be gone. It wouldn't take much of a slide to sweep the whole thing away."

"Let's have a look," he said, motioning for me to take the lead.

We no longer had a trail to follow. I picked my way up the steep slope, devoid of anything but sharp rock now, each of the thousands of rocks made slippery by the thin coat of snow. My approach too steep for him, Dad found his own route, tracing a series of switchbacks, stopping often as he climbed, and I had news for him when he reached me at the top of the pitch. "Still here," I said, pointing toward Pilot Knob. "Come straight down from what looks like the high point on the right there. Straight below it. It's right at the base of that big snowfield."

He found it. "Who in the world would have built something clear up there? It's impossible." He spoke between heavy breaths.

"Some crazy old bastard who thought he'd make millions up here. I don't think he ever got a tunnel started. The time I was here with Mike, there was an old woodstove and a metal bed frame inside it. Imagine packing them up. You want to see if we can get to it?"

He grinned at me. "Ready to quit already, are you?"

"Just checking," I told him, still sucking in air myself. "When we get there we can reward ourselves with lunch."

The slope swept up more gently now; only the final pitch in front of the old cabin looked truly steep. Behind the cabin, there seemed to be nothing but vertical rock—the rotten crag at the summit. The snow was deeper now, the firm placement of each step more difficult to judge, and it was almost an hour later before we sat on the loose boards we piled a few feet in front of the door—the derelict structure now a perilous parallelogram, listing so much it was hard to imagine it could remain upright.

It was late enough in the day already that the snowy summit of Pilot Knob cast the cabin and us in shadow. But surrounding us in three directions, the sharp and ragged peaks of the San Juans stood in brilliant sunlight. A few high clouds seemed to loiter near the summits, but there was little wind. We unpacked the sandwiches and cookies and drank hot cider from a thermos, keeping our parkas closed against the cold, our stocking caps back on now, protecting us from the weather rather than the erratic eyesight of hunters. I didn't want to resume our conversation about Mike now that we sat in front of the shack that he had fantasized could be his home. I didn't want to talk about our guilt again, to once again churn through the issue of what we might have done but didn't do. My guilt showed no sign of abating, and I doubt my father's did, but the more I talked about it, the more wasted and selfish that emotion seemed.

"In case you never get to to go, Dad," I said as I bit into my sandwich, "this is not all that unlike the view from orbit. The specifics are different, the vantage points, but the sense of it— the panorama, the feeling that everything below you is beautiful, calm, and orderly, all of it elegantly patterned, is very similar."

"I think this shack kind of spoils it," he said. "I'd just as soon it wasn't here. It's not that big of an intrusion, but without it, the view here would be of total wilderness. No sign of man whatsoever."

"That's similar too, in a way. At any given moment, you can usually see something manmade—highways, airport runways, the green circles of sprinkling systems. Even out over the oceans, you see the wakes of the big ships. Not the ships themselves but these wakes that must stretch for miles."

Dad smiled. "So the extraterrestrials will certainly be able to tell we're inhabited, won't they? Do you suppose they might already have telescopes so powerful that they can look and see the highways and assume there may be some sort of burrowing insects here?"

"And just where are they looking from?" I asked, enjoying his lighthearted speculation.

"Oh, that's your department. Heavens, I don't know. But didn't they think they'd detected true planets around some nearby star not too long ago?"

"Vega. Yeah, they did. But planets obviously don't necessarily imply people. In this solar system, Mars was the real hope, of course. The way it appeared in telescopes, the temperatures, distance from the sun—it seemed to have the best chance of having some sort of life. When the Viking landers started to dig and send back data, there were a lot of people, very informed people, who expected to see some sort of microbial life, at least. It was really a blow not to find it, in some ways. God, imagine what it would have done for funding if they'd found evidence of even the most elemental life."

"And your opinion of whether there is life out there somewhere?" He was baiting me, but his spirits were bright and we were avoiding grimmer subjects, so I gladly responded.

"When you consider the billions, trillions of stars, many, most of which may have planetary systems, meaning matter that can coalesce into the stuff of life, the likelihood that we're the *only* living planet, or the only intelligent planet is, well, it's infinitesimal. I mean, my God."

"But that's the fun thing to consider, isn't it? I'm sure you're right, Jack, that very probably there is other life in the universe, perhaps other civilizations. That doesn't seem all that mind-boggling to me. If they're there, fine—although I don't expect any encounters for a good long while. But the thought that really is dizzying to me is that we might, just might, be all there is. Hal and I used to talk about this a bit. What if, in all the enormity of the universe, among all those trillions of stars, we are it? If we are alone, the only—what's the word? biosphere?—if we're just possibly the only thinking, creating beings in the whole universe, well, it's a stunning possibility to consider, isn't it?"

"It appeals to your religious sensibilities, I can tell." I reached for the last cookie, split it, and offered him half.

The frivolity was gone from his voice now, replaced by an intensity that the subject seemed to demand. "Well, I am who I am, and that may be a part of it, but whether you think it's theological or cosmological or whatever, it's an equally astounding question. I mean, this is what's fascinating to me. What would be the more profound information to receive, if we could ever know it indisputably? That indeed there were other civilizations, other people? Or that, no, throughout the entire universe, life and intelligence existed only here?"

"Well, I think it would be the, the easiest... the possibility that would be the most gratifying to the human ego would be if we were all there was. But—"

"But wouldn't it also impose an enormous, well, responsibility? Ethically, morally, religiously—however you want to look at it—if we somehow knew, without question, that we were alone, wouldn't our perceptions of ourselves have to change fairly radically?"

"You mean that fact—assuming it could ever be proven—

would have to focus the whole issue of some divine plan?"

"No. You think this is the priest talking, don't you? No, even if we were just a quirk, just some chemical aberration that could only happen once, wouldn't that uniqueness, make us feel . . . feel perhaps that life was even more incredible than we had thought it was? That life's very existence—however impossibly it came to be—gave it a meaning that was even more profound? Just because of the odds against it ever happening?"

This was the father I hardly knew, the one I seldom spoke with, a man who privately delighted in the problematical issues of existence, but who kept his questions, his uncertainties, unspoken—perhaps because he was afraid they implied he was about to try to convert you, perhaps because he found them so fundamental, so crucial in some respects, that he reverenced them with silence. As I sat there beside him, I felt something akin to privilege—perhaps it was pride—to hear him speculating about issues that utterly surprised me.

"I remember a comment, but I can't remember who made it," I told him, "about how in a very literal way, humans represent the universe becoming aware of itself."

"It's true, isn't it?" he said, pulling his hat low on his forehead, the air seeming to grow colder now. "But I'd also argue that life in general on this planet—and thinking, human thought in particular—separate us from the rest of the universe in a pretty fundamental way. When matter evolves into life and life evolves to the point that beings are aware of themselves and can wonder about themselves and how they came to be, haven't those beings—here's a religious word for you—*transcended* their universe in some way? I guess what I'm trying to say is that I would think that even the most atheistic minds have to see something in our existence that is so improbable that it's wondrous in a spiritual kind of way."

"They'd probably just say it's wondrous in a wondrous kind of way."

"Fair enough. If they'd agree that there is such a thing as wonder, I'd say I'd made my point."

●

We built Michael's cairn on the saddle between Pilot Knob and Golden Horn—a chest-high, pyramidal pile of rock on the ridge between two peaks he had twice climbed. The wind we had been sheltered from below was strong and icy on the exposed ridge, and we worked quickly, gathering and stacking the sharp-edged rocks into a rough monolith. When we were finished, our gloved hands stiff and clumsy from the cold, Dad said a short prayer, blessing the simple monument and asking for the repose of Michael's soul. "This was a good idea," he said as we started down. "I'm sure the cairn will be here a hell of a lot longer than that cabin will."

We passed to the south of the shack and moved steadily down the talus slope, warmer now that we were moving again, our breathing easier on the descent, our progress still slow because of the slippery snow. A hundred feet or so above Ice Lake, Dad's foot lost its hold and he tore his hand on the edge of a rock as he reached back to catch his fall. When I climbed back up to him, his palm was so bloody that I couldn't get a good look at the cut, but he assured me that it was nothing serious, saying there wasn't much pain, wishing he hadn't warmed up so much that he'd taken his gloves off.

I wrapped his hand with a handkerchief he had with him and held it tight until the bleeding subsided. Then, despite his objections, I tore a piece of fabric from the tail of my shirt, wrapped his hand again and held his glove open for him while he gingerly pushed his hand inside. He was just fine, he said repeatedly, anxious to get going again, and we started down, Dad in the lead this time. We were happy to be rid of the snow by the time we reached the trees at timberline and the trail

down to the campground was firm and easy to negotiate—the
final miles of our hike quiet in the crescendoing cold, our heavy
steps in the early evening light a kind of numb and meditative
march.

A laughing group of hunters stood round a bright campfire
near the place where we had parked the car. Dad was reluctant,
but he walked over to the hunters with me and waited while I
asked if they could spare us any bandages. The man who spoke
said they had some large Band-Aids that they were glad to give
us, but nothing more. "I know we ought to bring better to
hunting camp, but it doesn't seem like any of us ever gets hurt
too bad. You think you're all right?" he asked my father. Dad
assured him he was and told him that we, too, should have
brought more in the way of first aid.

"This'll help," said a second man in a parka with a fur-lined
hood, skirting close to the fire as he walked toward us, holding
out a pint bottle of bourbon. "I swear by this stuff." Dad declined, but the man insisted, and the others assured him that
whiskey was something they had plenty of. Dad acquiesced
quickly enough that I could tell the bourbon sounded very
good to him, and he thanked them all with a flourish for their
medicinal assistance.

I drove on the return trip, taking swigs from the bottle the
first two times he offered it to me, then waving away his subsequent generosity, letting him use the rest to nurse his wound
and his obvious exhaustion. The heater quickly warmed the car
and I realized that I, too, was very tired. When we reached the
smooth surface of the highway outside Silverton, the leg-
jarring demands of the down-climb and the ruts of the gravel
road behind us, civilization seemed surprisingly welcome.
"Thanks, Jack," Dad said as the car accelerated. "That was a
good trip."

"Sure sorry about your hand," I said in reply.

"Oh shoot," he said, "please forget my damn hand. I'll be
fine."

There was a pleasant kind of cordiality in the silence as we drove, neither of us needing to say much now, each of us comfortable enough with the other after twelve hours together that the wordlessness seemed conversational, communicative. I was glad we had made the hike, pleased to have gotten into the high country after a long absence, pleased to have done something with my father other than to sit across from him in an easy chair, and to have done something sacramental for Michael. I hadn't shoveled dirt onto his coffin, but I had helped build him a sentinel pile of stones.

As we drove down the south slope of the pass, the warmth and the darkness inside the car secure and comforting, I told Dad I had gotten a new mission. I hadn't planned what I would say, and I was surprised that I was interrupting the silence, but the short burst of words were quickly out for him to hear. He didn't respond for a time; he stared into the headlights' wedge of light, then turned away from me toward his window.

"That's wonderful," he said after so long I had begun to wonder if I had made a serious mistake. His voice was soft, full of a warm paternal pride and pleasure, and I could tell that despite the week just past—perhaps especially because of it—he was glad to get the news. "How long have you known?"

"A little over a week. I found out just before I came up." I gave him the few details I had, told him it would probably be a year from now, told him I couldn't have imagined a mission I wanted more than the one that deployed the telescope. Finally, I said I did realize it meant I would see even less of the kids, and for some surprising reason, I also confessed that it might mean Jane and I would lose the relationship we had begun to build.

"You know, I really do think that life is more complicated now than it was in Mother's and my day," he said, speaking slowly, the bourbon evident in the subtle slur of his words. "I know there probably isn't any logic in believing that, but . . . all the complications of careers and locations, and lifestyles, goals.

It's tricky to hold it all together. I used to think people just aren't as committed to staying together as they once were. But . . . I'm pretty sure that isn't the case. Part of it, I suppose, is that people today are more demanding. They are less willing to put up with rotten situations. And that's all to the good, as far as I'm concerned. But the sad part is that even when they have something very good together, other aspects so often pose such complications. I don't know, Jack. You know I love Peggy very much. I was heartsick when you two . . . And Jane's . . . like a daughter. I so much want her to be happy." He took the last sip of his whiskey. "You're supposed to be able to get good advice out of old men like me, but all I can say is that I hope none of you kids ever has to have any regrets. I mean that at least you'll feel like you made the right decisions."

There didn't seem to be a particular response for me to make, and I drove on in silence for a while, enjoying Dad's verbose and emotional kind of drunkenness, appreciating moments like these when he seemed less like a father than a bald and round-bellied priest who, despite its sins and sadnesses, lived in and loved the world. I saw him close the cap on the bottle and lay it between our seats. He leaned back and sighed, as if to say that nothing was simple.

"Jane told me about the time when she was in the hospital," I said when we were closer to town, "about her asking you to get her some sedatives. She appreciated the fact that you weren't shocked by her asking. She said you said something about believing that in some situations it might conceivably be the right decision."

"Did I say that?"

"I've thought about that several times since Mike. You think it really might be the right thing . . . ever?"

He considered for a moment. "The fundamentalists see red whenever you talk about situational morals. But as far as I can tell, morals and ethics are situational by their nature. They are reasoned responses to events, to life; they don't exist in a damn vacuum. So no, I don't suppose I'd categorically say suicide is wrong, though it's hard to imagine when it'd be right. It's like what we were talking about this afternoon, isn't it? If this phenomenon called life is so precious because it's so improbable, you'd better have a hell of a commensurate reason if you choose to end it."

"In Mike's case, more than being terrified, you mean, being chronically afraid . . . nothing making sense?"

"I don't know, Jack. I just don't know. Is it things making so much sense that keeps the rest of us alive?" he said, shutting his eyes.

seven

Training for the new mission was much more like work than it had been before. My first flight had been a kind of quixotic dream, and training for it was a devotion, a fiercely single-minded commitment, an unhidden affair that had ended my faltering marriage. But this time, the shuttle orbiter was more than a dream machine; it was palpable, a spaceship built of nuts and bolts, an ungainly airplane that looked, up close, as if it were wrapped with movers' blankets, and I was a veteran passenger, one of the fortunate few who had defied gravity inside it and briefly escaped the earth. To do so again would be wonderful, but somehow the preparations for that second flight, unlike the first, had no sublime sense of destiny. I might indeed be destined to go to space again, but in the meantime I was destined to punch a tedious and often monotonous clock.

We spent long and exhausting days in the flight simulators, days spent dealing with aborted launches and engines that failed to fire, with simulated landings that only closely averted catastrophe—other days under the high roof of 9A, practicing the mission plan that would eventually be rote, Gina Rinaldi and I taking turns maneuvering the remote-arm simulator, endlessly lifting a big, sausage-shaped air bag marked "telescope" out of a painted plywood cargo bay. Sometime after the first of the year, Ron McFarlin and I would have to begin a series of trips to California to familiarize ourselves with the actual telescope and with the berthing adapter that would secure it in the bay, and in the months preceding the mission we would be lowered, time after time, into the water of the WEFT tank, where we would devise and practice contingent plans in case we should have to go out into the cargo bay to adjust the telescope manually or to free it from its cradle. Eventually, or so they told us, our year of training would end, and we would go to Florida and ride *Discovery* into space.

It had been hard to return to Texas, not so much because I began to pity my schedule and my solitude again as because the events in Colorado had held my attention there. Michael was always in my thoughts, but curiously, it was often the gangling boy covered with Band-Aids whom I thought about, not the man who had died in Denver. In the weeks after the funeral, alone again except for a couple of Saturday trips to Austin to see the kids, Michael, or Michael's memory, was my ready companion. I heard no voices, and I would have argued with Dad if he had suggested I felt the presence of Michael's spirit, yet there was, unmistakably, a sense of tenuous fraternity, of something ineffable that binds two brothers, which I had never experienced before. There were moments, to be sure, when this new sense of connection disgusted me, when I was sure that it was no more than my own self-absorbed effort to turn guilt into something soothing, something that would acquit me of my failure to have been a good brother while he was still alive. And perhaps that was part of it, but I wanted to think there was something more—some nascent sort of truce between Michael and me made possible by his death. No, Mike hadn't died for my sins, but perhaps there was a kind of redemption for both of us in the end of our years of resentments and misunderstandings. For the first time in a very long time, I was able to imagine Mike outside the context of how I was or wasn't being responsible to him, and the more I was able to think of him solely as himself—mischievous, jovial boy and mentally ravaged man—the more I missed him.

●

Peggy invited me to spend Thanksgiving with her and the kids and I accepted, although I wasn't sure I liked the idea of playing the role of the pitied Ex who remains included on family holidays. Mark MacArthur was in Arizona, visiting his parents—or more likely, I wanted to think, some woman he kept on the side—so at least I didn't have to deal with the awkward business of which one of the two of us would carve the turkey, and the day turned out to be a delight—Matt and Sarah and I kicking the soccer ball around in the little park near their house; the four of us playing Hearts and Go Fish at the kitchen table while the bird baked nearby; the lovely dinner that included creamed onions only because Peggy knew how much I liked them; then, after dark, *The Black Stallion* on the VCR before I put the kids to bed; Peggy and I sitting on the sofa, holding hands and talking, once they were asleep. She told me I was welcome to stay, telling me the sofa made into a bed, and I happily agreed to, postponing the three-hour drive until morning, seeing Peggy, her legs tanned and lithe and strong, in the old T-shirt she loved to wear to bed when she went to the kitchen to turn off the light, thanking her then for the day, aching to be getting into bed beside her.

I didn't see the three of them again until two days before Christmas. They were in Denver to spend the holiday with Buddy and Marge, and I stopped by for part of an afternoon en route home to Durango. Buddy offered me eggnog, reviling the Broncos for barely missing the playoffs as he filled my glass. Sarah was apprenticed to Marge in the kitchen, the two of them baking sugar cookies, Sarah in charge of pressing the star- and angel-shaped cutters into the firm, thin dough. Matt, suddenly grown introverted, it seemed to me, was sprawled on the living-room carpet reading Conan comics, and Peggy sat looking bemused in a rocker near the Christmas tree, knowing better than to try to do too much in her mother's house. I decided not to make much ceremony out of giving the kids their presents; I slipped them out of paper sacks and slid them under the tree without attracting the attention of Matt or Sarah. Peggy whispered that she would be sure they knew the gifts came from me. Before I left, Sarah asked me why I couldn't stay. My explanation that, if I did, Gram and Papa would have to spend Christmas all alone, seemed to concern her. "You mean 'cause Mike has died, too, huh?" she asked.

"Yes. That's right," I said, talking about him with her for the first time. "Without Mike, they'll be kind of sad this Christmas."

Mom and Dad's house didn't seem melancholy so much as simply quiet. Dad had a busy day at the church on Christmas Eve, and Mom and I decorated the tree—a little three-foot fir she had set on a folding card table covered with a green felt drape, a tiny, nondescript tree that seemed to be harsh evidence that this would be a Christmas spent without children. Jane and I went to midnight mass together. Dad's short sermon seemed unfocused, somehow absentminded to me, but singing the joyful, wonderfully familiar carols somehow choked me up; Jane noticed and squeezed my hand.

She joined the three of us for Christmas dinner the following afternoon, Dad mentioning the family's many fortunes during grace, his voice betraying the misfortune that bore heavily on his mind. No one mentioned Michael until Mom, serving plum pudding, told us it was for him. "The rest of you always preferred pumpkin pie, didn't you?" she said, "but plum pudding was what Mike really loved." Dad fell asleep during a Placido Domingo concert on television; Mom, her apron still on, sat rapt by the tenor's voice. Beside me on the sofa, Jane pinched my leg to get me to notice my father, who was now beginning to snore. We smiled at each other, hers the kind of smile she might have given to a sleeping child she had gone in to check on.

Despite the holiday hordes, Jane and I skied at Purgatory on the twenty-sixth, both of us tentative at first, a little rusty, Jane using only a single pole, holding her handless arm high and away for balance, skiing fast once she had gained some confidence, skiing better than me, looking agile and at ease on the snow as I followed behind her. "God, that was a good thing for me to do," she said as we drove back to town. "Skiing used to mean a lot to me. Kenny and I were pretty comparable skiers. We used to have these terrific days on the slopes, then we'd go home, both of us beat, and make love for a long time. I mean, not just fuck each other, but really make love. Occasionally we could still be entranced."

We drove out to Jane's ranch and I stayed for a drink and a dinner of the leftovers my mother had sent home with her the night before, but we didn't make love, nor did we fuck, before I held her and said good-bye, adding that I wasn't sure when I'd see her again but that surely I could manage to come through again before too long, Jane telling me to call her, for heaven's sake, if Texas seemed too lonely.

At the airport the next morning, both Mom and Dad seemed cheerful, relaxed, and eager to send me away in good spirits. It was the third day of Christmas, and my mother gave me a little bag with three pieces of fudge and three polished apples. They

were planning to visit Mary and her family at the end of January, and I told them that if by chance I had to be in California
at the same time, I'd finagle a way for us all to get together.
"Don't you get caught playing hooky," my father said as he
hugged me. "We want to be able to go to Florida in October to
see another launch."

I didn't get to see them in California a month later, not because I was stuck at home in Houston, but because I had gone
to the Cape to see a launch myself. Someone had decided that I
would make an appropriate escort for the contingent from the
University of Colorado who had come to watch their Halley's
experiments get lifted into space. I had argued that my training
commitments should come first—not particularly anxious to
spend several days in charge of thirty strangers and a couple of
former professors I barely knew—and John Young had even
gone to bat for me. But the decision was made, it seemed. El
Onizuka would deploy the CU experiments and I would make
sure that the experiments' designers enjoyed their front-row
seats. The place would probably be a zoo, more press, more
television people and VIPs in attendance for this launch than
for any since Sally Ride's first flight. A spunky schoolteacher
from New Hampshire would be part of *Challenger*'s crew this
time, and everyone was paying attention.

•

Some of the astronomy students joked with me about how
they didn't have to come all the way to Florida just to freeze
their asses off while we waited for the launch at the VIP viewing area. And it did seem like January in Colorado as we stood,
shivering, in the morning sun—the weather so cold that I cau-
tioned them all that we would probably have to wait at least
one more day to see *Challenger* climb the sky. What little I
knew about launch requirements made it seem certain that the

risks of ice damage and brittle metals were just too great. But
the loudspeakers never announced a scrub, and a great celebra-
tory cheer went up from the several hundred people surrounding us when the hold at T minus nine minutes ended and the
countdown resumed. Terrific, I told myself, the telemetry from
previous flights obviously tells them the temperatures are safe
—and at last I'm going to be able to watch this ship begin its
journey.

When the solid rockets ignited, their enormous crackling
roar reaching us seconds later, I couldn't have spoken a word.
The sight and the thundering sounds of that machine straining
to rise were stupendous. *Challenger* was my orbiter, after all; I'd
traveled three million miles in it; I'd sailed alone away from it
when I went to grapple the satellite, and, satellite in tow, I
returned to it gratefully, seeing it float in the blackness like the
safest harbor imaginable. This time it was leaving without me,
and in those speechless, emotional seconds, I knew how much I
wanted to go again.

I remember that I was about to turn away from the spectacle,
from the graceful arc of rocket smoke and the searing fountains
of exhaust, to see the reactions of the Coloradans, when the
fireball filled the sky. The external tank exploded with such
force that it was momentarily another sun, then the spot in the
sky where this new and cataclysmic sun had been was a growl-
ing, billowing ball of smoke, dark streamers of debris shooting
from it like fireworks and falling away to the ocean, the twisting plumes of the SRBs snaking on toward space.

Amid the gasps and shrieks, the wordless sounds of shock
and disbelief, of horror at this unimaginable image of hell
where seconds before only a shimmering spaceship had been,
came a shaken and uncertain voice over the loudspeakers: "Obviously a major malfunction." The public relations officer's
voice trailed away to silence; the bright numerals on the mission clock in front of us continued to tick—T plus one minute

and eighteen seconds, nineteen seconds, twenty...; then Canaveral workers who had been assigned to the viewing area
began to circulate through the crowd, their faces looking
blank, some faces looking frightened, their flat voices suggest-
ing we try to make our way to the buses.

For a long moment I didn't think, I didn't comprehend, I
didn't see what I was seeing. Then it was as though I were at
the point in the nightmare when I'm falling from the cliff and,
in a frantic change of focus, I break the fall by waking. But this
scene, this sudden apocalypse, would not, could not be
stopped. Despite the impossibility, *Challenger,* the tank, and the
solid rockets were strewn across the sky, a rain of hot and
smoking metal was falling toward the choppy waters of the
Atlantic, and I was wide awake.

Failed launches were nothing new. In the simulators I had
ridden hundreds of them—aborts in the seconds before liftoff
that sent us scurrying out the hatch and down a breakneck
escape slide in a bucket; aborts in the air—the main engines
mysteriously shutting down—that required us to jettison the
tank and the racing SRBs and to nurse the orbiter back to one
of several landing strips; aborts above the atmosphere that gave
us little choice but to burn the engines longer than planned to
nudge the ship into a shallow but safe orbit. But this terrible
contingency, total destruction at ten miles high, was one we
had never practiced. We all knew it was possible, at least in a
theoretical sense, but surely it would never happen to us—not
to a machine in which one of us was riding, not to friends and
admired acquaintances, not to NASA. Not now.

Yet the cold, clear morning was suddenly overcast with
smoke, clouded by debris that included seven people. I walked
toward the restraining rope at the far edge of the grassy slope in
front of the grandstands—away from the Coloradans, away
from everyone else, watching foolishly for the parachutes I
knew would not begin to open, searching the sky for the famil-

iar shape of the orbiter I knew no longer existed, praying, I suppose, by silently chanting *no!*

The weather grew hot and muggy somehow as I stood, watching, peering into the gray, gruesome finale of the hydrogen fire, seeing an end of innocence in the flames and smoke, seeing Michael again on a hospital bed, his neck purple and swollen, his chest no longer rising with his breath, imagining him standing beside me now in a worn white T-shirt, looking like a medicine man with his long dark braid that hung between his shoulder blades, tears streaming from his eyes, his large hand cupping the back of my neck, squeezing it in an effort to speak.

●

No one was talking when I got on the bus. The seat behind the driver was empty and I slumped into it. He closed the door behind me and slowly drove away, joining the cortege of buses that rolled south toward Cocoa Beach. As we passed the Vehicle Assembly Building—vans with blinking lights circling its perimeter as if there were actually something they could do—I stood up and tried to say a word or two to the astronomers and their students, whose years of patient planning and design had also burned up ten miles above us. "I...I guess there'll be some information of some kind when we get to Cocoa Beach," I said. "From what there was on the loudspeaker, I don't think anyone had any warning. It...well..."

"Do you think it's possible they survived?" asked the grad student named Cynthia, sitting a few rows behind me. Her voice was a sort of whisper.

"I don't see how they could have. It would have...no, I'm sure they didn't." I knew I couldn't say much more. "Probably...I hope, it was instantaneous. I think all they would have felt...the only thing they would have known is that they were outbound."

•

When we got off the bus near the Holiday Inn, I spotted Jim
Vandertag, an astronaut, who stood with a clutch of people on
a newly mowed strip of lawn, the people milling as if they had
no notion of what to do, speaking in funereal voices, Jim scanning the growing crowd. He pursed his lips when he saw me,
sucked in air, then let it go instead of saying hello. "Any
word?" I asked him.

He shook his head. "They've got planes up, looking, but I
don't think anyone expects there's anything to find. They want
everyone who's here to get back to Houston. You're on the list
of people I'm trying to track down. We're supposed to get to
Patrick as soon as we can. I guess there're enough T-38s here to
get us all home."

I found the Coloradans again and as I talked to them, telling
them good-bye, strangely saying I was sorry—an odd kind of
apology for the explosion that had ruined their day—my
words came to me easily now, but they sounded callous and
officious somehow, the initial mute shock giving way to the
same sort of emotionless attention to logistics that I had heard
from my father on the morning Michael died.

The seven or eight of us from the astronaut office who had
been at Canaveral for the launch put on flight suits in an old,
sea-stained Quonset hangar at Patrick Air Force Base, saying
little about the accident except to ask each new arrival if he had
heard anything, talking in subdued voices about whether there
were pilots enough to get us home, discussing the fuel loads on
the T-38s and the refueling stop at Pensacola, someone mentioning that there would be a van waiting for us at Ellington.
"God damn it to hell!" shouted Terry Conover out of the silence. He threw his flight bag against a bank of lockers, then
picked it up and marched out onto the tarmac toward his plane.
"Anyone who doesn't feel up to flying, please speak up,"

said Harvey Thomas, a shuttle commander and veteran of three successful flights. "It's been a bad enough day already." No one spoke up, and soon we made our way to the small jet trainers that were lined up wing to wing in the early-afternoon sun. Terry Conover gave our plane its preflight while I climbed into the second seat. "All set, Jack?" he asked through his headset while we waited in line, our engines idling. One by one the planes ahead of us screamed down the long, heat-shimmered runway before at last they lifted up. I told him I was ready. "Then let's get the fuck out of this place," he said, radioing for takeoff clearance, pivoting the needle-nosed plane into position.

The T-38 climbed through air that was still hazy, polluted by a disastrous smog, but above us to the west, visible through the clear shield that surrounded me, visible above Terry's red helmet, was sky that still knew no trouble.

●

Like everyone else in America that night, I watched the repeated replays of the accident on television, but each time, the outcome was the same. Each time, as the launch vehicle climbed through the thinning atmosphere, a tongue of flame seemed to curl from the right SRB, then to lick the long black underbelly of the orbiter, then to pierce the tank and to draw its fuel into a ferocious fire. Each time, the solid rockets, spiraling like the horns of a devil, continued to climb, as if to defy the catastrophe—or to mock it.

In the minutes between the video replays, I listened to politicians, ex-astronauts, scientists, and schoolchildren talk about what seemed to have happened, what they all by now had been forced to accept as fact. No one knew what might have caused the explosion; some were reminded of the Apollo 1 fire nine years and one day before; many knew members of the crew and talked about their dedication to their jobs, their commit-

ment to space; and I was disturbed to hear some of the com-
mentators—the President among them—call the crew
members heroes. Was death heroism's sole prerequisite? Did
you have to do nothing more than die to gain a kind of glory?
To call them heroes seemed hollow somehow, perhaps because
two of the people who had died as *Challenger* disintegrated
were friends, and I knew three others as colleagues in the office, knew all of them well enough to know they were full of
pride and pleasure at being able to do the kind of work they
did, full of faith in their machine and the reasons for riding in
it, each one of whom possessed special talents, of course, each
one of whom was spirited and alive. But their achievements,
their glories, for God's sake, were in their lives, not their
deaths. Was it a kind of collective guilt, a need somehow to
apologize for their sacrifice, that caused so many of us to
quickly canonize them? Would I have been a hero if this mission had gone to me instead of to El Onizuka? I didn't think so.
My death, like Michael's, could not have had such sudden sig-
nificance. *Remember, old man, that dust thou art, and unto dust shalt
thou return.*

Before I went home that night to my silent house, I had gone
with seven other astronauts—those of us who had stood in an
empty corridor outside our offices contemplating what we
should do, wondering if we should try at least to offer a few
minutes of awkward words—to the homes of the four women
who lived nearby who were newly widowed, each of them
mothers of children whose fathers had said they would be
home soon. At Jane Smith's house, which was full of friends
and neighbors who had gathered because at least they could be
together, we spoke our inadequate statements, then hugged
Jane in turn, telling her to let us know what we could do,
telling the three kids who sat together on a sofa, seeming baf-
fled, perplexed amid their sorrow, that their father meant a lot
to us. Mike Smith and I had been regular handball partners and
partners in crime on occasion when NASA junkets took us out

212 BEAUTIFUL ISLANDS

of town together. He might have been the best pilot in an astronaut corps full of very good pilots indeed. Had he been orbiting the earth at that moment, it seemed certain that he would have commanded some spectacular missions in his time. While I embraced Jane, holding her tight, saying nothing, she told me she hadn't seen me yet to say how sorry she was to hear about my brother. I nodded, but didn't say anything, didn't tell her how sorry I was that, like her, I had been in Florida and had seen what happened to the Mike who belonged to her.

Our next three stops were similarly short, identically painful. June Scobee met us at the front door and although she didn't say so, something in her demeanor made me think she appreciated our short, ceremonial visit. Cheryl McNair, amid her quiet crying, said Ron had gone to heaven. We didn't see Lorna Onizuka; she was in her bedroom, alone and trying to sleep, said friends.

Back at the astronaut office, we placed calls to Judy Resnik's father and to Michael Oldak, her friend and former husband, to let them know we shared their loss. J.R., I had always known, would have been easy to fall in love with. On her thirtieth birthday, Michael Oldak mentioned, J.R. had announced she would never get old.

The phone rang often once I was home. Peggy called, crying, to ask how I was doing. She said that because of Christa McAuliffe, Matt and his classmates had been watching the launch and saw the explosion. "He knew you weren't on it, but I think that in the chaos and emotion at school he became a little confused about whether you might have been. Here. Let me get him. I want to put him on." Matt was quiet. I assured him I was all right, told him I was at home in the house in Clear Lake, and that I wished I could be with him and Sarah and their mom. He asked me why it had happened, and I told him I didn't know. Sometimes horrible things happened, things that you couldn't explain.

Jane called from Colorado, sounding surprisingly shaken. "I just feel so bad for you, for everyone," she said. "I didn't even know the names of any of those people, and I feel like I did when Bobby Kennedy got shot." She wanted to know what this would mean—for me, for my mission. I said I didn't know. What I presumed but didn't say was that not only lives and machines had been destroyed; programs, policies, thousands of careers had surely been shattered as well. I was too stunned, too much in shock to try to imagine the future—in part because, at the moment, the future seemed unimaginable, made meaningless by the sudden explosion. Jane asked me to promise I would stay in touch.

Steve Hawley called. Like me, Steve was a mission specialist, and like mine, his father was a minister, pastor of a Protestant congregation somewhere in Kansas. Steve said a memorial service had been scheduled at the space center for noon on Friday. President Reagan would attend, as would families of the crew. He said someone had suggested that perhaps our two fathers would be appropriate speakers; I asked him if he had talked to his dad. "Just a few minutes ago. He said that if people agreed they wanted him to, he would do it. I told him I'd check with you and get back to him." It was hard to guess what my father would say; perhaps he would want to come, to be a part of this collective expression of grief; perhaps he would feel like too much of a token cleric—the man of the cloth who's always called on such occasions, but whose words are as empty as everyone else's. I asked Steve how quickly he needed to know and said I would try to reach my father.

●

"Yes, they are here, Jack," Mary said a few minutes later. She answered the phone on the fourth ring. "Gosh, I feel so bad for you. You must have known those people. Are you okay?"

"It's been quite a day," I told her. "How are you all?"

"We've just been watching TV all evening, but I'm turning the damn thing off now. I don't want to hear about it anymore. They keep showing these pictures of the teacher's parents as they watch the explosion. I can't believe they're that insensitive. Those poor people have gone from joy to this impossible shock, that kind of tragedy, in about half a second, and some fool thinks he has a right to shove a camera in their faces."

"The whole thing was pretty public. Matt watched it happen at school in Austin. Catastrophes don't usually get covered live like that, do they? Jesus, Marie . . . I almost feel like I did when Peggy left—like I'll do anything to keep what's already happened from happening. Like if I only promise to try harder it can all be reversed."

"Except it can't."

"No. It can't. Marie, I need to talk to Dad. I need to ask him something."

"Sure. I'll get him. I hope you're okay," she said. "We've got room if you'd like to get away for a few days."

Dad asked me how I was, asked me where I was, asked me if I had any idea how in the hell it had happened. "I pray they didn't know it was coming," he said, "—the crew."

"That's probably the way it was. I suppose if you have to die, it's not a bad way to go. You might as well die supersonic."

"If they had to die . . . I'm not sure they did, Jack. Accidents, tragedies like that, I don't think there's anything preordained about them."

"I just meant that—"

"No, I know what you meant. You're right. People shouldn't have to see it coming at them like a locomotive. Except, that's the way it was for Hal. He said something once about being glad the cancer gave him time to think about what was happening. I don't know. Maybe that's the more fortunate situation."

He didn't answer for a moment after I asked about the memorial service, his silence giving the weight of deliberation to what he was about to say. I, in contrast, always started to chatter in immediate response, thinking about what I said only between the syllables. It seemed a strange time to note that distinction between us—those seconds in which I waited for his reply. "Well, it's really very gratifying that they thought of me, and I suppose this is what I do for a living. The morticians and I are the death brokers, aren't we? We're the transition team, sending bodies and spirits on their way." His voice seemed to grow weary, to lose its tone of certainty. "But maybe it is time I retired, Jack. I'm getting tired of it. Maybe I've prayed over too many graves lately . . . I guess it was just six months ago that we buried Hal, then Mike in October. Now . . . I don't know. The deaths you feel personally—a close friend, a son—they take something out of you. You lose the facility you had. The words aren't easy, they don't seem to comfort and they certainly don't explain. I don't know what I could say, Jack. I could say what a gift it seemed to be that I hadn't lost my second son in that explosion. I could say that we lose seven people, more, in accidents all the time, then admit I'm really not sure why these deaths seem so much more cruel. I told you that day we went up to Mike's miner's shack that you'd better have a damn good reason if you do something to snuff out life. I don't know. Is space worth it? Is it worth the risk?"

"It's a risk; it isn't suicide. I don't know, Dad. Dick Scobee, Mike—Mike Smith—J.R., everybody, I have this sense that they're okay. I'll miss them. It'll be awful for their families, but . . . What seems so shattering for the rest of us is that this whole collective deal can obviously fall totally to fucking pieces. It's like we've been kidding ourselves. I feel foolish, like a total fool. Everybody talked about how we'd have a failure sometime, something serious. But now it seems like it was just sort of macho posturing or something. I think it's so shocking now because we never really believed it could happen."

Dad was silent again, perhaps unsure whether there was more for me to say. "Jack, I guess I'm going to ask you to decline for me. I'd like you to tell whoever it was that I do appreciate being asked, but the occasion calls for someone who can remind people that these were not vain deaths. I know they weren't, I really do, but I don't think I could say so with much conviction right now. What would come from my heart would be that I've seen a disease eat up the dearest friend I had, seen my son choke off his own life, now seen these very fine, very brilliant young people go up in a ball of fire—and none of it makes a damn bit of sense to me. I guess you should just say that your old man is praying but that he hasn't heard any answers."

Before we hung up, I told my father that as I watched the explosion that morning I had had a clear image of Michael watching it as well, his face reflecting a kind of sorrow that was overwhelming.

"I'm sure it was," my father said.

•

I tried to sleep but couldn't. There was continuing coverage of the accident on the all-night news but, like Mary, I had seen enough. I drank a beer in the darkness, then dressed and went out in the car. The streets were empty, but from a distance the lights in the buildings at the space center made the place appear to be bustling—as if a mission were in progress and controllers were keeping their nightlong shifts. I remembered the clock at Canaveral, marking mission elapsed time as if nothing had happened. Perhaps a mission *was* under way, Houston strangely out of radio contact but still hopeful. After all, there was no evidence yet, was there, that *Challenger* had returned to the earth? But I knew better, of course, knew that the grim-faced people working this night were part of a gruesome sal-

vage operation, or were desperately studying the morning's telemetry for some sign of system failure.

I suppose I was heading for Building 4, for the astronaut
office, where I assumed there would be some activity, perhaps
some news, some explanation, someone to commiserate with,
someone with whom I could share the troubled night. But for
no reason, I turned into the tourist parking area a few hundred
yards beyond the guard station and walked in the darkness
across the grass to the horizontal Saturn V, separated at its
stages to show each massive cluster of motors, the vehicle
stretching nearly four hundred feet from the probe atop the
command module to the exhaust bells of the four first-stage
rockets.

The dozen machines like this one that years before had been
lit like Roman candles had never failed; none had ever exploded. Each exquisitely crafted rocket motor had screamed
skyward only once; each spewed fire only a single time before,
its fuel spent, it was destroyed in its tumble back to the atmosphere and to earth, or before it was abandoned in the blackness. But each one always worked, ultimately delivering
twenty-seven men to the neighborhood of the moon. A
hundred people by now had been launched in the shuttle, all of
them but seven sent into earth orbit, then returned—the orbiter falling like a bag of bricks—to safe and dramatic landings.
Seven people, however, had been launched on a far different
kind of journey.

There was enough light from the moon, full just a few days
before, to allow me to see to climb up and inside the exhaust
bell nearest the ground at the base of the Saturn—this moon-
ship that never sailed. Rust had begun to tarnish the gleaming
metal, I knew, but in the diffuse light, it seemed shiny and new,
its surface smooth and glassy. The cone-shaped bell enveloped
me; it seemed like a strange kind of cave, and I reclined against
its curving walls, looking out at the quiet night. I couldn't see

any of the space center's buildings in my small circle of vision, couldn't see anything but the shadowed tops of the trees near the spot where the car was parked and beyond, the dark silhouette of a water tower.

The late-night traffic out on the Gulf Freeway was a distant and subdued rumble; occasionally I could hear a car pass nearby, probably driven by a space center employee, unlikely someone I knew but certainly someone in the grip of the day's grief like I was, someone heading home to try to get some sleep. I don't know how long I stayed inside the bell; I might have dozed, but I didn't sleep. I remember wondering whether one day some tangible symbol of the shuttle era would be on display here, its history heroic, inspiring despite what had happened a few hours before—or whether the ungainly airplane that could fly home from space but that once blew up while it was outbound, would become symbolic of an era when we finally had failed, our applied technology imperfect, our best people the terrible price. I wondered if even I might lose my devotion to that machine that had once taken me safely to a high and spectacular orbit. Did it matter, I wondered, whether I went again?

I didn't make up my mind before I crawled out from inside that rocket we could be proud of and rode home.

●

By Thursday afternoon, flowers left by local people and sent from around the country, lined the curbs of the streets leading into the space center. Traffic on NASA Road 1 moved slowly, seemingly reverently past the perimeter fences, as if the space center itself were lying in state.

I had spent Wednesday in the office, doing nothing except helping to keep the watch, hearing the bits of news that seemed to implicate the solid rockets in beginning a chain reaction that resulted in the exploding tank, passing along my father's regrets that he would be unable to attend the service.

Thursday was much the same. There was no work to be done—our immediate tasks and perhaps our jobs themselves suddenly had been placed on hold—yet most of us wanted to be on hand, to ride out the shock and the uncertainty together, to memorialize the crew with some measure of solidarity and with the appearance, at least, that the program would continue.

On Wednesday evening, I had stopped by Jane Smith's again, finding her so composed, so seemingly resilient that I worried about what might befall her later, then had gone to a potluck dinner at Bill and Becky Grimes's, a group of us who often socialized holding a kind of wake, I suppose, getting together because solitude seemed inappropriate, forgoing much merriment that night, still talking about little else but the accident and the friends we had lost, finally beginning to talk about when—or if—our several subsequent missions might be flown.

I was getting ready to go out for a bite to eat with Steve and Caroline Ehrlich on Thursday evening when I heard the front door open and heard Peggy inquiringly call hello. Sarah ran round the corner into the hallway where I stood; I scooped her up and held her and we walked out to see Peggy and Matt, standing in the foyer like visitors, unsure whether they should come farther into the house.

"Austin seemed too far away," Peggy said, hugging me. Matt was a little reluctant to embrace me, but he acquiesced. "I hope you don't mind us coming without calling. We just decided after the kids got home from school. We wanted to be with you," she said.

"No. No, hi. I'm glad you're here. I thought I might head over your way on Saturday, if I—"

"How are you?" Peggy asked, holding my hand, her voice soft but insistent, demanding an answer other than "fine."

"I'm okay. Really," I said. I would have willingly told her more if I could have, but I didn't know how to describe the black sort of vacuum into which we all had been thrown, all of us untethered by the accident, all of us adrift and sorrowful not only for the seven who had perished but for the careers, the commitments that four days ago had seemed so secure. "Better now that you're here." Sarah had already abandoned us; I could hear the television in the other room. Matt wanted to know if he could go say hello to Jesse Carroll, a friend who lived down the street.

"Well, first let's talk to Dad about dinner," Peggy said to him, then turned to me. "You have plans, I can tell."

"Because you can't imagine me cooking a meal for myself." I grinned.

"No, because you absolutely never wear that particular pair of pants unless you're going out." She sounded as if she were married to me.

"I was just going to have something quick with Steve and Caroline. Ninfa's or something. I'll call and cancel. They won't mind a bit."

"No. The three of us can—"

"They'll understand. We can go get a hamburger or something."

Caroline said of course she understood when I called, and we took the kids to Fuddrucker's, focusing the conversation on them, forgetting for a while the events of my week, talking instead about Sarah's box turtle, recently adopted, about her tap lessons and her struggle with arithmetic, about possibilities for Matt's science project and the reasons why we probably wouldn't get to go skiing that winter. Before we left the restaurant, Matt mentioned watching the launch at school, seeing the explosion. "Some kids cried," he said. When I asked him if he had cried, he said no. "But I was scared. I thought maybe it would be a bomb and kill all those people watching where we watched you go up. I didn't want everybody to get killed."

I told him that by the time explosion occurred, the shuttle was already far away from the launch site, farther than it prob-

ably appeared to be on television. "Yeah," he said, "it was just
the astronauts."

When I went into her room to check on Sarah that night, her
bed was empty and I found her curled in a blanket inside her
closet, a place where she had often played and sometimes slept
before she moved to Austin. She called it her playhouse when
she spent afternoons inside it; at night it was a tent where she
would go camping. Matt had closed his door—Peggy said this
new need for privacy had begun only recently—and I didn't
look in on him.

Peggy and I had a drink in the living room, sitting opposite
each other, each of us slouched in one of the overstuffed chairs
she had declined to take to Austin, Peggy relaxed, almost at
home, but somehow still a guest. "It must seem so strange,"
she said. "Everyone here must just be in a daze."

"Yeah, that's exactly what it seems like. Everyone's at work,
but we're just going through the motions."

"You're not still training, are you?"

"No. That's on hold for a while, I'm sure. We're not going
to fly again for a year, at least. I won't for two years maybe.
Everything's entirely up for grabs. Nobody knows what we'll
do. Even the people who were planning to retire—there'll be
pressure on them not to leave now, not to look like they're
bailing out of a sinking ship."

"Is it going to sink? You keep hearing people on TV say how
it has to continue."

"And it will. Oh, I'm sure it will, but it may be very different. Once they figure out what happened, there's bound to be
some kind of redesign. If it's major, Jesus, it could be three or
four years before... And with just three orbiters now, the research is probably going to have to take a backseat to the military bullshit—we'll all be flying Star Wars missions. The
telescope'll get launched, someday, I'm not worried about that,
but... I don't know. They got any positions open for mediocre
astronomers at that university of yours?"

"You don't want to be a professor, do you?"

"Oh...no. But I wouldn't mind being a little closer to the kids, the three of you. I've thought about that a lot in the last three days. But you'll probably get married again one of these days, and then I'll really be the odd man out. Once there's a new dad on the scene, I'm not sure I—"

"I don't have any marriage plans, Jack. You don't have to worry about being replaced. Mark and I are...well, we're not seeing quite so much of each other."

"Why not?"

"Oh, partly because I've been pretty cautious, I suppose. Partly, I know, because he's beginning to realize that I'm an old lady with two children and that the situation imposes a few limitations. He thought that we simply had to make a trip to Cancún sometime this winter, and when I told him I just didn't see how I could leave the kids, he got rather bent out of shape."

"I thought this was the great intimate, understanding relationship," I said. I'm sure I said it sarcastically.

"Don't gloat or I'll just be quiet about it. It is a good relationship. And we do understand each other, I think, but it... well, relationships are not simple, are they?"

"You mean old Jack Healy isn't the only son of a bitch to live with in this world?"

"Jack," she said.

"I'm sorry. It was just...the hardest part for me has always been the presumption that this writer is everything that I wasn't."

"I never presumed that."

"I did."

"Well, you were wrong," she said, smiling as if to add that I had not been a total hardship.

"Listen," I said. "I'm not sleeping on that sofa, and I'm not very interested in finding blankets for you. There's plenty of room in the bed. Why don't you just swallow hard and join me. I promise to stay on my side."

RUSSELL   MARTIN   223

"It's strange enough just to come back to the house. I don't think I belong in that bed anymore."

"I didn't say you belonged. Just pretend it's a field trip."

"For your information," she said, "I do miss this place sometimes." I told her I didn't believe her for a minute.

Peggy was surely asleep; beside her, I read for a long time— Carl Sagan's novel about the first contact with intelligent life beyond the earth. For some reason, Sagan's fictional notion made me think that Dad's thesis was definitely the more astonishing. What if we really were *alone,* the only life, the only death, the only beings conscious of beginnings and ends? I turned off the light and soon slept, oblivious until I was aware, sometime in the empty hours of the night, that Peggy and I were entwined, pressing ourselves together, waking as we groped for each other, waking but not pulling away, Peggy saying nothing but my name as she pulled off her nightshirt.

I wanted to cry, to shout, to tell her how much I had missed her as I pressed inside her, her body so wonderfully familiar, her rhythms and responses still so attuned to mine, her body made so new and lovely and alluring by its absence. It wasn't a dream; we were awake and making love, talking now, whispering, telling each other what we wanted, yes, what we had to have, Peggy clutching me, holding me, shouting, crying, me telling her I loved her as she came, then coming too, telling her I didn't mean to say that as I shuddered and became still.

She lay with her head on my stomach, her hand between my thighs, neither of us sure what to say. I combed my fingers through her hair, knowing indisputably at that moment that although it often possesses such maddening, monotonous sameness, there is something in an enduring relationship, in a marriage, even in this failed marriage of mine, that is sublime because it has such history. Peggy and I had made love—how many times?—two thousand? ten thousand? We had always been good at saying the stupidest, cruelest things, at fighting in the evenings to the point of fatigue, then, despite the anger, responding to our separate passions as we went to bed, our bodies finishing the fight, turning it into something warm and intimate and forgiving, forgetting what had been at issue as we fucked.

I wanted to forget the year just past, to forgive the dashing English major and the move to Austin, to apologize for being obsessive about my job, for caring more about going to space than about giving myself to the people who probably loved me. I wanted to say out of the silence that I would give it up, that I could free myself from my obsession if she could take me back, but I said nothing, my hand still caressing her hair.

"Jack," she said, sounding sleepy, "why did we do that?"

"You forced yourself on me."

"Did I? I couldn't have. I'm not the sort who sleeps around."

"I believe this has happened here before. I was beginning to wonder if it ever would again."

"Oh, God," she said, "why do I always complicate things? You'd think I could figure out a way to keep something straightforward sometime. I came over . . . I just wanted to be with you. I didn't want you to have to wait this out by yourself. Making love with you wasn't part of the picture."

"I know. Nothing lately ever is. Maybe there's a lot of sunspot activity right now—ruining the weather and screwing up everyone's lives."

"You've had to deal with some difficult things. I still care about you enough that I feel guilty that I haven't been around. I guess I still feel sort of responsible for you."

"Peg, the hard stuff hasn't happened to me." I scratched her back. "El Onizuka got the Spartan Halley mission instead of me, did you know that? I might have been on the *Challenger* crew, except that George Abbey wondered if my marital problems might not get in my way. Jesus, I feel like I always stumble through, like I have this dumb luck that I don't really deserve."

"You'd be happier if something really horrible happened to you?"

"No, but I . . ."

"I'm not sure it's lucky to be an astronaut right now. I mean, not knowing what will . . ."

"Yeah, but I'm not the only person in the country who might be out of a job, am I? And, God, I've got a family. That's all—"

"Jack. I'm not sure this . . . tonight . . . changes anything."

"I know," I said, certain that it had. But I let it go at that. I didn't sleep again till the sun came up.

•

I don't remember much about what the President said on Friday, except that he talked about heroism again, and he assured us we once again would fly. I remember that I was impressed by Steve Hawley's father, who didn't talk about heroism, who spoke about how we struggle to understand events that seem so meaningless, losses that seem so cruel, who said that questions about whether things transpire with a purpose or only somehow happen are at once scientific and religious, and fundamentally deserve to be asked. What I remember most is simply that I stood with Peggy and the kids among all the other current astronauts and their families in a section reserved for us, all of us silent on the flat, grassy quadrangle at the space center, the winter day cool and blustery. I remember that I felt nothing more than numb, really, until the four T-38s screamed low overhead in the Lost Man formation, the fourth plane, piloted by Steve Ehrlich, pulling into a nearly vertical climb as it passed above us, the planes' engines showering us with an enormous emotional roar, my hard tears at that moment the first I had shed since the accident, since my brother Michael died.

•

The space center closed following the memorial service, its thousand or so employees sent home as a gesture of respect. We went home as well, staying after the service—exchanging somber greetings—for only a few minutes, traveling as a foursome for the first time in over a year, returning to the house together. While we were changing clothes, I suggested to Peggy that perhaps we should drive down to Galveston later, let the kids splash their feet in the Gulf for a while, then feed them shrimp at one of the little cafés on The Strand. "It's fine with me if we just stay here," I said, "but maybe it'd do us all good to stare at the waves for a while."

"I . . . should have mentioned last night that we have to leave this afternoon," she said, stopping in mid-turn toward the bathroom, realizing I had assumed they were there for the weekend. "I . . . gosh, Jack, I didn't think to tell you. Matt's got a soccer game in the morning, and I have plans for tomorrow night."

"Oh."

"We just, well, they wanted to see you and I did too, at least for a little bit. We wanted to make sure you were all right."

"He can miss one game, can't he?"

"He could but . . . I need to get back too."

"So stay till tomorrow morning. That'll give you plenty of time."

"We can stay till five or so," she said, hoping to mollify me. "It's a long drive."

"I know how long the drive is. Stay till tomorrow. It'll make it easier." I wasn't quickly seeing it Peggy's way, as she had hoped I would, and she didn't want to argue.

"Jack, I really am sorry I didn't say anything earlier. I should have. But this way Matt can go to his game and I can get a few odds and ends accomplished."

"And you and your man can have a great evening together."
There wasn't any energy in what I said; I was being spiteful,
but somehow I couldn't get angry. I desperately wanted them
to stay, to sustain this illusion of family, and now hearing that
they would not seemed only to deflate my latent meanness, my
ready sarcasm.

"It isn't... no, it's not just so I can go be with Mark, for
God's sake. Don't start in on me, Jack, please. We just should,
we really should."

"So you and I won't end up sleeping together again, is that
it?"

"That... no, that isn't it. You aren't so terrific that I couldn't
resist you if I wanted to." She tried to smile, to turn this into
something comic, but the comedy was awkward. "That wasn't
a mistake last night. I don't feel like it was. It was wonderful
for just what it was, for when it happened. But... I don't
know, you jerk. I care about you so much. You know I do. But
I can't just come marching back because we discovered that
something still connects us. We didn't have to make love again
to know that. We've—I've known it all along, but that alone
isn't enough to make it all perfect again, to change everything.
Jack, I've got a life in Austin now. The kids and I aren't just
over there till the dust settles."

I stood there in my stocking feet, looking shattered, I suppose. I thought I knew her so well, that I was so sensitive to
her moods and emotions—certain that we each felt more than
simply some kind of connection. I had assumed, stupidly, that
each of us had salvaged something during that timorous night,
that unlike everything else that was ending, we might have
scratched out a means for the two of us to survive. I wanted to
go to Peggy, to hold her so tightly she'd change her mind, to
cry and to tell her there was just too much hollowness without
her and Matt and Sarah, to say, no, nothing had been too difficult to bear except losing the three of them to Austin. But I
didn't say anything. I couldn't—couldn't draw the breath to

speak the words I wanted to. Peggy went into the bathroom, but didn't close the door. She disappeared from the mirror's reflection when she sat on the toilet, then standing again, I watched her change into jeans and a T-shirt and I watched absently as she combed her hair.

"So," she said when she came back into the room, "when are we going to see you again?"

"You're breaking my heart," I said. She turned to look at me, her face at that moment reflecting the rueful years that had brought us both to this, exhibiting the same kind of sadness I had seen in her eyes when she came to Durango to say goodbye to Michael.

"Didn't that happen a long time ago?" she asked.

"I didn't need this today," I told her, my self-pity casting my voice in a kind of whine. "God, I didn't need this."

"Can you come over next weekend? Matt would love for you to see one of his games."

"I don't know. Who knows what's going to happen around here. A week's way too much future to think about."

"Okay."

"I'll call."

"Can I have a hug before I go?"

"You're determined to tear me apart, aren't you?" I hugged her and held her a long time, smelling her, my lips pressed against the warm skin where her neck curved into her shoulder. I had never loved her so much, yet she was going away again.

I offered to go fill her car with gas while she helped the kids get their things together; I was strangely willing to assist them in getting under way, feeling defeated, too tired somehow to protest. The three of them were standing in front of the house when I returned, their bags beside them. I pulled into the driveway, loaded the bags in the back of the car, got Sarah seated and buckled up, telling her I wanted to meet this turtle, then gave Matt a quick hug. "I hope everything gets better," he said, seeming somehow grown up. I told him I hoped so too.

Peggy was already in the driver's seat, her door closed. I leaned into her open window and pulled her head toward me, still desperate not to let go. "Will you call us as soon as you know something?" she asked. I told her I was beginning to doubt that I would ever know anything, then stood like some kind of fool, some sort of satellite father, on the cracked concrete driveway. They drove down the street and the car disappeared as *Challenger* had, safely turning the corner but nonetheless shattering it all forever.

•

The one thing that was absolutely certain was that I wasn't going to stay alone in that awful house, haunted by memories of much happiness, haunted by constant reminders of how I had failed. I went into the house, got a sweater, my wallet, three beers from the refrigerator, then drove away with a melodramatic squeal of the tires, the moment demanding some sort of theater. I got on the Gulf Freeway, which was curiously quiet for a Friday afternoon, and headed for Galveston, driving in the thin traffic through the flat and swampy coastal plains, through the humid haze punctuated by billboards and service station signs mounted on swaying steel towers. So I would go to Galveston alone, stare at the gray, listless little waves by myself, watch them roll in from the open water as reminders that it is all so goddamned relentless.

The beers were gone by the time I crossed the causeway that connected Galveston Island to the state of Texas, the fifty feet or so of altitude on top of the arching ship bridge enough to lift me briefly out of the haze. I bought more beer at a U-Totem on Broadway, then followed it all the way through town, past abandoned warehouses and small, derelict, windowless groceries and fish markets, past the shingled, salt- and hurricane-battered houses with screened second-story porches, past the old cemetery whose high, narrow headstones and mausoleums

seemed to tilt in the island sand. At the seawall, I turned left
and drove out to East Beach, empty at the end of January except for a few crazy old farts combing the sand with metal
detectors, looking for pirates' booty, I suppose, praying for
buried treasure. I drove along the wet, packed sand between
the dry dunes and the water, past a treasure hunter who waved,
then turned the car toward the surf and stopped at a place
where no one was searching. I got out of the car, peed beside
its open door, then sat on the warm hood, quart of beer in
hand, my back angled against the windshield, a cold and ma-
rauding wind blowing in off the Gulf of Mexico. The kids
couldn't have waded into the water, I told myself, not as cold
as it was; they wouldn't have been happy here more than a few
minutes, and Peggy would have sat in the car.

It was hard to believe that only a week before I had spent the
day lifting the dummy telescope out of the mock-up of the
cargo bay, practicing my role as Gina's backup, blithely convinced that things went well in the space business, before I
went off to Canaveral to watch the launch. The world had been
utterly transformed in that week, hadn't it? It still spun on an
inclined axis, still orbited the sun; its moon still moved around
it, the seas still rose and ebbed with the pallid moon's pull. Yet
everything was somehow different. *Challenger*'s crew wasn't
composed of seven heroes so much as seven harbingers of
change, seven men and women whose deaths now meant that
if we went to space again, when we went to space again, we
would not assume success but would hold our breath against
the frightening chance for failure. The lesson had been a cataclysmic one—everyone within range of a television set had
seen it, the lesson burned into a billion retinas by the ball of
fire—the grim lesson that nothing is guaranteed.

I didn't know. Perhaps it would be better now for people to
understand the risks viscerally, to know in their guts that this
was more than just some patriotic extravaganza staged by Hol-
lywood producers. It was technological wizardry, true, but

until four days ago, it was wizardry that always worked. If we would now better understand how risk gave achievement its meaning, how it was death that made life matter, then Christa McAuliffe was an extraordinary teacher indeed, and her six fellow spacefarers just might have been heroes.

Yet I was afraid—really frightened for once in my life that *Challenger*'s legacy would only be cynicism, proof that these space nerds had spent all our money only to fuck up royally, that the orbiter's loss, the loss of its crew, would simply mean the end of something, the aching and vacant end, no more meaningful than my dissolving marriage, something that once worked, then burst irreparably into pieces.

My God, how dumb it was of me to think that Peggy and I could share a bed a single time after a year of separation and that our sex could bridge the space between us. How could going to a hamburger joint, then standing together in our best clothes, listening to eulogies and the crushing noise of jet engines, somehow make us a family again? Peggy and the kids had lives in Austin, she had finally said, lives that included me only as some sort of cousin who came on occasional weekends. *That* was the reality now, and no amount of whining or posturing or romanticizing the past could change it.

I wouldn't see Michael again, wouldn't be able to tell him I now had a small notion of what it meant to be a brother. I wouldn't see Mike Smith, J.R., El, and the others again, wouldn't be able to go on with them in boozy conversations about what it meant—how it was so exquisitely stunning—to encircle the watery earth. I wouldn't get the kids up each morning again, watching them stir out of sleep and wake into adolescence; I wouldn't fall asleep each night with Peggy, the two of us troubled and tired yet somehow content. All of that had ended now. There had been a time when I didn't have any of those people, those pleasures, and, well, now I'd have them no more.

Remember, old man . . .

I sat on the hood of the car till the beer was gone, till my face was frozen from facing the weather. The sweater had given me a bit of protection and I had curled my hands inside it. The waves had swelled a little in the wind, but they were still unimpressive, still just the steady slap of the gulf onto the grieving continent. I drove downtown in the twilight, bought a paper and ate alone in a diner on The Strand where the four of us might have eaten. The city was quiet after dinner; I walked Mechanic and Market streets, peering into the dim little bars and tobacco shops where black men with gray hair sat at tables playing dominoes. I thought I might go in and get drunk in one of the places; their slow demeanor—the world inside them unchanged in twenty years—seemed inviting. But I decided that some white asshole from Houston, ready for a bit of blackout drinking, would rather unfairly bring them up to date. So I drove out to the seawall again and stopped at the Galvez Hotel, beneficiary of a recent facelift, a sprawling plantation of a place, a refurbished reminder of Galveston's salad days.

Fat men who looked as if they remembered the antebellum South sat in large chairs in the lobby, children in swimming suits ran through it toward the pool. The bar in the seaward wing was quiet; the bandstand was crowded with supine instruments and silent sound equipment. I switched from beer to scotch—it seemed time to take this mission seriously—sitting one stool away from a woman who looked as if she might have undergone a facelift herself, her skin smooth and tanned, sweeping back from below her jaw as tightly as a teenager's. She wore a pleated skirt and a Navajo silver squash-blossom necklace that had come from my part of the planet, and she raised her glass in a kind of greeting as she caught my eye.

"I was out on the beach for a while," I told her, amazed that I felt like talking. "I trust this will warm me up."

"What in the world were you doing out there? Waiting for your ship to come in?"

I smiled a thin and rueful sort of smile. "No, just watching the water, I guess. Seemed like a good idea at the time."

"This is a funny town to come to by yourself," she said. "I haven't been down here in I don't know how long. Except for this place, it all looks like it's been beaten down pretty hard, doesn't it?"

"You from Houston?"

"River Oaks, yes. West Texas before that. Alamogordo, New Mexico, before that. Nowhere at all before that." This woman had a head start on me. She was drinking a martini and it certainly wasn't her first; we were already discussing her childhood. "You?"

"Houston. Clear Lake. Near NASA."

"Oh, Lord," she said, "I just feel so bad about that. I could have cried driving by that exit on the way down. I don't know. It's like Kennedy, isn't it? The best and the brightest, as they say. Whole town of Houston feels like it's lost its own, I guess. I'm trying not to think about it. I just came down here to get the hell away and kiss my cares good-bye. You too?"

"Oh...I suppose. Didn't feel like staying at home anyway. Do you need a drink?"

"That would be very kind of you," she said, moving her glass toward me, sliding onto the stool that separated us. I motioned to the bartender—the universal sign language that orders another round. "Home. Now that's an interesting word, isn't it? I've got a house big as a church up there; I've got European paintings and fancy Italian tile and big old Persian rugs you could set a trailer house on, but I don't have a home. That's something entirely different. A home is where two people make their lives together, and that I don't have."

"I'm sorry. Did you lose your husband?"

"Did I lose him? You mean as in did he die? No, I didn't lose him, but he's lost. He's long gone. Out in Odessa, I guess, there or Midland, it's all the same. He's in drilling mud. Sold drilling mud to damn near every outfit in the Southwest before the bust. Has his main deal there in Odessa, used to fly out there once a week or so. Shoot, I knew he had a sexy 'executive assistant' out there that he couldn't resist, but I never troubled him about it. That was just his little peccadillo and neither of us ever mentioned it. I figured, well, at least he's home five days a week and doesn't bring home diseases, you know. But it turns out that he thinks he has to marry her. Says it's true love and that's all there is to it. He came home on Wednesday with his big announcement, sat me down at the breakfast nook just like it was nothing more serious than having to sell a piece of jewelry to pay back taxes or something."

"Son of a gun," I said, imagining in the emotion of the alcohol what a tactless bastard he must have been.

"You just don't even know what to say," she continued, sipping her martini between the long sentences. "You try to provide a good home; you keep yourself up and always play the happy hostess for his oil cronies. I'm an attractive woman; I have had my own temptations in my time, and, my Lord, I'm only forty-goddamned-four years old. I'm not some kind of artifact. And she's not so much, either—kind of trashy, to tell you the truth. She may be something special in bed, but frankly, that was never something Cal and I had trouble with. I feel like I've been traded in because my tread's worn out, for crying out loud." She was silent for a moment or two, letting the whole sad story wash over both of us. My God, I thought, liking this woman in part because she wasn't some professor's wife, wasn't an electrical engineer or a physicist, the sort of woman who wouldn't have considered spilling her heart to a stranger in a bar, liking her because we had so much boozy heartache in common.

"Well, that's it in a nice little package," she said. "I got the 'Dear Liz' letter, he headed back for Odessa, then I came down here yesterday because I'd be damned if I'd stare at all his crap cluttering up the house."

"Your name is Liz?"

"Yes. Elizabeth, really, but it's always been Liz to every-body."

"I'm Jack," I said, extending my hand.

"Jack. John? Would you mind if I call you John? Seems like everybody in the world has a nickname, me included, and I get so tired of it. Most people have such pretty names really, then they get called Liz all their lives."

"I'll call you Elizabeth, if you'd like."

"Would you? You're a dear man. What do you do, John?"

I told her I worked for NASA, told her I was an astronaut for reasons that must have been strictly confessional; I wasn't trying to impress her, although she was right—she was an attractive woman. Yes, I said, I knew the people who had died in the explosion, some better than others, and no, I wouldn't be afraid to fly again. But I wasn't sure I would. I had been scheduled for a flight that year, but now I didn't know. Maybe I'd get out, find some sort of job, something intriguing to do. "What kind of work do you suppose I could do?" I asked.

"Could you be an airline pilot?" Elizabeth suggested. "I don't think they have to work very hard, and they get to go to some fun places."

"I'm not a pilot. Only about half the astronauts are pilots anymore. Maybe I could be a flight attendant, serve cocktails and yell at people when they pushed their call buttons too often."

"No. I don't want you doing that. That's just waitressing in the sky. You want to go into business? A man like you could get his own 'executive assistant' pretty easy. I assume you've already got a wife."

"Why do you assume?"

"Oh, the nice ones always have. If you were single you'd already be telling me how well equipped you were. Really. You wouldn't believe how forward those characters are. A friend and I occasionally go out to a club on Westheimer. The lines we hear, I tell you. And kids?"

"Two kids."

"Are you separated yet?"

"What makes you think we aren't together?"

"Well, with the shuttle... I don't know. I'd just guess you'd be at home if..."

"You ought to go to work for the *Enquirer*. You've got a talent for it."

"Marriage is something else, isn't it?" Elizabeth said. "Two people tie the knot, thinking the moon sets in the other's eyes, then they end up fighting in court over who gets the big color set in the living room. I thought Cal was the finest man in all the world at one time, thought lucky was my middle name."

When the bar began to get busy and the band members climbed onto the platform with club sodas in their hands, we ordered fresh drinks and adjourned to a table on the enclosed veranda, close enough that we could still get service, far enough away that the band's amplifiers wouldn't make us shout. I followed behind Elizabeth, deciding as I watched her walk that Cal was a foolish man.

Elizabeth had no children, she told me—trouble with her plumbing, as she put it. She wasn't sure which one of the two of them had regretted that circumstance more. And when we talked about what would happen to her now, she began to get tearful, not out of fear so much, I don't suppose, as sad acknowledgment of the lives of the divorcees she knew—too many cocktail lunches alone with the girls, too many nights at home alone watching "Dynasty."

"My trouble is that I fell for that homemaker crap years ago," she said, her words a little slurred now. "There isn't a job I could do that I could get paid for. Well, there's one, isn't there? but I don't think that's my cup of tea. About all I can do now is hope some lonely man comes along who's decided he still needs a wife. He'll be in oil—seems like everybody I've ever met except you is in oil—and he'll probably smoke stinky old cigars and have the fattest stomach you ever saw. And all the gals in my shoes always accept that circumstance because, like I say, they don't have any alternative, and they act like they just love him to pieces."

"I won't become a flight attendant if you won't do that," I said, making a drunken deal. "Don't hook up with anyone you're not in love with. Really."

"If everyone waited till they fell in love, good gracious, there'd be even more lonely, sad-sack people in this world. I don't put love at the top of the list."

"What about what you said about people sharing their lives together?"

"Well, yes, I do think that's worth working for—something Cal just shoved down my face—but don't confuse that with love. Sticking together is just deciding that this old world isn't too pretty on your own. That, all things considered, it's worth it to have somebody who'll sit across the table from you night after damn night. Love... I'm not sure what love is. I think it's a little bit like a mental illness. You feel like it's just going to eat you up; it's all you think about. You think it's the only thing in the world, really, but it's only you—the two of you, if you're lucky—who knows it's there. Nobody else has any idea what you're talking about. Sometimes you get over it, kind of like a cure, and sometimes... I don't know."

I wasn't so drunk yet that I didn't think of Michael when she mentioned mental illness. But Michael's disease wasn't akin to love. Surely not. No, at last I had an inkling of what Michael felt, what he thought in the midst of his malady. The tears I had imagined Michael crying as *Challenger* exploded were a kind of final confirmation of what he had always known, weren't they? Everything he was devoted to—friends, family, the traditions of the church, the snow-battered miner's shack— was somehow less than he had hoped it would be. Michael's dreams demanded absolutes, but what he encountered in his life were fragile commitments, tenuous faiths, destinations that never got him home.

"I suppose Mike understood a lot more than I thought he did," I told Elizabeth in a vacant kind of voice. She didn't seem to notice that what I said made no sense; she was still considering love.

"Who's Mike?" she asked, now assuming she had missed something I'd said.

"My brother. He died a few months ago."

"John," she said, taking hold of my arm, "I'm so sorry. I sure am."

"When he died, one of the saddest things was that I didn't think he'd ever had a chance to sort things out, to make sense of things. I thought everything must have been total confusion for him. Now... well... Maybe the confusion, the mess wasn't inside him so much as in everything he encountered. Hell, he probably always knew exactly how it all comes out."

"John," Elizabeth said. She was sorry that my brother had died, I could tell that she really was, but she wasn't interested in what he did or didn't understand. "John, you're a gentleman. You are not in the oil business and you are the first gentleman who I've ever been tempted to invite to my room for a nightcap. I have a bottle of wine open. Nothing fancy. But after Cal a couple of days ago, I don't believe I could stand to invite you if you were to decline. If I were to invite you and you were to say no, well, this would be quite a week, wouldn't it?"

"I'm sure I'd accept such an invitation," I said in a slur of words, feeling a rush of anticipation as Elizabeth stood and held out her hand, inviting me with the gesture.

She kissed me as she closed the door to her room—the passion of our separate loneliness as determined as the passion of the alcohol. While I poured two glasses of wine from the bottle that sat on the bureau, Elizabeth went into the bathroom. When she returned, her skirt was gone, her heavy necklace was off, and her blouse was open. She looked at me as if to say, "You get by however you can," as she stepped out of her slip and dropped her bra straps over her shoulders. "The weather is cold, dear John," she said, standing in only small lace panties, her childless belly smooth and flat and unmarked. "It is cold and we might as well try to stay warm. I don't think I'm interested in going out to look at the waves."

I'm not sure I will ever understand what I saw as I looked at Elizabeth, Liz to everyone else, standing supplicantly in front of me like that, looking fragile and somehow frightened, beautiful but afraid of being abandoned. For some reason, I couldn't focus on how handsome she was, how she was offering me something exquisite that surely I wouldn't refuse. All I could think of was how I couldn't do what Cal had done, couldn't make love with her now, then leave while she slept, or tell her I'd call her sometime as I buttoned my shirt in the morning, couldn't fall in love for an hour or two, then endure another ending. "I . . . I think you're lovely," I said. "And I think you're terrific and I think Cal is a son of a bitch. I want to make love with you, God, I really do, but we shouldn't. We shouldn't for me and we shouldn't for you."

She reached for the bedspread and pulled it toward her to cover herself. "I . . . I'm sorry," she said, her sad eyes looking at me unbelievingly. "I thought that . . . I'm sorry, I . . ."

"God, I don't know. Maybe we should. God, I'd love to lie on that bed with you, but, Jesus, then I'll never see you again and you'll just think of me as some creep that you encountered on a vulnerable night."

"I feel like a stupid teenage slut," she said, now looking blankly away from me. "God, I am no good at this, am I?"

"No, you're terrific. You really are. You've been wonderful to me tonight, but . . . but that's all the more reason for me not to . . . I like you too much."

"I'm the one with my clothes off, asking for it like some kind of tramp."

"No, you . . . don't you see what I'm . . ."

"Go," she said in the saddest voice I have ever heard. "I'm sorry, John. I apologize and I wish you'd leave me alone now."

"I've just. . . I've just had to say good-bye to too many people lately. I don't want to . . ."

Elizabeth sat on the edge of the bed, the spread under her arms. "I wish you happiness, John. If you'll wish that for me, we'll call it even."

I went to the bed and sat beside her. "I feel like this is the stupidest thing I've ever done. God, you're so . . . and the last thing I mean to do is hurt you or to . . ."

She didn't want to look at me. "What you mean is to be decent, and that's fine. I guess I was just going to forget decent for a while. Trade it for something with a little more life to it."

"Please. Let me stay. I want to; I'm crazy, I don't know." My refusal seemed so mean in that instant, so wrong. For heaven's sake, all that mattered was a little life, wasn't it?

"No. Really. You should go. I like you too, but I wish you would." I tried to kiss her, but she turned her head away. "Okay? Please. You've been very kind to me, but you're right. It would just be something that neither of us would be very damn proud of. Good-bye, my friend. Good luck." There was a remorseful kind of smile on her face when she looked at me, but there was also a look of painful certainty, something that convinced me I had to go.

"I'm going to hate myself for about five years," I said as I stood.

"No, just maybe till tomorrow afternoon," she said. "It's funny, isn't it?"

I called Elizabeth's room from a phone in the lobby, letting it ring, aching for her to answer, imagining that if I could only make it up to her, if only she would let me come sleep in her bed, I might survive the night. Finally she answered, saying "John" as she picked up the receiver. "John, go have a good life. Do. I'll meet you back here in ten years and then maybe, if it seems like a good idea, we'll make love like nobody's business."

She hung up and I walked outside. I followed the seawall down to the Seventh Street fishing pier, and at its point, lit by the garish street lights behind me, I stood looking into the dark water and the steady wind until I vomited, the wind blowing some of the thin gruel onto my shirt. I found the car when I got back to the hotel and got into it, determined to drive off of that sorrowful island, but somehow I couldn't start the engine, not because I knew I shouldn't drive, but because—suddenly, brilliantly, out of a kind of desperation—I realized that in the morning I would wait in the dining room for Elizabeth until she came down for breakfast. She would forgive me in the warm sunlight and we would spend the day together and make love through the long next night. We would share our lives together and fall in love in a way that would never end.

eight

I never saw Halley's Comet. I didn't even try to get a glimpse of that celestial traveler whose visit should have seemed like such glorious good fortune. *Voyager 2,* the small but intrepid spacecraft whose own journey had been under way for nine years, had passed within spitting distance of the planet Uranus three days before *Challenger* exploded, yet I never saw the photographs it sent home, never saw the images of that island, so distant that the sun must appear there as only a bright dot in the blackness. Somehow, I wasn't interested. I guess I didn't care to know.

I never saw Elizabeth again, didn't meet her at breakfast, didn't fall in love. I thought I loved Jane—or that I could quickly love her if she would let me—and I knew I loved

Peggy, but it was love that seemed static now, settled, something that at last would no longer trouble me. By the end of
March, I knew it was time to see the lawyer.

The Air Force lost a Titan 34D in April, the workhorse
rocket exploding after takeoff, its white-hot debris showering
coastal California. Two weeks later, NASA lost an unmanned
Delta above Canaveral, its flight controllers destroying it when
its main engine failed and it began to skitter out of control. We
had utterly lost our skill with rocketry, for God's sake. We
could no longer escape to space.

Throughout the spring, the information that reached us at
the space center grew grimmer. It was indeed a seal in a joint
on *Challenger*'s right solid rocket that had precipitated the accident, a seal too cold to seat—solid fuel gruesomely burning
through it—a seal that had been suspect for *five goddamn years,*
we discovered. In its headlong efforts to send shuttles into
space like buses bound for the county seat, NASA had somehow ignored this fatal flaw. The agency's far-flung bureaucracy
had somehow shrouded the knowledge of the suspect rocket
joints from the astronaut office. Although we hadn't known it,
twenty-four times we had gotten to space only by the skin of
our teeth. Yet we were as much a part of NASA as the fuel-
systems engineers and the starched-shirted bureaucrats. Was it
our hubris as well as theirs that had led to that high image of
hell?

We went to work, but there was little work to do for a long
time. Most of us were eventually assigned to studies of dozens
of shuttle safety issues; we sat at tables for months of meetings;
memoranda were dutifully written. In May there was a rumor
that we would begin to train again before long. Mission assignments, for the most part, would remain the same; the telescope would be launched on one of the first three or four
flights—a year hence perhaps, maybe two—and I would be
welcome, or so I was told, to fly with it, to ride retooled solid
rockets up and out of the atmosphere.

In the meantime, I decided to take some accrued vacation time. I had a divorce to take care of; I owned a house I was anxious to sell. I wanted to lose a little weight and to temper the drinking that had become my avocation. I wanted to smell the summer cottonwoods at the edge of Jane's little creek; I wanted to taste her again on the broad plain of her bed. I thought I might consider a move to Colorado.

•

Peggy and I had lunch in Austin on the day we signed the papers. We met downtown with a certain solemnity, making it official in a glass-walled office with a view of the capitol dome; then we escaped the lawyers, eating by ourselves in the dining room at the Driscoll. We drank gin-and-tonics to toast this occasion we long ago had never imagined, and we assured ourselves that Matt and Sarah would somehow always connect us, keep us abreast of each other's lives, keep each of us from forgetting that the other once had mattered so much.

"I suppose we should go Dutch," Peggy said, smiling, "but why don't you let me get this today? I'd like to."

"Sure. Thank you. As long as it doesn't represent making anything up to me. Let's be finished with that crap."

"No. Maybe I'm just feeling flush. I mean, you have just legally committed yourself to sending us a lot of money every month—that or having your legs broken. I feel like I can afford it."

"If I end up finding anything else, surely it'll pay a little more. God, it'd better."

"What are you looking at?"

"Nothing really. Nothing right now. I'll probably go see some people at Martin Marietta when I'm in Denver this summer. If I'm feeling particularly adventurous, I might even go to Boulder and stick my head into the astronomy department."

"What about the college in Durango?"

"Oh, I don't think any of those guys ever leave. Besides, other than the odd bonehead stargazing course, I'd have to try to teach physics, and that would be some kind of spectacle. Maybe I'll go to seminary—take my dad's place at St. Mark's."

"Sure you will," she said, rolling her eyes toward the heaven neither of us was sure was there. "If that happens, I promise I will personally make the pilgrimage and confess all my darkest sins to you."

"I'm sure I'll be shocked."

"One of them will be recurrent sexual fantasies about my ex-husband."

"Please," I said, feigning surprise.

"You don't ever have fantasies about me?"

"I don't admit to them," I said, smiling ruefully. "I'm a little gun-shy." She looked into her empty plate. "Peg...I know I've always been a jerk about him, but I hope you and Mark pull it off. I mean, I hope that it works for a long time."

"Mark is dating a woman who works for the legislature, the daughter of some heavy hitter from South Texas—very chic, no stretch marks." She looked at me as if to confirm that I could say "I told you so."

"I'm sorry. I really am sorry. It's all a big goddamn mess, isn't it?"

"I'm all right. I still see him occasionally, but there's no more pretending about it being the big one."

"Yeah."

"As if there is such a thing. I don't know."

"Don't stay alone too long," I said. "I'm pretty sure that's not the answer. I mean, you may not find the one in all the universe, but, damn it, you just might. If you do, tell the son of a bitch he sure got lucky."

She reached for my hand and took hold of it. "If I do," she said, "I'll tell him I got lucky twice."

"We've had our luck, haven't we?" I agreed.

I drove home from Austin feeling sad and somehow euphoric at the same time, as if, like Elizabeth, luck once had been my middle name.

●

Three days later, I drove back, this time all the way across the curve of Texas, stopping in Dalhart to call for an appointment on the following day with the head of the division at Martin Marietta that had developed the manned maneuvering unit. I spent a short night in Colorado Springs, then drove to the Martin Marietta plant in the redrock foothills southwest of Denver. I was early, and I pulled the car onto the shoulder of the road a few hundred yards in front of the security station. The morning was clear and still cool; I rolled the windows down and thought about what I would say, how I would tell Fred Glickman that I needed to get back to Colorado. No, I'd tell him, I wasn't abandoning the astronaut office. I'd explain that Owen Garriott had already resigned and that several others of us were considering following suit. We all wanted very much to be part of a resuscitated space program, but we weren't sure we could wait for years like worried relatives for the program to begin to breathe on its own again. Even going to space, I would say, wasn't worth such an anguished wait.

But I couldn't convince myself. The words I spoke into the dashboard of the car didn't sound believable to me and I didn't think they would satisfy Fred Glickman. He would tell me, I suddenly realized, that he could not comfortably hire me away from the agency that had been his best—his only—customer in recent years, especially in the wake of the accident. He would tell me to shake off my indecision, to quit whining and get back to work. "Accidents happen, for cripe's sake," I could hear him say. "It's time for us all to quit this breast-beating and to get on with it."

"No, it's not breast-beating," I knew I would try to say, but then I also knew I didn't even want to begin the conversation. I turned the car around and called his office from a pay phone in Littleton, apologizing to his secretary, saying something had come up.

I didn't drive to Boulder, didn't look up the astronomers I last had seen in Cocoa Beach to ask them casually whether they could put me to work. But I did drive to St. Andrew's.

John Long was in New York, a young man in a denim cassock told me, but I found Lucy in the kitchen when I walked down the stairs to the basement. She turned off a large mixer when she saw me, remembering who I was, smiling as though she welcomed the visit, shaking my hand with both of hers. "What a surprise," she said. "I did not expect to see you come down those stairs. How are you?" I told Lucy I was fine, and told her I had often thought of her and Father Long during the months since I had seen them. "Oh, gosh, I've been thinking of you," she replied. "That accident like to broke my heart. All those precious people, may they rest in peace."

"It's . . . it's been an interesting time. Seems like ages since I saw you last. You look good."

"Oh, I'm fine. My little boy's going to be a grown-up here one of these days and that scares me a little, but we're doing fine. I do miss Michael." Her voice trailed away, as if she wasn't certain she should have mentioned him.

"Me too. Me too," I said, trying somehow to say more. "How's Father Long?"

"He's out trying to scrounge up some money for us. The diocese says it can't spare any more, but people have to eat, don't they? He had a couple of appointments back East with some foundations started up by old-line, old-money Episcopalians, you know what I mean. He said he'll try to make it sound as best he can like we try to convert people after supper. If they thought we were just feeding folks, shoot, they wouldn't want any part of it."

We moved to one of the long folding tables in the dining room, the tables already covered with fresh butcher paper in preparation for the evening meal, painted benches pushed beneath them. "You're still serving quite a few meals then?" I asked as I pulled out a bench and sat down across from her.

"Summer's are light, really. The weather's not too hard on people. There are more options of one kind or another for them. But we stay busy down here. I think we average about forty or fifty dinners. Maybe fifteen or twenty stay to spend the night. Sometimes in the cold weather though, this place is just jam-packed."

"How much help do you have?"

"I've got a man who comes in at noon, and he stays till everything's cleaned up, seven-thirty or so. We get whoever's handy here at the church to help serve the meal, so it's not too bad. Sometimes when there is plenty of help, I can get out of here as early as five o'clock."

I watched Lucy as she spoke; she looked older since the last time I had seen her, but she was prettier somehow, and her face reflected a kind of self-contentment that made me envious. "Doesn't sound like an easy schedule."

"Oh, it's okay," she said. "I don't go out and party much, it's true, but I don't think I'd do that if I had scads of time. No, you can't ask for much more than doing a job that maybe helps somebody. That's the best kind of work a person can have. And guess what?" She grinned impishly at me, then took me into her confidence like a schoolgirl with a secret to tell. "I am seeing a man. No kidding. He's a teacher at East High. He's divorced but doesn't have any kids, and he's as good to Simon as you can imagine. He also is very pretty to look at." She pretended to swoon, touching her hand to her throat.

"Congratulations." I returned a smile.

"Oh, it's not to the congratulations stage yet, but it sure is fun. I can't tell you how long it's been since a man set me to stir like that. I feel kind of silly, but, oh, my, it sure makes you see why people do the things they do, doesn't it?"

I told her it certainly did. And when I left a few minutes

later, I stepped briefly inside the church and put some money into the collection stand, a slim and apologetic offering for the misfortunate people who ate at St. Andrew's and the people like Lucy who were lucky enough to feed them. Then I tried to imagine my future as I drove across the rugged hump of the Rocky Mountains.

●

I phoned Jane from Pagosa Springs to see if she was at home, to see if she would welcome a wayfarer on a moonless summer night. "You're not supposed to be here for two more days," she said, half shouting into the telephone. I told her my contacts in the Denver area had been quick to make. "Well, you happen to be in luck," she said. "For the first time in a long time, there isn't a handsome man here telling me he can't resist me. So you might as well come along."

Jane was wearing cotton pajamas when she met me at her kitchen door. She told me I was forgiven for arriving at such a late hour as she hugged me, and she said that I didn't look much different now that I was divorced.

"I feel different," I said, sitting down at the kitchen table, taking the beer she offered me. "I really do. Always before, I could pretend to anyone, and to myself for that matter, that I was a family man. We were just 'giving each other some space' or whatever. Now I guess I'll have to admit that I'm *divorced,* and I definitely do not feel comfortable saying it. The word sort of sounds like leprosy or something."

"No it doesn't. It just sounds like you've switched halves. You've left the half of the population who have pulled it off and joined the half who are miserable failed slime-balls."

"Well, when you look at it that way . . ."

"I like you better this way," she said, looking wide awake and somehow seductive in the oversized pajamas that must have belonged to Kenny. "I don't have to feel like a jerk for maybe stealing you away from someone who I think I would have liked."

"You would like her. Peggy's . . . I think she's going to be great. I'm sure she'll shine now that I'm out of the way. But her English major dumped her, which pisses me off. I always knew that guy was no good. I hate to think of her by herself for too long, but maybe next time she'll meet someone who knows what a fortunate bastard he is."

"And you? How's the solitary life for you these days?"

"Okay. I've had two offers on the house, and if we decide to take a beating and accept one of them—which is what we ought to do with Houston in the midst of the great depression —then I can get out of that place."

"Where would you live?"

"Oh, I don't know. I won't really worry about that until I figure out what in the world I'm going to do. If I'm not going to wait out my mission, then I've got to say so pretty damn quickly so they can slot somebody else."

"You're going to go on that mission," Jane said, sounding aggravated by the suggestion that I might not.

"What makes you so sure?"

"Nothing. Except the fact that you've never quit anything in your whole life."

"It's totally different around there now," I said, becoming serious. "It's a different place. You sense this kind of self-doubt in all these people who've never had anything but success before. I mean, everybody talks gamely about getting right back on the horse, but there's something else that isn't said."

"Is that the way you feel? Some idea that maybe your odds wouldn't be so good?"

"No, I really don't think it's fear. When that thing flies again, it's going to be safer than it's ever been. Really. No, it's just this sense that maybe the accident woke me up. Before it, I had this, Jesus, this awesome sense of purpose about working for

NASA, about the shuttle program, everything. Now...I
haven't totally changed my mind, but I...I've been ignoring a
lot of other things, haven't I? I know I couldn't do that forever,
even if I really wanted to. Maybe now is the time to get out—
now while everything is being regrouped anyway."

"You could live without a second space trip?"

"My God," I said, "the fact that you ask that must show
how single-minded I've been about it. Of course I ought to be
able to live without another flight. Jesus, if that's all there was
to live for..."

"Well, there was a time when...It isn't really all that different from living for skiing, or to make big bucks, or to have
babies or whatever," Jane said. "People get obsessed. I don't
know. Maybe you have to get carried away to really succeed at
something."

"That's a depressing thought."

"Why?"

"What are you obsessive about?" I wanted to know.

"I've never succeeded at anything, have I?"

"Of course you have."

"Don't be patronizing," Jane said, standing up, walking out
the door to the open porch. I followed her, then stood silently
beside her, looking beyond her shadowed barn into the starry
darkness. "Probably life makes a lot more sense when you stop
worrying about the big plan," she said, "—whether you're
doing what you were meant to do, that kind of crap. You
probably shouldn't even try to succeed at simply being happy.
If you do, you end up looking for some sort of gauge all the
time. How do you decide what's happy, for heaven's sake?"

We didn't discuss ourselves that night—our tentative romance, our strange tumble of emotions—nor did we for the
longest time thereafter. Perhaps we were afraid to, I don't
know; perhaps we finally assumed it made sense to leave some
things unsaid, some issues peaceably unsettled.

•

I woke soon after dawn on the following morning. The horses were grazing, filling their bellies before the heat rose, and the air was still damp and chilly in the cottonwood shadows beside the creek. I took off my clothes and waded in, thinking I'd try to swim in the small pool held back by a coffer of rocks. But the water was too icy, stinging my skin and suddenly numbing it. I stood thigh-deep in the water, holding my breath, making myself stand there until I could bear it, until the pain became just a memory of pain, until I couldn't tell where my skin stopped and cold Cherry Creek began. Then, in a single motion, I squatted down, dunking my head and my back beneath the surface, and bolted for the shore. I moved into the sunlight to dry. The Episcopalians baptize infants by sprinkling a few drops of water on their foreheads, but by God, the Baptists dramatize the sacrament, I thought as I stood on the damp grass, my eyes closed, my face turned toward the fiery deity that I was certain of.

When I got back to the house, Jane was up and she was dressed. She was wearing her prosthesis—the shiny hook—the long sleeves of a snap-button western shirt covering its straps and socket. I watched her use it while she made coffee. "You're good at that," I told her, my legs hiked onto the kitchen counter. "I'm impressed."

"Wait till I wear it to bed sometime. I've got some tricks like you wouldn't believe."

"Are you wearing it most of the time now?"

"When I'm around here, I am. It really does make it a lot easier to get things accomplished. It's a pretty clever contraption, I've got to admit."

"What about the one that looks like a hand?"

"Decided against it. I never could get very good with it and I figured to hell with it. If I'm going someplace where I really don't want to drag the hook along, I just go without. Besides, with the hook you have to wear long sleeves or you give away all your secrets. I can tell that that's going to be a pain this summer." Using the prosthesis, she purposefully picked up the saucer beneath a coffee cup and carried it over to me. "See?" she said coyly, proudly, "the damn thing works. It ain't high fashion, I grant you, but it sure beats feeling like part of you is missing."

•

On Sunday, Jane and I managed to make it to church. At my parents' house the day before, my mother had mentioned secretively that it would be a special service for my father. She had already written to Mary in Ecuador, she said, telling her the news. But I had to wait until the following day to hear my father announce that he was retiring. He would stay on as long as needed to allow the parish to find his replacement, he said, and no, he and my mother would not move away. They would retire in the town that had been their home for more than thirty years. "I'm taking suggestions for hobbies," he told his friends sitting before him in the pews. "This is not a day I've done much planning for."

In the homily that followed, my father rambled nostalgically, then finally focused his comments on God's grace, calling it His miraculous favor, as I recall, a kind of divinely proffered fortune, bestowed as no enticement, no reward. He said that grace was perhaps the greatest gift of all, and I wished I knew precisely what he meant. We had been sitting near the front of the nave, and at the close of the service we waited a long time to leave, standing at the end of a queue of people, almost every one of whom stopped at the door to hug my father, to say something special to him. He hugged Jane at last, and took my hand, smiling brightly, his red cheeks wet. "Oh, gosh," he said, "I'm finally all cried out."

•

In the afternoon, we lounged on the grass in their backyard, my father's bare round belly reminding me of the Sunday a year before when he had wished he had no children. Jane lay on her back in shorts and a sleeveless shirt, her arms spread wide, her right arm ending in a slender stump instead of a silver hook. My mother was near us but in the shade, reclining on a chaise.

"For the longest time, I assumed that someday we'd live somewhere else," my mother said, "that Dick would answer a call from another parish. But once you kids were gone, it didn't make any sense to start over again. This is a funny little town in so many ways, but, well, I'm not sure it really matters where you live."

"Mother can only say that because she's never lived anyplace too terrible," my father said.

"We should have a party," I said. "This is quite an occasion, after all."

"No. Sitting doing nothing is just fine with me," my father said. "People tend to have coronaries in the midst of their retirement parties. Besides, I may have to work for a good long time while they find someone to take over for me."

"Very big shoes to fill," said Jane, hiking herself onto her elbow, smiling at him.

"Not at all," Dad said. "I hope they find someone with some real vision this time."

"Dick," my mother said.

"Seems like all the fellows my age either retire full of disillusionment or they retire as absolute saints."

"You mean you haven't got your sainthood letter yet?" I asked, pretending astonishment.

"Not yet. And, well... I guess I don't really fall totally into either of those camps. I hope I don't. I don't regret this life—

having been in the clergy—not for a minute. But it's a crazy business. You pretend for years that you truly understand the spiritual life, that the religious impulse, faith, the whole works, are as accessible as auto mechanics or something. But the truth is, you just do it by feel. You close your eyes and pray. If you ever open your eyes and think you understand something, well, that's what grace is, isn't it?"

•

Michael's cairn had survived the crush of snow and the punishment of the winter's wind. From the basin below the ridge, I could see that it still stood, but I wanted to climb up to it. Jane wasn't sure she should try to scramble one-handed up the slope, and she waited for me near the miner's shack, more nearly horizontal now, but also still surviving. I piled a few more rocks on the little monolith, turning them till they were seated and secure. I didn't pray, but I told Mike I envied him the vantage point, thanked him for keeping watch.

•

Two more summers passed before, at long last, we launched the shuttle with the telescope tucked inside the bay—the vehicle sent skyward by an agency much changed from the one I worked for on my first trip—one that will remain a bit bowed, certainly cautious, everyone cognizant now of something we somehow always should have known, aware of fragility, versed in failure.

Standing on the marsh grass at Canaveral, Matt, Sarah, Jane, and my parents anxiously watched the solid rockets fire for two minutes before they burned out and fell away to the Atlantic. Seven minutes later, I could almost hear their five exultants sighs as we shut down the main engines and sailed into orbit.

I made my second—and my final—trip to space. And I still wondered what I should do with myself down there during the minutes when I idly watched the sublimely spinning earth. I didn't have a job awaiting me, but George Abbey, John Young, and a few others already knew my resignation would follow the flight. Yet for the first time in my life, I actually seemed to enjoy my indecision. In the reach of time since Michael's death, since a blind kind of innocence was consumed in *Challenger*'s awful fire, since Peggy and I had forged a liberating sort of truce, I had come to realize finally that certainties are as elusive as the light from meteor showers. Few things are ever sure, and nothing is easy to answer. My father was right. In the end you do it all by feel. You search for verities, you work to find securing answers, not because they are certain to be found, but because searching is all any of us is good at somehow.

We deployed the telescope without a hitch—its solar panels unfurled, its antennas extended and aligned, its exquisite mirror outbound. Now, the telescope is at work at last, looking beyond the black place where *Voyager* travels toward Neptune, far beyond Halley's streaming tail, peering ever so distantly into the swarm of vagrant gases and sociable dust that somehow coalesce into islands, into the sea of matter and energy and grace.